William Dalton

The Wolf Boy Of China

William Dalton

The Wolf Boy Of China

ISBN/EAN: 9783743336605

Manufactured in Europe, USA, Canada, Australia, Japa

Cover: Foto ©Andreas Hilbeck / pixelio.de

Manufactured and distributed by brebook publishing software (www.brebook.com)

William Dalton

The Wolf Boy Of China

THE

WOLF BOY OF CHINA.

By WILLIAM DALTON.

ILLUSTRATED.

"SOMETHING IS LEARNED EVERY TIME A BOOK IS OPENED."

Chinese Proverb.

PREFACE.

THIS little work has been cordially recommended, not only for young readers, but for those of larger growth. The descriptions of the Celestial Empire are fascinating; the adventures and 'scapes hair-breadth are exciting enough to make every body who reads it wish to go to China almost as earnestly as Robinson Crusoe made him long for a Desert Island and a Man Friday. Having submitted it to our little friends Mary Lizzie and her cousin Eddie for perusal, and had their hearty approval, this American edition is offered to the public.

CONTENTS.

CONTENTS.

THE WOLF-BOY OF CHINA.

CHAPTER I.

A BOY, having once caught a mouse, kept it in a large square box, where, after a short time, it had a young one; as this little creature grew older, it was petted and made so much of by its young master, that, not knowing the value of liberty, it became perfectly contented with its position in mouse life; and not-withstanding the endeavors of its mother, an old mouse of considerable experience, to explain that there was a world outside the box, the little minx was so conceited that it would not believe one word she said.

One day, however, the boy, to amuse himself with the gambols of the two mice, placed a board inside the box, when the little mouse, thinking it very good fun, ran up to the edge; but when it saw the great room, it trembled with fear, and ran back to its parent, crying, "O mother, there is such a big place outside; surely it must be the world you have so often told me about." Well, although it may scarcely be believed, instead of wishing to roam at liberty, the selfish little thing felt so contented with its little box world, that it remained there till it reached a good old age, without doing any harm, it is true, but also without taking its fair share in the troubles and anxieties of its brethren of mouse-world.

For thousands of years the Chinese lived as selfishly as this mouse. The Almighty has blessed them with a land so extensive, beautiful, and productive, that, although their numbers are nearly equal to one third of the population of the world, they have existed prosperously for thousands of years, without being compelled to beg, borrow, buy, or steal, a necessity or luxury from any other people on the face of the globe. Indeed, had Noah's ark rested in China, (as the Chinese declare it did,) and left a pattern of almost every animal, plant, art, invention, and even law, making it a land of patterns, for the purpose of setting the world up in business again after the deluge, it could not have been a more wonderful country than it is. And although the Chinese are not thought to be so brave or talented as Europeans, they have been clever enough to do what most people find a difficult matter, — keep their own secrets, — and also to anticipate many of the great discoveries and inventions since claimed by Europeans; such, for instance, as gunpowder, canals, (or artificial water-roads,) the magnetic needle, paper money, and even printing, which was practised by them at least five hundred years before it was known in England; even our comic old friend Punch was born in China, where he is still known as Pun-tse, (the son of an inch.) So, you see, these people (who look so ridiculous on our plates and dishes, for the simple reason that, having paid very little attention to the art of drawing, they have caricatured themselves) have really some reason to be proud of their race.

The cleverness and industry, however, which helped the Chinese to make so much of the manifold blessings bestowed upon them by God, also made them arrogant and conceited, and moreover, with respect to every thing out of China, very ignorant; to such an extent, indeed, that for thousands of years they believed China to be the chief and central nation, upon which all others were dependent. As a proof of this belief, it is related that, when some of their most learned men first saw the French missionaries, they asked if they had such things as cities, towns, or houses in Europe. This question so amused the Frenchmen that they laid before the learned Chinese a map of the world, at which they were not a little surprised and confused, especially as for a long time they could not find China: at last, however, they took the whole of that half of the world which contains Europe, Africa, and Asia, for China, and the rest of the world for America. The Frenchmen let them alone some time in their error, till one of the Chinese desired to have the letters and names on the map explained to them. "You see," said the Frenchmen, " Africa and Asia; in Asia here are Persia, the Indies, Tartary." "But where then is China?" cried the Chinese. "This little corner of the earth," said the missionaries; "and see here the bounds of it." The Chinese looked at each other with astonishment, saying, in their own language, "*Siao te kin*," "It is very little."

It is also remarkable that, amidst the rise and downfall of empires during their own vast historic period, the Chinese have been able to keep themselves to themselves; for though the population is so vast, they have ever been too fond of peace and repose to attain much knowledge of the art of war, and consequently must at any time have fallen an easy prey to any of the fighting kings of history, had their existence been known. For their safety from such great robbers as Alexander the Great, Julius Cæsar, and Alaric, they have to thank Heaven, which not only placed them in a corner of an out-of-the-way portion of the world, but made them contented with their lot, so that they were never known to any of those crowned gentlemen whose especial line of business it was to plunder more peaceable people than themselves. When, however, it became known that the Chinese possessed in abundance such commodities as tea, silk, and many valuable and curious manufactures unknown to other people, the merchants of Europe endeavored to trade with them; but, with few exceptions, for a very long time they were rudely repulsed by the Chinese, who were too haughty either to buy or sell with foreigners. It was fortunate for this arrogant race that *conquest* (which, by the way, is a fine word for robbery) was out of fashion; for any one of the nations whose merchants asked so politely to purchase goods, was sufficiently strong to have helped itself had it so willed.

At length, after a great deal of persuasion, the emperor permitted Europeans to trade with his people, provided they confined themselves to certain *places* on the sea coast, one of which was *Canton.* The great art in selling is to offer your customer something that you know he will buy; and there is nothing that the majority of people will buy sooner than that which will gratify their senses. The Europeans imported into China large quantities of opium, a deleterious drug, which lulls pain and drives away care, but by slow degrees saps and undermines the health, and ultimately destroys life. And as in all countries, so in China, numbers of foolish people were to be found ready to purchase a few hours' pleasure at the expense of a life of misery, opium became very popular; opium eaters and smokers increased daily by thousands, and the merchants made large fortunes by its sale. The habitual opium smoker soon becomes sickly and emaciated, and, as the Chinese say, "like a paddy-bird in figure, and a pigeon in the face."

So rapidly did this pernicious habit run through the ranks of the lower order of people, that, out of a thousand soldiers who were sent to battle, more than *two hundred* were sent back by the general; the vile habit had rendered them unfit even to serve as "food for powder." The emperor, to save his subjects' lives, issued an imperial mandate, in which he ordered both buyers and sellers of this pernicious drug to be severely punished, and every ounce of opium to be destroyed — an order which nearly ruined the English merchants, who had large quantities in their warehouses at Canton. The consequence was, that the English sent an army and a fleet to China, for the double purpose of avenging the merchants, and com

pelling his majesty the emperor to permit his people
to swallow as much opium poison as they chose. `But
for this war, I should very probably have had nothing
to tell you about *Lyu Payo, the Wolf-Boy*, whose adventures came about as I will now relate.

Some few years before the outbreak of the war,
Captain Richardson, an English officer, then stationed
in India, obtained two years' leave of absence, which
he determined to spend in China, for the purpose of
studying the language; by the time his leave had expired, he had learned to speak Chinese fluently, and
was about to return to his regiment in India. Whilst
travelling through one of the provinces on the sea
coast, an insurrection broke out among the people,
and the rebels had so far succeeded that a party had
obtained possession of the governor's palace; and, as
the captain was very fond of fighting, he at once put
himself at the head of a body of straggling soldiers,
and entered the palace just in time to find the ladies
of the family in very great danger from some rebels
who had taken possession of their private apartments;
the governor's wife and daughter had fainted, and a
very beautiful lady, their companion, was being very
roughly used. After a short but gallant struggle, the
captain and his party succeeded in driving the rebels
from the palace, and were then relieved by the governor himself, who came up with a large body of soldiers. When the rebellion was suppressed, the governor gratefully invited the captain to stay with him
for a time. During his visit, he became on very
friendly terms with the ladies, and especially with the
one he had rescued from the rebels. The name of

this lady he discovered to be Sang, and, although he had found her in waiting on the general's wife as a slave, she was really a lady of rank, who had been taken prisoner by the general, after a battle he had fought with her countrymen, a brave race, who live among the mountains, in the province of *Kwei-chou*, and are called by themselves the *Miao-tse*, but by the rest of the Chinese people, wolf-men and women; and a very wonderful race they are; for although living in a part of China which is surrounded by many millions of their enemies, they have remained perfectly independent, from time immemorial, notwithstanding the conquest of the empire by the Tartars, who compelled all the Chinese, except these Wolf-people, to shave their heads, and forever after wear long tails — which, by the way, proved a capital thing for the barbers, of whom there are no less than seven thousand five hundred in the city of Canton alone. But as I shall have a great deal to say about these Wolf-people by-and-by, I will proceed with my story. So pleased was the captain with Sang that he proposed to marry her: the general, out of gratitude for his service against the rebels, gave his consent, and, after the ceremony, he returned to India with his new wife. Some time after, when the opium war broke out, Captain Richardson returned to China with his regiment, but this time he was accompanied with a wife and little boy. All through the war, he fought very bravely against the Chinese; but when it was closed, he resolved to give over soldiering, and become a merchant in Canton.

So far I have given you the history of the father

and mother of *Lyu Payo*, whose real name was Herbert Richardson; but his mother, upon her return to China, insisted upon his being called *Lyu Payo*, because it meant *Lyu the Treasurer*, and she had resolved that her boy should be the treasurer of all her happiness.

CHAPTER II.

"THE GEM CANNOT BE POLISHED WITHOUT FRICTION, NOR MAN PERFECTED WITHOUT TRIALS."

GOOD actions are sure sooner or later to meet with their reward; and so the captain found. During the war it had been his good fortune to save the life of a Chinese merchant of the name of *Tchin;* who in consequence became his friend, and very impatient for an opportunity to repay the obligation. This opportunity now offered, for, as an English merchant, the captain would have been shut up in a close factory — the only portion of the city where the Chinese permit the *Fan-kwei,* or *foreign devils,* (as they call Europeans,) to carry on their trade. The good and grateful Tchin, therefore, who had large warehouses of his own, in the best part of the city among the natives, begged of the captain to become his partner and take up his residence with him; an offer he the more readily accepted as *Tchin* some time before had embraced the Christian faith. Thus the captain became a merchant, with a good wife, a good friend, and a very dear little son; and no one could have been happier.

As Canton is a large and densely crowded city, where people of all nations meet for the purpose of trading and making money, a vast number of the very worst and most wicked of the Chinese gather together for the purpose of plundering and cheating the numerous strangers who daily arrive. The city of Canton covers a vast space of ground; but as the houses are all built of wood, and the streets are so narrow that but one sedan chair can pass at a time, great fires are no rarity. These conflagrations, however, frequently arise from the wickedness of incendiaries, who secretly set houses on fire with the hope of being able to plunder and rob during the confusion of the conflagration.

Now, it so chanced, when Messrs. Tchin and Richardson had a larger stock than usual of valuable goods in their warehouses, a fire broke out, how, no one knew; and although all the fire engines, which resemble large tubs, were soon on the spot, it was found impossible to extinguish the flames. At the time, little Lyu unfortunately happened to be there: as soon as the alarm was given, the captain sent him away in a sedan chair, under the care of his nurse, and endeavored to prevent that portion of his property saved from the flames from falling into the hands of thieves; but so great and rapid was the destruction of the property, and so little was rescued, that he believed himself to be ruined, and greatly he grieved for his wife and partner; as for himself, he was young, clever, and persevering, and hoped to retrieve his fortunes. When he found that he could do no further good, he hastened to console his wife, who, he knew, must have heard from the nurse all about the fire; but, on reaching home, you may imagine his surprise and alarm to find that neither nurse nor Lyu had arrived, and Sang, who had heard of the fire, in a state of distraction; still, while her husband was

absent sl.e had buoyed herself up with the hope that
the boy might be safe under his care; but when she
saw him return without him, the Miao-tse blood within her became aroused, and she raved like a mad
woman, calling out loudly against the wicked Tartars,
who, she declared, had taken the boy and sold him into
slavery. Whatever the captain may have thought,
he was too sensible a man not to know that to give
way to violent grief would be but to increase his misfortunes; and so for a minute or two he laid his head
upon his hand, and began to think seriously what was
best to be done.

His first idea was to ask the advice of *Tchin;* but
then the good merchant as yet could not have heard
even of the fire, for he had started early in the morning on a long journey down the river, and could not
possibly return till late in the evening. His next
thought was to go to the police *mandarin*, or magistrate; but as he was about to do this, the nurse, and
the two coolies or porters, who had carried the chair,
made their appearance, and threw themselves at his
feet; the nurse with grief, the coolies with terror,
begging for forgiveness.

The captain then really lost his temper, for he
knew from their countenances they were rogues; and
he bade them rise, threatening to have them bastinadoed if they did not tell him what had become of *Lyu.*
Terrified at this threat, and perhaps more so at the
appearance of *Sang*, who looked terrible in her anger
and grief, the coolies said that, while they were carrying the boy through Hog Lane, one of the narrowest
and filthiest streets in Canton, they had been pounced

upon by a dozen of the *Chaou-chow*, a people half pirates, half fishermen, who cried aloud for the miserable little *Yaou-jin*, *Lâng-jin*, that is, dog-man, wolf-man, to be given up to them to kill, because his mother had married a red-bristled barbarian, and that the *Chaou-chow* then knocked them down, took the boy out of the sedan, and ran with him towards the Floating Town on the river.

The captain believed this story, but he believed also that the coolies were connected with the child-stealers, and knew a great deal more than they confessed; he therefore very coolly took one of the rogues by the neck, and threshed him with a large bamboo cane till he roared again, and threatened to have them placed in the Cangue, which terrified them into a confession that the child-stealers had agreed to give them four *taels* (about twenty shillings) each for every boy or girl they could carry through Hog Lane. Then the captain, who really felt much alarmed for his son's safety, sent for some strong cord, and secured the men to one of the pillars which supported the apartment, telling them they should remain there while he went in search of Lyu, and that, if he did not succeed in finding him, they should be given over to the police mandarin; then telling Sang to inform *Tchin*, in case of his returning first, that he had gone to search the Floating Town, he left the house.

On his way towards the city he met a boatman, whom for a small sum of money he persuaded to change clothes with him. Thus disguised, he proceeded to a tea shop near the river, called for a dish of tea and a pipe; and, as he had the appearance of a boat man who had been lucky enough to have earned some money, several men came round him grumbling for want of work, and the captain treated them to opium and strong waters, when, taking him for one of their own class, they became very communicative about the great fire, and moreover about the many children that had been recently missing. Then, to put them the more off their guard, he carelessly gave it as his opinion that the lost children had fallen into the river by accident; at which one of the men laughed, as if he knew more than he cared to say. This was enough for the captain, who, secretly beckoning to the boatman to follow him, left the tea shop, and walked on till he came to another, where he treated him to strong waters till he became half stupid: he then made him a small present, and began to converse about his misfortune, informing him that he had sustained a great trouble in the loss of his only son, and that he should henceforth be disgraced and miserable, for he should leave no child behind him to perform the customary ceremonies at his funeral, or to sweep and strew his tomb with flowers. Now, as no calamity can be more terrible to a Chinese than this, the man so sympathized with the captain as to hint plainly that several stolen children would be taken down the river that very night, and that his son might probably be among the number. Having obtained this information, which fully justified his suspicions, Captain Richardson thanked his informant, and left him, with a promise to keep secret the source of his information. Indeed he had no wish to disclose it, for he knew that the boatman was not connected with the kidnappers.

The Floating City, which the captain soon reached, is one of the curiosities of the world: it is on the River *Pekiang*, one of the most beautiful streams in China; at Canton it is about as wide as the Thames at London Bridge, and for many miles it is covered with boats of all kinds, but chiefly those called *Sanpans*, or family boats, of which there are (imagine it if you can) upwards of forty thousand, in which some two hundred thousand men, women, and children pass their lives; very many being never allowed by law to go on land, or even to marry with people on shore. They are a species of above-water fish, living in an aquatic town. It is said that these water people are a separate tribe, called the *Tan-hoo*, and descended from the Mantchow Tartars, who conquered China; and notwithstanding that the number of these people is so great, and their floating houses so close together, so regularly are they arranged side by side in straight and transverse lines, like the streets in London, and so admirably are they governed by the mandarins, that no confusion is to be seen, and rarely even a quarrel.

The captain's first notion was to search among these water houses; but finding it somewhat difficult to get any information respecting the object of his search amid the population of forty thousand vessels, he hired a horse, and galloped along the banks of the river till he got far beyond *Foshan*, a town about fifteen miles from Canton; then, leaving the animal with the keeper of a tea shop, he proceeded to the river-side, borrowed an open boat, and, to make his disguise the more complete, adopted the lazy but ingenious custom of the Chinese boatmen, which was to lie nearly at full

length in the stern of the boat, guide the rudder with
one hand, manage the sail with the other, and row by
means of his left foot, which he pushed against an oar
fastened in the side, and with a pipe in his mouth he
glided down the river, when, although his mind was
tortured with anxiety for the safety of his son, he
could not but feel a sensation of pleasure as he viewed
the surrounding country.

It was a beautiful sight: on both sides of the noble
river the country was low, but interspersed with artificial hills, crowned with lofty and luxuriant fir trees;
the level ground along the banks thickly but taste-
fully planted with peach, orange, and plantain trees,
varied here and there with the noble mulberry, the
pride of China; the fragrant sandal, or shittim wood
of holy writ; and the curious but useful tallow tree,
which supplies the natives with candles; then again
the rich fruits, the muscle plum, the dragon's eye, the
lemon, the citron, and far-famed pomegranate; and
the vast rice fields, spreading into the far distance,
and shedding a cool light, as if in bashfulness, at the
rich, deep golden oriental sun, which was gradually
waning before the shades of approaching evening.
All this pleasure to the heart, delight to the eye, and
food for the mind, was soothing to the troubled brain
of the captain; but was there no drawback to this
delicious scene? Yes, indeed, a hideous one; for his
floating oar would occasionally strike against the corpse
of some poor female child, which had been allowed to
fall, or, what was equally possible, thrown into the
river, by the selfish parents; and then the captain
would shudder with horror, and thank Heaven that

he had been born in a Christian country. But here
I must caution my young readers against too readily
believing all that has been said about little girl
drowning in China; for, bad as it is, and often as it
occurs, it is still considered barbarous by all good men
even in that country, although their cruel law permits
the practice. It was growing dark, and the captain
was keeping a good lookout in the direction of the city;
and while he had been contemplating the scenery, and
breathing the delicious fragrance with which the air
was impregnated by the rich fruits and trees around,
he had not perceived that his boat had floated near to
a huge raft, some three hundred yards in length, made
of trees lashed together, on which was erected a small
hut, constructed of bamboo poles and matting; when,
however, he did notice it, he observed a woman and
several boys preparing to catch fish in the following
ingenious manner: the mother was fastening to the
side of the raft a long, narrow plank of wood, which
glittered with white, shining japan, which by a gentle
slope reached the top of the water, so that when the
moon arose the light would be so resplendent on its
shining surface that the fish in their gambolling and
sportive leapings would mistake the glittering surface
for their native element, and fall either on to the
plank or the raft.

No sooner had he reached the side of the raft, than
the woman called to him by name, and he at once
recognized her as a person to whom, some time before, while living in Canton, he had afforded some
little charitable aid, and he was delighted, for he knew
that she would, if possible, assist him in his efforts to

recover his son; he then got on board the raft, and told her the story of Lyu's disappearance. For a minute or so, the worthy woman beat her breast in sorrow, but then more wisely set about thinking what was to be done, and soon remembered that she had that day seen at Canton a *Tan-kea* boat very suspiciously move from its inner position to a more convenient spot for departure without being observed; this, she had little doubt, was the kidnappers' boat, and as it was getting dark, would soon pass the raft on its way down the river. Then beseeching the captain to be patient and ready, by means of a long pole she pushed the raft farther across the river, stationed one of her boys at each end to watch, and made a bowl of tea for the captain, who then took out his pistols, and examined the priming, to see that they were fit for use.

CHAPTER III.

"THE GODS CANNOT HELP A MAN WHO LOSES OPPORTUNITIES."

IN less than an hour, the captain heard the plash of oars, and, looking through a crack in the wall of the hut, he saw a large tan-kea approaching the raft. These boats are very common in the Chinese waters, and strongly resemble the half of a huge egg; it is indeed to this resemblance that they are indebted for the name of *Tan-kea*, or egg-house boat.

As the tan-kea came nearer, the captain's heart beat high with hope — the hope that Lyu was on board; and with the rapidity of thought, he caught up a boat-hook and waited for its nearer approach. As for the raftswoman, she silently thrust her pole into the bed of the river, and pushed the raft sufficiently across the stream to obstruct its farther passage. The tan-kea was rowed by a woman, who, as her craft neared the raft, began to ply her oar more vigorously, and, at the same time, keep a keen lookout at its movements; she could, however, perceive nothing suspicious on the raft, as the captain had hidden himself within the hut, where, like a tiger watching for its prey, he waited till the tan-kea came within reach of his boat-hook, when he threw it on to its side, brought it close to the raft, jumped aboard, pistol in hand, and in another moment stood in the cabin.

Quick, however, as he was, the owner of the *tan-tea* was no less so, for no sooner did he enter the cabin than he heard the click of a pistol, and found himself confronted by a savage-looking Tartar sailor; the weapon had missed fire, and before the man had time to draw another, he was lying on his back with the captain's hand upon his throat, and knee upon his breast. While wrestling with the sailor, he had not observed another person in the cabin; it was fortunate, however, that he glanced around when he did, for a miserable woman of the lowest river class was creeping towards him with a long knife in her hand: perceiving her in time, the captain pointed his pistol at her with his disengaged hand, and threatened to fire if she moved one step farther. At that moment, he heard a low, moaning sound from behind a curtain which hung across the end of the cabin, and his heart almost leaped into his mouth. Could it be the voice of Lyu? He called; there was no answer, and, his anxiety quickening his invention, he placed his pistol between his teeth, and, keeping his eyes fixed upon the crouching woman, dragged the sailor across the vessel, placed his knee upon his chest, and, taking a large silk handkerchief from his pocket, bound his arms behind him, and then with a piece of cord fortunately at hand he tied the man's legs together, and threw him into a corner, like a great bundle of wickedness as he was; then serving the woman in a similar manner, he tore down the curtain, and to his horror beheld not only Lyu, but six other boys, lying senseless on the floor, like so many drunken men. Great was his fright at first, for he thought them dead; he soon, however, found they were only under the influence of some narcotic drug, which had been given them to render them incapable of making themselves heard, while passing through the crowded parts of the river.

After glancing at his prisoners, to see that they were secure, he ran on deck to obtain the aid of the raftswoman, whom he found with her brave boys, wrestling with the steerswoman of the tan-kea.

When the captain boarded the tan-kea, the brave raftswoman and her boys followed, and sprang on to the helmswoman like an enraged lioness, and held her down on deck till he reappeared; when he carried her below, and having made her as secure as the other prisoners, with the help of the raftswoman he carried the six boys on to the raft, and, by dashing water in their faces, soon had the satisfaction of seeing them revive.

His next difficulty was to secure his prisoners till morning, for, as they formed but a part of a large gang, it was probable the others were lurking about on the river, and would attempt a rescue when they discovered the dangerous position of their comrades. After some consideration, he wrote a few lines in pencil on a leaf of his memorandum book, and sent the raftswoman in his own boat to Canton, where she could readily find a cooly, who, for a few tchen, would deliver it to his partner, Tchin; but as at least two hours must elapse before her return, he fastened the tan-kea to the raft, and, taking the six boys into the hut, gathered from them an account of their adventures. All they knew, however, was, that they had been met by an old woman in Canton, and beguiled by her on board a pleasure boat, where she treated them with sweetmeats and tea, after which they could remember nothing till they recovered their senses on the raft.

For some time the captain chatted with the boys, to prevent them from being frightened by the darkness of the night, but at length the moon arose and glistened upon the water, and one of the brave raft-boys left his post to announce that the "fish were jumping," and the captain took them to the japanned board at the edge of the raft, to see the stupid fish cheated into catching themselves. The finny creatures were gambolling in confidence in their safety from their enemy — man. Soles, cod-fish, and carp, one after the other, leaped from the river, and tumbled upon the board, mistaking it for a more brilliant portion of their native element, and were immediately picked up by the boys, and thrown into a basket, in readiness for their morning's meal; but in the midst of the sport, the moon disappeared, and it was so dark they were compelled to return to the hut, leaving the raft-boys, as before, to look out for mischief.

An hour had scarcely elapsed, when the watch-boy crept slowly into the hut, with the news that another tan-kea was gliding down the stream, and before the captain could cock his pistol, he heard a low whistle, and, at the same instant, the raft gave a sudden jerk, which nearly threw him off his feet; in an instant, however, he left the hut, and saw the crew of the tan-kea board his prisoners' boat, enter the cabin, cut the cords, and set them at liberty. This was the rescue he had feared; but now, knowing that it was useless attempting to fight against such odds, he made an effort to cut the raft adrift from the tan-kea; but, before he could effect his purpose, the enemy had gained a firm footing on the raft, and, while two of them secured his arms, the others endeavored to retake the boys, who, although they kicked and fought very bravely, were soon overpowered and carried to their old prison, the tan-kea. When the thieves had secured their young prisoners they threw a rope to their comrades, who held the captain, by means of which they fastened his arms behind his back, and were about to force him after the boys; but, in the midst of the struggle and the darkness of the night, they had not perceived the cautious approach of a war junk, which came alongside and threw out two lanterns over her prow, and exhibited to the captain a deck crowded with soldiers under the leadership of his friend Tchin.

Enraged at the prospect of losing their prey, one of the thieves struck the captain with his knife, when Tchin, alarmed at his friend's danger, foolishly fired his pistol, and hit the assassin in the left arm, which so maddened him that he again plunged his knife into the side of the captain, who, being near the edge of the raft, reeled over into the river.

At this catastrophe Tchin was about to plunge into the water after his friend, but the lanterns suddenly fell from the junk and were extinguished: this had been effected by the crew of the last tan-kea, who, during the struggle on the raft, crept up to the junk and cut them adrift; when, taking advantage of the darkness, they pulled away so hard, that by the time fresh lanterns had been slung, they had placed a great distance between themselves and the war junk.

Much as the escape of these rogues vexed Tchin, the good man was too anxious about the fate of his friend to order a chase; so, contenting himself with the impossibility of the escape of the remaining tan-kea, which had been taken possession of by a party of his soldiers, he offered a large reward in silver for the discovery of the body, for he made no doubt that his friend had been drowned; but great was his sorrow when, after a long search, the boat parties returned to the junk without the object of their search. However, as it was no time for idle sorrow, he went on board the captured tan-kea, where, to his delight, he found Lyu and the other boys, and moreover had the great satisfaction of seeing the kidnappers lying on the deck, where they had been thrown, bound hand and foot, by the soldiers.

Thus was his sadness streaked with one ray of sunshine; for although he had lost his friend, he had rescued six poor boys from slavery, and was about to save many others from a similar fate by bringing the vile boy-stealers to condign punishment. That same day there was great rejoicing among the mothers and fathers of Canton; for not only was the cause of the disappearance of so many children discovered, but some of the rogues themselves were known to be in prison awaiting trial. When the trial came on, as if to prove the falsehood of the axiom " that there is honesty among thieves," one of these wicked wretches gave evidence against his companions in crime; and, among other things, confessed that for a long period a gang of men and women, called " Water Rats," had obtained their living by stealing and selling children to the pirates, who again sold them in a distant province for slaves; and that this gang had stolen four hundred children in one year. By means of this man the rest of the kidnappers were captured, and sentenced to cruel deaths by the several judges before whom all great criminals have to pass in China, where the law is so merciful in all cases but high treason, that sentence of death has not only to be confirmed by each separate judge, but afterwards submitted to the supreme monarch himself. Now, tho emperor, who felt deeply for the kidnapped victims ordered the thieves to be marched slowly between the boys of the city, who might beat them to their hearts' content with thick bamboos, and afterwards to be beheaded; a severity which, it was supposed, would forever put an end to kidnapping. The better plan, in my opinion, would have been to have abolished slavery throughout China; for if no one were permitted to buy slaves, it would be of little use to steal them for the purpose of sale. After the punishment of the child-thieves the emperor testified his approval of Tchin's conduct in the affair by presenting him with a very handsome sum of silver money. Nor did he forget the raftswoman, whom he ordered to be provided for, for life, at the public expense.

CHAPTER IV.

"A WISE MAN ADAPTS HIMSELF TO CIRCUMSTANCES, AS WATER
SHAPES ITSELF TO THE VESSEL THAT CONTAINS IT."

IF any thing could have consoled *Sang* for the loss
of her husband, it would have been the recovery of
LYU PAYO; for a long time, however, she was so distracted with grief, that, like her countrymen, she
would have sought the pagan remedy — suicide, but
for her firm faith in the teachings and example of
the Saviour, and the sympathy of her kind friend
Tchin, whose Christian counsel sustained her in her
troubles, and enabled her to submit to the dispensa-
tions of Heaven.

As for Tchin, so deeply was he grieved at the loss
of his friend, (which he in some measure attributed to
himself,) that he determined to leave Canton, and
return to his native place near Pekin — a plan he was
enabled to carry out, as the emperor's bounty saved
him from the ruin that had fallen on the captain's
family by the destruction of their property.

Accordingly he told *Sang*, that, as his own wife
and daughter had died some years before, he would
adopt her and *Lyu* as his children; and although it
would vex his brother and sister-in-law, neither of
whom was aware of the deaths of his wife and
daughter, it did not matter, for they were not by any
means so good as they should be.

3

He further arranged that *Sang* should pass for a widow, whose husband had left her and her son so poorly off that she had been obliged to take up her abode with her father; and as *Sang* was much attached to the good merchant, she very readily consented to his wishes. It was further agreed that *Lyu* should be educated and brought up as a Chinese, but in the Christian religion, in order that he might be safe from the jealousies of the people in the interior, who would never tolerate him if they discovered that he was of the blood of the Miao-tse. These preliminaries being settled, *Sang* attired herself in the most spotless white, (the deepest mourning in China,) which she vowed never to leave off till she had found her husband, for she still believed him to be alive.

They then took ship, and, after a long and stormy voyage, arrived safely at the city of *Hang-tcheou*, at which place they rested for a few days, and then took their passage for Pekin on the Imperial Canal, the largest artificial river in the world, being five hundred miles in length, which, as they could not travel more than ten miles a day, promised them a fifty days' journey; however, knowing nothing of railroads, they did not care for this so much as you might, who can manage to get over the same number of miles in two days. As they were about to go on board the boat, a military mandarin rode up to the bank of the canal, and ordered them to stop, as the imperial tribute barges were approaching; and, as Tchin knew they would take more than a day to pass, he resolved to return to the inn; however, to please *Lyu* he remained to see the sight.

These tribute barges were very large and numerous, and many of them covered with highly-polished japan, and ornamented with golden dragons. The first of these ships — for they were really too large to be called boats — was much larger and grander than the rest, and crowded with gaudily dressed soldiers armed to the teeth: this was the great mandarin's vessel, and distinguished both at the head and stern by four beautifully painted lanterns, on which were painted, in letters of gold, KIN-TCHAI-TA-GIN; that is, "the great envoy from the court;" but, as you will soon see, the *great tax-gatherer* would have been more appropriate. Then there was a large ship filled with soldiers and an immense floating kitchen ; of the rest, some were filled with sacks of rice, wheat, millet, loaves of salt, sacks of beans, bundles of straw, beautiful silks and satins, raw silk, calico, linen, cloth, velvet, damask, japan varnish, oxen, sheep, hogs, geese, ducks, wild fowl, fish, herbs, fruits, spices, and all kinds of wine ; and, with the exception of a kind of head or poll tax paid in money, this is the manner in which the people in different parts of this vast empire pay their taxes : indeed they have no other means of making their payments, as they have no coin except the small pieces of copper with square holes in them, called tchen, and yet the want of a coinage of silver and gold is not from ignorance, but sheer obstinacy ; for not only did they once possess a coinage of the precious metal, but also a species of bank note, as you will see from the following account by *Marco Polo*, who travelled in China six hundred years ago.

"With regard to the money of *Kambalu*, the great

Khan may be called a perfect alchemist, for he makes
it himself.   He orders people to collect the bark of a
certain tree, whose leaves are eaten by the worms
that spin silk.   The thin rind between the bark and
the interior wood is taken, and from it cards are
formed like those of paper, all black.   He then causes
them to be cut into pieces, and each is declared worth
respectively half a livre, a whole one, a silver grosso
of Venice, and so on to the value of ten bezants.   All
these cards are stamped with his seal, and so many
are fabricated that they would buy all the treasuries
in the world.   He makes all his payments in them,
and circulates them through the kingdoms and provinces over which he holds dominion ; and none dares
to refuse them under pain of death.   All the nations
under his sway receive and pay this money for their
merchandise, gold, silver, precious stones, and whatever they transport, buy, or sell.   The merchants
often bring to him goods worth 400,000 bezants, and
he pays them all in these cards, which they willingly accept, because they can make purchases with
them throughout the whole empire.   He frequently
commands those who have gold, silver, cloths of silk
and gold, or other precious commodities, to bring
them to him.   Then he calls twelve men skilful in
these matters, and commands them to look at the
articles and fix their price.   Whatever they name is
paid in these cards, which the merchant cordially receives.   In this manner the great sire possesses all
the gold, silver, pearls, and precious stones in his
dominions.   When any of the cards are torn or
spoiled, the owner carries them to the place whence

they were issued, and receives fresh ones, with a deduction of three per cent.

"If a man wishes gold or silver to make plates, girdles, or other ornaments, he goes to the office, carrying a sufficient number of cards, and gives them in payment for the quantity which he requires. This is the reason why the Khan has more treasure than any other lord in the world; nay, all the princes in the world together have not an equal amount." The Chinese were therefore the first people who adopted bank notes, the use of which, however, I may add, has long been discontinued, a few only having been preserved as curiosities.

On the first appearance of the great man's barge, all the soldiers from the neighboring stations were drawn up along the banks of the canal, the inscribed lanterns hung out from the barge, and a signal gun fired by the soldiers, which was answered by the guns at the neighboring stations. At the sound of the guns the laborers in the fields, and about the town, began to scamper like mad, and the soldiers to pursue them like hunters after so many wild beasts; and no wonder either, for the mandarin, finding he had not sailors enough to row his vessel, ordered the *lanterns* to be hung out as a signal for the soldiers to catch him a few hundred peasants; and, as the latter understood this, they endeavored to make their escape at the report of the first gun; a great number, however, were caught, driven down to the banks in flocks, like sheep, and harnessed to the barge by means of ropes; when the music struck up, the great tax-gatherer hauled down his lanterns, the soldiers fired a salute, and all went along merrily except the peasants, who, having neither animals nor money, were compelled to pay their taxes in labor. I do not think it would be so casy to make English peasants pay taxes after such a fashion; so you see, we foreign devils, as the Chinese call us, are better off than the long-tailed children of the Son of Heaven, as they call their emperor.

Having seen enough of the sight, the travellers returned to their inn, and on their way *Lyu* was sadly frightened by a troop of dogs which were howling and scampering after a man, who was at last seized by one of the animals and thrown to the ground, when he would have suffered severely, but for *Tchin*, who ran to his assistance and beat off the beast, which, after all, was not so much to blame, for the man was a *dog-butcher*, and was carrying a fresh-killed dog to a customer for his dinner, when the animals set upon him, and endeavored to rescue their dead companion's body. This dog-eating is very common among the lower order of the Chinese, who have a taste also for cats, rats, and mice.

The next morning they were permitted to set off on their journey to Pekin, and for the first day or two saw little but houses and dense masses of people, (who swarm in China as in no other nation; some of the highways even being crowded to inconvenience.) They floated on the canal through many miles of rice fields, and day by day watched the husbandmen and their wives toiling at times on flat plains, at others by the side of mountains; not one inch of ground do they allow to be unused. Labor is considered sacred by the people, and is patronized by the great emperor himself, who, by way of encouragement, occasionally turns up the earth with a golden plough. Nor do these hard-working, badly-fed husbandmen forget ornament in their utilitarian labors, for they plant the rice in various tasteful devices, and even cut the mountain sides into terraces, one above another, to the number of twenty, and sometimes thirty.

After twenty days they arrived at the city of *Nankin*, once the residence of the emperor, and the capital of the empire. Here Lyu first saw the celebrated *Porcelain Tower*, which is of great height, and as fantastic in form as if a vast number of school boys had subscribed to build a monument to the glory of some master who had given them more holidays than lessons. It is large at its base, and runs up *nine stories*, each story decreasing·in size as it rises: moreover, it is hung over with small bells, which keep tinkling in the wind, very much, I should think, to the astonishment of the sheep, who must mistake it for some phantom friends.

At this place they remained to witness an agricultural festival. The streets were hung with tapestry; triumphal arches were erected at different places, and covered with lanterns of every shape and hue. As they entered the city they met a grand procession: the governor of the province was crowned with flowers, and carried in a beautiful sedan-chair, preceded and followed by flags, lighted torches, and bands of musicians. After the great mandarin came six litters, painted and adorned with silk tapestry, on which were figures and representations of illustrious persons who had made the practice of husbandry famous. Then followed one litter so large that it required forty men to carry it; on this was an immense clay cow, with gilt horns, and covered with ornaments: behind the figure stood a little boy with one foot naked, who kept beating the cow, as if to make it go on. After the cow came all the husbandmen of the neighborhood, followed by a number of clowns most grotesquely dressed. When the procession reached the governor's palace, the cow was stripped of her ornaments, her inside opened, and a quantity of small clay cows taken out and distributed among the husbandmen; the large cow was then broken into pieces, which were distributed among the people. The governor then closed the ceremony with a long lecture on the importance of husbandry, after which the people roamed about the city, which was brilliantly illuminated with festoons of lanterns of all shapes and colors.

The next day they proceeded on their journey, and in another twenty days came in sight of the city of Pekin; the sun shone beautifully upon the yellow tiles of the imperial palace and the public buildings, making them glitter like fields of burnished gold. Another hour and their tedious canal voyage was at an end, for they had reached Tchin's house, which was situated in a small village within a mile of the western wall of the city.

On their arrival, *Tchin's* brother *Hieul* and his wife *Chang* very warmly embraced him, and made many professions of love for his daughter and adopted son, as they took Sang and Lyu to be — too many Sang thought to be genuine. Now, Hieul had once been as well off in the world as his brother Tchin, but being a great spendthrift, he soon wasted his fortune, and would have become a beggar but for his good brother, who not only allowed him an income, but had lent him his residence during the many years he had been away at Canton.

Notwithstanding their brother's kindness, this wicked couple were discontented, and had longed to hear of Tchin's death, for, as he had but a daughter, who would be provided for by marriage, they made no doubt of inheriting his property: you may therefore imagine their vexation when they found that, although their niece, as they believed Sang to be, had been married, her husband had died leaving her so poor that Tchin had been compelled to install both her and her son beneath his roof. Hieul and his wife, therefore, hated both from the moment they saw them, and resolved to effect their ruin at the first opportunity; and, like most bad people, the more they hated the more they pretended to love. Still they all managed to live together for about two years without quarrelling, during which time Lyu made so much progress with his learning, that Tchin loved him as if he really had been his own son, which, being apparent to Hieul, caused him so much vexation that he again flew to his vile habits of drinking, opium-smoking, and gambling; and on more than one occasion found himself in trouble with the police mandarin, who would have had him bastinadoed but for Tchin, who, by means of a handsome bribe to the magistrate, obtained a remission of the punishment.

CHAPTER V.

"IF MEN WILL HAVE NO CARE FOR THE FUTURE, THEY WILL
SOON HAVE SORROW FOR THE PRESENT."

ABOUT two years after Sang and Lyu had taken up
their abode with Tchin, a crowd of persons had assembled together in one of the wide, open spaces in
Pekin to see a man suffering the punishment of the
cangue. This frightful instrument of torture has been
said to resemble the stocks, in which it was formerly
the custom in England to fix drunken and disorderly
people; but the two are not to be compared, as the
Chinese instrument is by far the most cruel.

The cangue is a species of collar made of two oblong pieces of wood, which, when put together, form a
square as large as a small drawing-room table; each
of the pieces is hollowed out where they are to join, so
that, when locked together, there is a hole just large
enough to admit a man's neck; lower down there are
two smaller holes for the hands.

It was in one of these instruments, weighing at least
a hundred pounds, that the man's neck was fastened,
with his face downwards, looking at his hands, which,
being also confined at the wrists, he was unable to
move. Along one side of the cangue was the word
" *Gamester* ;" on the other, " *Disturber of the family
peace*," — which some of the mob repeated aloud, jeer-
ingly ; while others taunted the unfortunate wretch

with his former pride; all of which he was obliged to bear without any relief but that of closing his eyes. Whatever had been his crime, he seemed to be fully punished, for he had worn this horrible instrument for more than a month; being compelled each day to walk the streets and public places, accompanied by an officer, who held a whip in his hand, with which he would, from time to time, lash the exhausted wretch to prevent his sinking to the earth.

At the time the crowd were jeering and taunting the poor fellow, he had, from utter failure of strength, been permitted to rest the cangue on the ground; indeed, had the whipper forced him onwards, he must have died, as many do, beneath the punishment. It was a heart-rending sight; for, as the people taunted him with the vile habits which had brought him to that pass, he closed his eyes and bit his lips till the blood ran. O, how his heart must have bled with shame, that he, a gentleman, should be placed in such a purgatory, unable to hide his face, and compelled to endure the gibes and jests of the vilest of the city vagabonds!

The feelings of multitudes are sometimes changed by the merest trifle; and so it happened now, for suddenly there was a movement among the crowd, who, rude as they were, made way for a little boy, who passed through, followed by a slave, carrying a basket; when he reached the cangue he affectionately laid his hand on the head of the sufferer, whose eyes glistened with delight, and voice trembled with emotion as he murmured his gratitude to the boy, who took a basin from the basket, and fed him with bird's-nest soup, all the while looking so piteously affectionate, that the jeering people became silent with shame and approbation.

After the soup the man appeared refreshed, and attempted to walk; but no sooner did the horrible instrument touch his bleeding shoulders than he shrieked with agony; the weight had become more than he could bear; and he would have fallen but for the boy, who instantly placed himself beneath the cangue, so that the weight was removed from the prisoner's shoulders to his own head, and thus they walked onwards amidst shouts of applause from the crowd.

"A miracle from the gods!" said a man to his neighbor, "that so vile a wretch should have so blessed a son, and so brave as to care nothing about the people around."

"Ah," said another, "do you not know that no day has elapsed during the month without a visit from that good boy?" adding, "but let us follow them to the tribunal; to-day the term of his punishment expires: let us go and see how he will take the bastinado;" for we all know that every punishment in China begins and ends with a beating. Thus supporting the weight of the cangue, the brave boy tottered on to the Hall of the Tribunal, where they found the mandarin at a table, with a small case of reeds before him, and by his side six men with large bamboo sticks in their hands. When the criminal entered, the mandarin removed the official seal, the attendants lifted the cangue from his shoulders, and he shrieked with joy at the relief, but fainted immediately afterwards from excessive weakness; but, accustomed to such scenes,

HICUL IN THE CANGUE.

Page 44.

the mandarin quietly waited till the culprit revived, and then, counting twenty of the reeds, threw them one by one on the floor ; when the officers stripped the prisoner, and were about to give him four heavy blows with a bamboo cane for each reed ; but the boy threw himself at the feet of the mandarin, and prayed of him to remit the punishment.

The mandarin was so much astonished at the presumption of so young a boy in daring to address so great a man, that he stopped the punishment, and begged of the whipper, who had had charge of the prisoner, to tell him who he was ; and when he heard all that the boy had done for his relative, the great man was so pleased that he not only remitted the bambooing, but sent him away with a handsome present. Need I say that the brave little boy was Lyu Payo, and the criminal that same Hieul who had been endeavoring to do Lyu and his mother so much injury, but whom, humiliated, shame-faced, and weak, Lyu now assisted to his home? If any thing could have sponged the black spots of envy and ingratitude from Hieul's heart, it would have been the amiable and noble conduct of the boy ; but then, as the Chinese proverb says, "You cannot get ivory from rat's teeth ; ' and so Lyu afterwards discovered.

CHAPTER VI.

"WHAT IS TOLD IN THE EAR IS OFTEN HEARD A HUNDRED MILES OFF."

THE Chinese, who burn incense whenever they wish to ask a favor of their pagan idols,—which, by the by, are as numerous and ridiculous as mountebanks at a fair,—have a saying, that " while at their ease men burn no incense;" but when trouble comes " they clasp the feet of Fo." (This Fo is the chief of their false gods, and, according to the belief of the Chinese, must be a species of Harlequin in a very large way of business, for they assert that he has been born eight thousand times in eight thousand different shapes, as a man, a woman, and every kind of animal, bird, reptile, &c.; a transmigration, they believe, happens to the soul of every man, which, according to the goodness or wickedness of the living person, will, after death, pass into an elephant, goose, rat, or snake.) So with *Hieul*, who, when in health and prosperity, thought not of Heaven, but, when lying upon a bed of sickness, covered with shame and disgrace, began to ponder over his past wickedness, and promised *Tchin* to reform and become a better man ; and even to renounce his false gods and become a Christian. This, however, was from mere terror ; for, having faith in the worse than silly doctrine of the transmigration of souls, he feared that he should one day become a rat or snake, and pass through another life hunted and despised, with the power of uttering nothing better than a squeak or a hiss.

'As, however, *Lyu* read to him the word of God, this foolish superstition gave way, and he took heart, feeling grateful for the moment at a chance of escaping from *ratdom* and *snakedom*, and readily promised to cast aside his idolatry and wickedness. In what manner, however, he kept this promise we shall soon discover.

For the succeeding two years so affectionate did *Hieul* and *Chang* appear to *Lyu* and his mother, that complete happiness reigned in the house of *Tchin*, who was delighted at his brother's apparent reformation; and during this period little else was thought of but the education of Lyu, who made such progress in his studies that he promised to become a great scholar; nay, his master said, even "a great tree in the forest of pencils," as he called the great college of Han-Lin, and perhaps a *colao* or minister of state.

Although Sang was pleased with her son's abilities, she detested their learning as much as she did the Chinese and all their habits and customs; for she was proud of her own brave Miao-tse race, who for hundreds of years had lived in their mountains under their own princes, manners, and customs, in defiance of the Tartars, who, two hundred years before, had taken possession of every other part of China, and made the people shave their beautiful black hair from their heads, and adopt long, plaited tails, in order that the conquered race, who were so much more numerous than themselves, by not being able to distinguish

one race from the other, should be ignorant of the real
weakness of their conquerors. And notwithstanding
that at the present time a Chinese clings to his tail
almost as much as to his life, when the order was first
issued it was regarded to be such a disgraceful badge
of slavery that thousands of people preferred death to
its adoption. Now, as the Miao-tse, or, as the Chinese
call them, Wolf-men, were the only people among the
four hundred millions in China who dared to wear their
hair all over their heads, it made Sang's heart bleed
to see her handsome boy with his head shaved, and a
long tail growing down his back, and therefore, however she might have forgotten in time her Miao-tse
hatred for the Tartar-Chinese, this terrible tail stood
always before her as a badge of slavery, which she
dared not cut off, for the emperor would become so
alarmed at the audacious act that he would assuredly
order the boy to be beheaded ; yet, again, if Lyu ever
chanced to go among her own race, they would kill
him as a disgrace to their blood.

Now, as this terrible tail was always before her, she
could not help talking about it to Tchin, and sometimes
so angrily and loud that the worthy merchant feared she
would be overheard ; and if the mandarins discovered
her to be a Miao-tse, nothing could save her or her boy
from destruction, for the Chinese rulers hated and feared
the Miao-tse more than the Miao-tse hated them, and
you will soon find that the good Tchin was not far
wrong in being so cautious.

Some two years after Hieul's punishment, and the
day before the annual festival of the Feast of Lanterns,
for which the whole of the people in Pekin were

making great preparations, Tchin, Sang, Lyu, and Hieul's wife, Chang, were sitting together, talking of the approaching feasts and amusements; Chang's little tongue rattled away about the pleasures she was going to enjoy, for a neighbor had told her that the lanterns would be more clever, the theatrical shows and the jugglers and the grand fireworks more numerous and grand, than usual.

"Does my sister know for what reason?" said Sang.

"Is my sister Sang ignorant that the Son of Heaven and Lord of the Earth, the Imperial King of Kings — *may he live ten thousand years!*" (and here Chang bowed her head nine times as she mentioned the emperor's name,) "has received a present from the great Tien, for which the whole world will burn incense at the festival in rejoicing?"

"Of what my relation says I know as little as these chopsticks," said Sang, pointing to two long pieces of ebony tipped with silver, which the Chinese use instead of forks; but adding, "What in the name of our ancestors — *may they be reverenced!* — can such a present consist of?"

"Ten thousand heads, niece," replied Chang, clapping her hands. "Yes, ten thousand tail-less heads of the Wolf-men, those less than dogs." At this moment there was a sound on the gong at the door, and Chang ran out to meet Hieul and tell him the joyful news.

It was fortunate that Chang left the room, for she would have seen Tchin turn pale with terror, the eyes of Sang flash with anger, and moreover, Lyu clutch his fists in dumb show at this cruel news. The murder-of so many of her brave race was so great a shock to Sang, that after her first outburst of rage and terror she swooned, not a little to the surprise of Hieul and Chang, who at that moment entered the room; the latter, however, removed her to her own apartment, and endeavored to bring her round.

Then said Hieul, "The news is great, brother Tchin: the 'Flying Horse' arrived this day from Quang-tong province, with intelligence that the Wolf-dogs have dared to rise in rebellion against the Yellow Dragon, but that the rebel-killing general, the great Yin-Lin, with his war-tigers, has made the whole nation smaller than the dust, by laying no less than ten thousand of the thieves' heads at the feet of the Son of Heaven."

Tchin was too full of sorrow to reply; and although he could not blame Hieul for his joy, as all peaceable Chinese feared the terribly warlike Wolf-people, they were the kindred of his adopted son and daughter, for whose safety his heart was filled with grief and fear; but, as he dissembled his feelings, Hieul continued:—

"And what is more, brother, his fragrant majesty has published his Dragon will that the whole of the Miao-tse dogs shall be exterminated, and for this purpose has issued a proclamation under the vermilion pencil, that fifty pieces of silver shall be given for the head of every Wolf-dog, man, woman, or child. O, brother, would for the sake of my empty girdle that Tien would throw a few of these vermin across my path!"

This, as you may suppose, did not a little alarm Tchin, who felt thankful he had not intrusted Hieul

with his secret, for he knew that the fifty taels would
be quite sufficient inducement for him to have betrayed
both Sang and Lyu to the mandarins.

When Hieul retired to his own apartments he found
his wife very merry, dancing about the room, as if she
had heard good news. " O, husband," said she, " Tiea
is good to us at last, for he has not only placed one
hundred taels under our very noses, but put you in the
way of getting a government appointment, perhaps a
mandarin's button."

" What in the name of the five virtues, Jin, E, Le,
Che, and Sin, possesses the woman, that she speaks so
foolishly of picking up taels and mandarins' buttons?
Surely she has been drinking the pearly wine, and lost
her wits!" said Hieul, throwing off, as he always did
in his brother's absence, every semblance of Christianity.

" No, husband, it is not with wine, but joy, that I am
intoxicated, as you shall see; but first inform me if
your indignation is not tempestuous at these Wolf-dogs,
whose vile heads are now worth fifty taels each."

" Truly, wife, for once you utter wisdom; for could
I but find any of these dogs, our fortune would be
complete; but, alas! such fortune belongs not to
Hieul the unfortunate."

" Indeed it does, and therefore be thankful to Fo
that he has delivered two into your very hands; at
this moment they are beneath this very roof."

" By Fo, the woman has been drinking deeply to
make her tongue wag so simply," replied Hieul incredulously.

" Let my husband believe, or not believe, my words

as he will, but this I tell him, that his pretended niece and her son are both of the wretched Miao-tse blood, and were adopted by the artful Tchin to despoil his brother of the succession to his property."

"What words are these that sound so like truth?" said Hieul.

"Words poured into my ears by Sang herself, who prayed that I would keep her secret, as if, indeed, I had no regard for my husband's promotion. Now, cannot my husband do a service to the Lord of Heaven, and at the same time reap his just reward? for truly he will not only get the taels, but the fortune of the artful Tchin, who will assuredly be beheaded for his treason to the Imperial Dragon."

"Silly wife! the wily Sang, for some subtle purpose of her own, has been laughing at you," replied Hieul. "Yet," he added, "it is true that she possesses not the golden water-lilies of the flowery land, but rather the ungainly feet of a barbarian."

"It is true, husband — by the vermilion pencil it is true! for but yesterday, when passing the window of one of the inner apartments, I observed Sang and your brother Tchin in close converse, and heard her giving way to her wolfish anger, and blaspheming against the Imperial Dragon for compelling her boy to wear such a badge of slavery, as she called the graceful tails of the celestial people. Tchin endeavored to soothe her, and told her that if her words were heard she would bring ruin upon his household; and to-day, after recovering from the swoon into which she was thrown by your news of the vengeance that had fallen upon her people, the foolish creature related to me little by little her whole history."

"Surely, wife, thou art too credulous — this cannot be — for have you not heard that these Wolf savages have their feet shod, and wear tails like cattle?" replied Hieul.

"Shall it be said that my husband is so unreasonable as to believe what is only affirmed by the coolies and common people? Once more I say that they are of the Miao-tse, and, moreover, that Sang completed an alliance with one of the western sea-devils who came from an island in the sea called Britain, and who have so lately been swept from the flowery land by the barbarian-exterminating generals of the Yellow Dragon. This alliance makes her doubly hateful in the eyes of the mandarins, before whom you must drag her, or be no longer worthy to offer up incense at the name of the Dragon Emperor of the Earth."

"Even if this be true, am I a dog that I should devour the happiness of my brother, whose heart flows with milk, and who has so long kept me in the flowery path of prosperity?" said Hieul.

"Rat's flesh and tea leaves!" cried the angry Chang. "Can my husband wish to sacrifice at my tomb before the time appointed by Fo? Would he make himself less than an unfatted dog, or be so ungrateful to the gods as to make a hole in his lap while they are filling it with fortune? Truly it is as vain to talk to him as to pour water on a duck's back."

"Would my wife have me strip two skins off one cow? Have I not already had more from my brother than he could afford? How could I sacrifice at the tomb of our common parents, were I to hunt him to death? Surely my wife has lost her prudence, and remembers not that it is well to swim with one foot on the ground," replied Hieul with affected indignation.

"Truly my husband practises well the axiom, that 'he who would rise in the world should veil his ambition with the forms of humility;' though he cannot hide his desires from the wife of his bosom, who can read in his noble countenance that he is planning to do even now this thing so that it shall not bring obloquy upon his head. Let me remind him 'that the gods cannot help a man who loses opportunities;' and more," added the little vixen passionately, "that if he refuses, his wife, who is too wise 'to let the moth of fortune shed its silk without winding it round her finger,' will do it for him."

"Put up thy anger, wife, for it is as useless as the waves of the ocean without wind; and we will weigh well all that we have said; but cease not to be cautious, or we may win a cat and lose a cow."

Chang then left to attend Sang, and Hieul to call upon an intimate friend of his, the son of a mandarin of the third rank; for what purpose you will discover hereafter.

CHAPTER VII.

"EVERY DAY CANNOT BE A FEAST OF LANTERNS"

AT the commencement of the Chinese year, about the end of February, the people hold their great holiday and festival of the Feast of Lanterns. The courts of law are closed, all business is stopped, and the people do nothing but make and receive presents, and give themselves up to rejoicing. The smaller mandarins pay visits of respect to their superiors, children to their fathers, and servants to their masters; the very poorest of the poor don the best dresses they can buy or borrow, and think of nothing but visiting each other, performing plays, telling stories, and feasting.

Every house in the cities, and every boat on the canals and rivers of their vast empire, is hung about with hundreds of millions of painted lanterns, and at night the most costly and ingenious fireworks are let off for the amusement of the people; indeed, the expenditure of time and money is so great, and the mirth, joy, and pleasure so general, that no great national festival in the world can be compared with the great festival of the Feast of Lanterns.

Of the origin of this festival the Chinese tell several interesting stories, one of which is, that—

" There was once a great mandarin who had a most

beautiful daughter, and one day, as she was walking by the side of a river, she fell in, and was drowned. The afflicted father with his family and servants ran to the river, and, that they might be better able to find the body, caused a great number of lanterns to have lights put in them. All the inhabitants of the place thronged after him with lighted torches ; and, although they could not find the body, the mandarin was so much pleased with the anxiety of the people to help him, that he ordered them to go the next year with their lanterns, and make the same search, and so on each year until it became an established custom."

Another story is, — " That about three thousand years ago there lived an emperor of China named Kio, who, although very clever and a great hero, was given to pleasure and wickedness of all kinds, and, moreover, so extravagant with the people's money, that, out of a mere whim, he built an immense tower of diamonds and pearls, and all the most costly gems he could buy or steal, and filled a bath large enough to hold three thousand people with the most expensive wine. Now, as some of his best friends even thought this was going a little too far, they tried to persuade him to become more moderate ; but he did not seem to care about their advice, and, moreover, ordered them all to be put to death, which, of course, prevented people from being too free with their advice for the future ; after which he became more extravagant in his wishes ; for, not contented with a castle built of precious stones instead of bricks, and gold and silver instead of iron and wood, he wanted to find out how to make life longer — he, in fact, wanted to cut off

Death's head. To do this, he made arrangemens to forget that there were any changes of season, either of years, days, or nights, and commenced by building a palace in which the light of day should never be seen; and instead of the sun, he ordered, as an improvement, a vast number of lanterns to be hung up, and kept lighted night and day.

"He then shut himself up with his queen, and remained there till the people could no longer bear the hardships which they had to undergo in consequence of Kio's extravagance, and determined to let a little daylight into the palace, and so stormed and pulled it down, sending Kio to get his living by begging. As Kio had not been brought up to that line of business, he soon died of starvation; and to preserve the memory of the tyrant's defeat and death, and as a slight hint to succeeding emperors, the people hung out lanterns in every one of their cities every year on the same day, till it became a national festivity." Which of these two accounts is the true one, I will not venture to say; probably neither. But to proceed with my story.

The day on which the conversation we have recorded took place between Hieul and his wife was the last of the holidays of the festival of the new year, and the next, being the full of the moon, was the great Feast of Lanterns; and, like every body else, big and little, in China, Lyu was looking forward to a day of great enjoyment, for Tchin had promised to accompany him to see the sight and amusements. The good merchant, however, happened to be taken ill, and so he was only accompanied by Hieul, who was dress—

out in the very height of Chinese foppery; he had a bran new silk gown and girdle, from which hung his fan-case, tobacco-pouch, flint and steel for lighting his pipe, a pair of long ebony chopsticks, tipped with silver, a new watch-case handsomely embroidered by his wife Chang, a very fine purse, and a beautiful new porcelain snuff-bottle and silver spoon to take the snuff with; and, as he came into the room with all these articles hanging and jingling from his girdle, with his cap on his head as a matter of politeness,— for in China it would be considered very rude to take off your hat on entering a room,— he looked very much like a fat drum major prepared for a long march; but to be fat in China is considered to be very elegant and handsome; a thin man is called a short weight,— which Hieul certainly was not,— he was too indolent for that.

I had forgotten to tell you that his nails, which shot out from his fingers like a ship's bowsprit, were so long that they were supported by a kind of splint scaffolding; and when he put himself together and was all complete, it puzzled the boy to know how he had come by the money to convert himself into such a two-legged curiosity-shop: be that as it might, he had never found Hieul so kind to him as that morning; and although, when they reached the Temple, within the gates of the city, he spoke rather angrily to him for not burning incense before the three precious Buddhas, he soon recovered his temper.

On coming out of the temple Hieul determined to try his luck for the new year, and so sent Lyu to purchase a couple of long candles, which he lighted by

means of the flint and steel in his girdle ; then, hold·
ing one as uprightly as possible in his hand, he gave
the other to Lyu, and started off as fast as he could
run, telling him to follow, and, if they could continue
at the same pace all the way home without extinguishing the light, that they would be fortunate for the rest
of the year. Now Lyu, being a Christian, had no
faith in this silly superstition; but, as he saw so many
persons running on the same foolish errand, he thought
he would do the same by way of a bit of fun.

Well, off they ran as fast as their legs would carry
them, Lyu, being the youngest, keeping ahead, except when he stopped to laugh at the comical sight
of Hieul, who was so fat that he could never get
beyond a sort of puffing, panting, spasmodic waddle:
his long tail fluttered in the wind like a streamer, the
knickknacks in his girdle jumbling and clattering together, and his eyes starting with anxiety to prevent
the candle from being extinguished; for all the world
like some fat old pig scampering from its mistress
with the household keys round his waist. And so
they ran for a full mile, till they reached Tchin's
house, when, after adjusting his dress, Hieul returned
thanks to Fo for not extinguishing the light, and there-
by promising him a year's good fortune.

As for Lyu, he had been so much amused at the
fun that he had not been so successful; his candle
had become extinguished before he had run a dozen
yards; and as he had no faith either in Fo or his
promises, Hieul could not persuade him to try again.

When Hieul had readjusted his dress they again
set out for the city, now crowded with holiday folk

and Hieul· bethought himself that his head had not been shaved for a day or two, and so beckoned to a barber whom they saw on the other side of the street with his shop upon his shoulders, and two long pieces of iron in his hands, which he kept clanging together to attract the attention of customers.

This man had a long pole thrown across his shoulders, in the front of which hung a can of water, a basin, and some towels ; behind, to balance these, was a stool with drawers, containing an iron pan full of water, which was kept boiling by a small charcoal furnace.   As soon as he had found a customer he chose a convenient corner of the street, adjusted his instruments, placed the stool for Hieul to sit upon, and commenced to shave his head, clean his ears and eyes, crack the joints of his arms and legs, and shampoo his body — a queer kind of operation, you will say, to be performed in the public streets.

It is, however, a common custom in China for people to transact their business in the open air ; indeed, in a country where at least two hundred millions of heads are daily shaved, it would be difficult to find sufficient shops for the barbers alone.   The crops mown from such a number of heads must, I should think, form heaps larger and more numerous than haystacks in England.   This hair is all bought up by the farmers, who use it as manure for their land.   The barber is one of the most prosperous tradesmen in China, except at the death of the emperor, when, as every man in the empire goes into mourning and keeps his head unshaven for three years, they starve for want of work. Let us, however, hope that in the days of prosperity many are prudent enough to provide against evil times.

Having silently prepared his implements and commenced operating, the worthy barber addressed his patient, saying, " Has his fragrant honor, the essence of gentility, heard the news — news that ought to wring the hearts of all the children of the Son of Heaven ? "

" Perhaps the accomplished head-shaver will pour this news into his customer's ear while performing his kindly offices," replied Hieul.

" Know, then, that our supreme parent, the most illustrious Ten Thousand Years, the Emperor, had two beautiful daughters, as delicate as the white lily, and as fragile as the youthful shoots of the bamboo; the one, the Princess Lah-loo, was the child of his empress; tho other, of a favorite wife, named La-see. Now, La-see, whom, since she is disgraced, I may call very artful, pressed her daughter into the notice of his majesty, and, moreover, took every opportunity of scandalizing the Princess Lah-loo, who was as learned and accomplished as a doctor of Han-lin.

" Now, both these young ladies had been devoting their time to the production of some beautiful needle-work, which was to be examined on a certain day by the emperor himself; previously, however, to the day of examination, La-see had, by much malice, endeavored to prejudice the mind of his majesty against the Princess Lah-loo ; and, moreover, by her cunning, managed to make it appear that the princess's beautiful work was that of her own daughter, and that the badly executed work of her own daughter was that of the Princess Lah-loo.

"Now, as the princess was a great favorite, the supreme mind of the emperor became so enraged at the sight of the bad work, that a devil got in his leg and made him kick it against the princess as she knelt to receive his blessing; and the blow from the majestic foot of the Son of Heaven fell so harshly on the royal lady's forehead, that she was removed from the celestial presence in a state of insensibility, and in less than two days afterwards journeyed to the yellow stream."

"The death of this royal princess, then, will rob my worthy friend of his trade, by plunging the empire in mourning," said Hieul.

"The flower of gentility speaks not correctly," returned the barber; "for the emperor has commanded that the circumstance should not be known; but your servant is happy to relate that the cheat of La-see was discovered, and she herself banished forever from the presence of the Son of Heaven."

After Hieul had been shaved to his satisfaction, and he had paid the barber, they went to the borders of one of the large lakes and saw the boat-racing. Not far from this lake were some high hills, upon which hundreds of men were flying kites: not the wee bits of paper or calico that are called kites in this country, but made of silk, and ingeniously contrived to resemble real birds, butterflies, fishes, flying-dragons, and other creatures, which are not only constructed so as to fly three or four times as high as any kite you ever saw, but by means of round poles, which are supplied with vibrating cords, made to hum like a top as they ascend through the air.

Lyu greatly enjoyed this kite-flying, for the players

caused them to fight each other in the air, in imitation
of the old English sport of hawking; the winner of
the game being he who brought down his opponent's
kite. Lyu was so delighted with this healthful and
amusing sport, that he determined to try his hand at
making one at his leisure — an example I should ad-
vise my young readers to follow.

It was a rare day's enjoyment; for one half the
people seemed bent on seeking amusement, while the
other half were equally anxious to amuse them.
There was every kind of sport, some very cruel —
such, for instance, as cricket-baiting. This being a
favorite game of Hieul's, he purchased a cricket from
a man who warranted the insect to be well trained for
fighting, and then challenged any person in the crowd
for half a tael to find another cricket that could beat
it. The challenge was soon accepted by another
cricket-baiter: challenger and challenged sat upon the
ground, and with the ends of their chopsticks irritated
the little creatures till they fought each other to death.

As this cruel sport is very common among the
Chinese, Hieul was not worse than his countrymen;
however, as he neither won nor lost, he determined
to try his hand at a gambling table; for, although he
had been so severely punished for gaming, he was too
weak-minded to resist the temptation; so Lyu was left
to wander about by himself.

His attention was first called to some conjurers who
were performing all kinds of wonderful feats, one of
which was to place a china basin upon a thin, flexible
ratan cane, and make it spin round upon its bottom
with immense rapidity, when he threw it in the air,

where it continued to spin, at times falling within a
foot of the ground; then rising again, it would dance,
curvet, and cross the circle, all to the tune of a drum
or gong, which was beaten the whole time. Then he
had a look at Pun-tse — our own Punch, as funny in
China as in England — and a circle of some dozen
people, who were playing with a shuttlecock, which the
players threw from one to the other by hitting the
shuttlecock with the sides of their feet, by which
means they kept it flying quite as long as you could
with a battledoor.

Then there were craniologists, who were delivering
lectures upon the good and bad qualities of the mind,
as exhibited by the state of the head, eyes, nose, and
forehead; fortune-tellers, who, for a few coppers, would
promise any person, silly enough to believe them, that
he would some day become a great mandarin; and a
host of tinkers, tailors, and shoemakers, carrying on
their trades in different spots around: there were den-
tists also, and quack doctors, and teachers of the game
of chess; indeed every possible means of extracting
money from the pockets of the holiday-folks, who, like
holiday-folks in other countries, require very little per-
suading to part with their money. However, the only
money spent by Lyu was in the purchase of a book
of historical stories from a wandering librarian, which,
as he was by this time very tired, he took to a retired
spot, and sat down on the grass to read.

He had not been seated many minutes before Hieul
came up, and, in a very surly manner, told him to follow. The truth was, Hieul had lost all his money by
gambling, and was very hungry, and, moreover, with-

out a copper coin with which to obtain refreshment it was therefore fortunate that Lyu had been more prudent. They had not many yards to go to find a restaurateur; and, as travelling eating-house keepers are not common in this country, I will describe this one. He was a tall, stout man, and carried his whole kitchen and shop balanced on his back, holding it with one hand, while with the other he teased the fire, crying aloud the splendid quality of his ready-made dishes. His whole apparatus was about nine feet long, made of bamboo wood, parted into different divisions; the one at top containing basins, dishes, plates, and chopsticks for those who did not happen to carry their own in their girdles; a lower division was filled with wood for the purpose of feeding the fire; immediately beneath this was the fireplace and kitchen, which consisted of an iron pan covered over by a wooden tub, and let into light plaster work upon the fire; so that he could boil, stew, or fry, according to the taste of his customer. In another division there were half-dressed dogs, cats, ducks, meat, vegetables, dried herbs, pepper, and salt.

Although not usual for persons of respectability to take their meals at these peripatetic dining rooms, Hieul and Lyu were too hungry to be particular; besides, it was holiday-time, and so they picked out a retired spot, and heartily regaled themselves; after which they went to see the grand procession which was expected to pass through the middle of the city.

When they came to the square of the Tribunal of Justice they found a crowd of people assembled around a large chair, something like a hencoop, with bars of bamboo, each bar being pierced from the outer side with a vast number of long nails, the points of which came through some three or four inches in length, giving to the interior a resemblance to the hoop of daggers through which equestrians leap at fairs. In the centre stood a half-naked man, in such a position that at each movement of the chair his flesh became pierced by the nails. The two coolies who carried it had just begun to walk when Lyu and Hieul came up; and as the nails pierced his flesh, and the blood began to flow in small streamlets, the foolish fellow made a merit of this self-torture, for he was a begging bonze, or priest, of Fo, and this was the means he adopted to obtain money; he was, moreover, good-looking and modest, and held his head down humbly as he cried, " Will not the children of Tien have compassion on a devoted bonze, who, for the good of their souls and those of their ancestors, was, in a dream, in the middle watch of last night, ordered by the God to take to this holy chair, and not leave it till every one of these thousand nails should be purchased at sixty tchen apiece. O, children of Tien, if you buy any of these sacred nails, which were forged by Fo himself from the souls of the wicked, the act will become a source of happiness in your houses, long life to yourselves, and, in addition, you will be performing an act of heroic virtue; for the alms that your priestly servant asks is not for himself, but for Fo, to whose honor it is designed to erect a temple."

After this address he appeared very melancholy and woe-begone, and began to roll round and round a string of beads which hung from his neck, and cry aloud, "O, mi, To, Fo — O, mi, To, Fo!" And such was the lamentable want of the light of Christianity in the hearts of these poor idolaters, that the copper tchens, sixty of which are equivalent to about sixpence of our money, soon poured in showers into the priest's chair, and for which he gave the nails in return.

Now, notwithstanding that Lyu was a mere boy, and moreover in the midst of a crowd of pagans, who, at the smallest imagined insult to their religion might have killed him on the spot, the spirit of the true and only God was in his heart, and the teachings of our Saviour in his mind, and gave him courage to rebuke the wicked bonze; so, going close to the cage, he said, "Will the bonze of the idol Fo permit the youngest of the one true God's children to speak to his heart? Give not thyself, O bonze! such useless torment in this world, for fear thou gettest greater in the next: leave that idolatrous and wicked cage, and come forth to the true temples of the God of the Christians, there to learn heavenly truths, and hereafter scatter them by thy eloquent breath, which, although poison in a bad, may prove blessed in a holy cause. Do this, and I will buy the whole of these nails if thou wilt build a temple of truth in thy own heart."

"A black dragon, a fan-kwei!" cried the enraged crowd as if with one voice, and pressing around Lyu, who bravely stood with his arms a-kimbo and one leg pressed firmly against a stone, frowning defiance at them; and they would have killed the boy had not the priest cried aloud, "Waste not thy breath; disfigure not the shape of thy dragon eyes upon this boy without a father, for truly, if he had one, he would have been better taught; the spirit of the fan-kwei is within him, for the purpose of trying my patience.' Then, as if nothing had happened, the bonze turned to Lyu with a hypocritical smile, and said, " I thank you, boy, for your advice, and doubt not you intended well; still, I shall be under greater obligation if you will purchase some of these nails. The act will help thee on thy journey, for, although you know it not, you are about to take a long one. Here," he added, turning on one side, " take *these* nails, good youth; which, upon the faith of a bonze, are the most holy in my chair, because they give me the most pain."

" Come, boy, buy, buy, buy !" raved the crowd: still Lyu frowned defiance at them; and Hieul, perceiving the people were becoming very angry, plucked Lyu's purse from his girdle, gave the bonze a handful of copper coins, and, at the same time, whispered something to the bonze which made the boy wonder how the two should be on such intimate terms with each other.

The bonze then passed on to another street, and Hieul and Lyu to see a play that was being performed at a large theatre in front of one of the public buildings.

LYU'S ADVICE TO THE BONZE.

Page 67.

CHAPTER VIII.

*"TO SPOIL WHAT IS GOOD BY UNSEASONABLENESS IS LIKE
LETTING OFF FIREWORKS IN RAIN."*

BY the time they came out of the theatre it had
become quite dark; there was little or no wind, and
as they were upon hilly ground, which sloped downwards through a long street and terminated with a
large lake, which was literally covered with boats,
they had a fine view of the illuminations.

The whole city was deluged with light and tinted
colors, the reflection of which on the dusky clouds
might have been likened to a rainbow partially enwrapped in a vast celestial mantle; the variegated
colors sparkled and played on the glittering yellow-
tiled house tops, as if myriads of glowworms and
will-o'-the-wisps had been at their gambols.

From roof to foundation the fantastic houses were
speckled with lighted lanterns of every possible shape
and hue, as if each householder had endeavored to
outshine his neighbor in costliness and ingenuity;
some of the lanterns were round, some square, others
oblong, but all more or less ornamented with moving
figures, either of huntsmen galloping after game, soldiers engaged with an enemy, ships in full sail, tigers,
lions, dragons, windmills turning, fishes swimming, or
monkeys dancing and swinging.

Across the streets, suspended from house to house,

were festoons of lanterns — the same with the triumphal arches; the boats on the lake were surrounded with thousands of floating lanterns; others of a smaller size were so arranged about the vessels as to seem to be crawling the decks, up the masts, and all over the rigging; thousands of men and boys in full dress, and ladies in masks, crowded the streets and squares, all swinging lanterns; many would every now and then stop to give expression to their delight; yet the greatest sight was to come, for the Son of Heaven, the emperor himself, who so rarely shows himself to his people, had promised to pass through the city, to give the signal for the commencement of a great display of fireworks.

Then was heard a great shouting, and a large body of mounted life guards in yellow uniforms, with steel helmets and gilt spears, the heads of which were wrought in the shape of tigers' heads, came prancing through the street, driving the people into the middle of the road, to make room for the imperial procession, which was just returning from the temple, and on its way to the field of fireworks. No sooner did these soldiers make their appearance than the crowd bowed, or made an effort to bow their foreheads to the ground, for they dared not look up while the emperor passed.

The life guards were followed by twenty-four drummers, and as many men with wooden trumpets a yard in length, and hung with golden bells; then twenty-four men with long staves of red and yellow, followed by two hundred soldiers, one half of whom carried halberds, and the other half red japanned maces, decorated with golden flowers; then hundreds of others, each carrying a lantern shaped like a lion, tiger, bird, or fish; these were accompanied side by side by as many more, with lighted torches, which looked like a forest of flaming trees in procession, with its wild beasts in a state of madness, and endeavoring to escape; then came a large body of soldiers with spears ornamented with tufts of rich silk or the tails of leopards and foxes; then came four and twenty banners, on which were painted in gold the signs of the Zodiac, followed by two hundred men, who held aloft, upon gold sticks, fans carved with birds and wild beasts; then followed twenty-four gorgeous umbrellas of yellow silk magnificently embroidered with gold, then four hundred life guards in yellow uniform, wearing the emperor's crest (a dragon) embroidered on their chests; after them, at a long distance, on a beautiful white steed, rode the Son of Heaven himself, magnificently dressed in an azure-colored silk dress, embroidered with dragons and decorated with costly jewels; but as the mighty potentate rode through the ranks of his people, he moved his celestial eyes neither to the right nor the left, for it would have been beneath his majesty; indeed, had he looked, it would have been of little use, as his trembling subjects were performing a series of double knocks on the ground with their foreheads; it was with the certainty that they would have been put to death, or at least severely bastinadoed, if they dared to look him in the face.

The supreme monarch of China, or "Ten Thousand Years," as his people call him, was supported on either side by a great lord of his court, who carried an immense umbrella, around which were ten white horses, without riders, but with harnesses sparkling with costly jewels.   Then came a large body of spearmen and the pages of the bed-chamber, who immediately preceded the lords of the yellow and red girdles, or princes of the blood; then the lords and great officers of the imperial court, attired in cloth of gold, so speckled with precious stones that each shone like a galaxy of stars in the heavens.   After the ministers of state rode five hundred gentlemen of the palace, attended by a thousand footmen in red gowns embroidered with flowers of gold and stars of glittering silver; these were again followed by thirty-six men, who carried the emperor's state chair.   The procession terminated with elephants drawing wagons, and a thousand civil and war mandarins in their robes of state.

Such is the magnificence with which the Emperor of China is compelled to go abroad on grand occasions; it is, therefore, scarcely to be wondered at that he so seldom dazzles the vision of his beloved black-haired race, as he delights to call them.   It would be as difficult for you to imagine as for me to describe the grandeur of this procession as it floated through the prism of light that then glorified the city of Pekin.

By the time this immense procession had passed Lyu had become thoroughly tired, which was little to be wondered at, as he had been kneeling with his forehead bent to the ground the whole time; so that he made up his mind to forget all about the fireworks and go straight home; but, to his vexation, on again reaching his legs, he missed Hieul, and this too in the midst of that great body of people, the greater portion of whom were very surly, for the " Light of the Empire,"

by causing them to kneel in such a vast crowd, had
made many of them extinguish the lanterns of which
they were so proud: however, he determined to force
his way through the streets and get home as soon as
possible.

He had not proceeded many yards when he met the
bonze he had seen that morning in the cage, and who,
to his surprise, spoke kindly to him; and, perceiving
he was faint and tired, invited him to drink from a
porcelain bottle he pulled from beneath his long black
gown; and, moreover, asked the boy to accompany
him to see the fireworks — an offer Lyu did not refuse,
especially as he felt so much refreshed after the beverage; and the sight well repaid him for his trouble.
They were fortunate enough to get near the raised
platform which stood in a lake of water, from which
they saw vast quantities of noble rockets thrown up
into the air; then immense globes, which, after revolv-
ing for some minutes, suddenly burst and shed showers
of variegated lights, out of which started birds, winged
horses, dragons, and other animals of blue, yellow,
green, and crimson, which flew about in chase of each
other, and in mimic rage spitting forth colored fires
changed into other animals, which again spit forth fire
in other shapes; then the trees in the gardens on one
side of the water became suddenly illuminated with
animals and insects of glowing fire that played about
the leaves and branches, from which again darted a
pale blue flame that instantaneously faded into darkness,
and threw out hundreds of bunches of grapes, that
hung from the branches and shone like myriads of
party-colored gems.

After some minutes the light was so suddenly ex
tinguished, that the audience, especially the ladies,
screamed with terror, and had scarcely recovered,
when, at the sound of a huge gong, an immense ser·
pent of colored fire arose on the water, and, as it
floated, gracefully curled its large body, which was
speckled with jets of tinted fire, into circles ; from its
eyes gushed a liquid flame of crimson, giving a terrible effect to its green, writhing body. From its mouth
flowed streams of blood-red flame, intermingled with
balls of blue fire, which, dropping into the water, became metamorphosed into little boats and ducks that
floated far and wide over the lake.

During the whole of the exhibition bands of in-
strumentalists played sometimes soft, sometimes harsh
music, causing the vast audience now to groan with
sadness, then to scream with delight and wonder.

When the fireworks terminated the bonze persuaded
Lyu to accompany him to a wine shop to obtain refreshment; and they walked a long distance, till they
got beyond the city walls, when, the bonze taking a
by-path, they soon came to a miserable cottage made
of bamboo poles, and roofed with matting of the same
material. This alarmed Lyu; but he had gone too
far to think of returning: his companion made a
slight sound on the door-gong, and a woman made her
appearance; but so old and vicious-looking, that she
made the boy tremble, brave as he was.

They were shown into a long, narrow, low-roofed
room, lighted by a single paper lantern, where there
were several tables, at each of which sat a group of
two or three men, whose shrivelled limbs, bony fingers, sallow face, squeaking voice, boiled-gooseberry

eyes, and unsteady gait, when they attempted to walk
across the room, made Lyu feel sick at heart. Each
of these men had a wine cup before him, and in his
mouth a large-bowled pipe that he appeared to smoke
with great relish, and a sensation of delight that every
now and then sent a spark of vivacity into his dull
eyes. At the sight of the priest they all arose and
performed several respectful bows, after which the
bonze sat with Lyu at a spare table, and ordered some
refreshment.

When Lyu had taken a glass of wine, it suddenly
occurred to him that he had done a very silly thing
in trusting himself with a stranger; but then he could
not well have done otherwise; however, in a few minutes he felt so comfortable that he forgot all about his
trouble. Then the smokers began to chat with him,
and he seemed to like them better; then the priest
pressed him to drink more wine, after which he
thought these emaciated-looking wretches really, upon
the whole, very jolly fellows. The bonze, too, became merry, and, by way of fun, caught hold of one
of the smokers' pipes, put it to Lyu's lips, and dared
him to smoke; when, like a great many other foolish
boys, not liking to be dared, he puffed away at the
pipe, and soon felt a delicious sensation of ease and
quiet creeping over him, so much so, that in a very
short time he paid no attention to any thing the bonze
said, but, feeling drowsy, laid his head on the table,
and went fast asleep: shall I say where? — in an
opium-smoking house, among the vilest and worst
characters in the great city of Pekin; where sellers
and smokers of that drug, if discovered, are punished
with death.

CHAPTER IX.

"TO CONTRIVE IS MAN'S PART; TO ACCOMPLISH IS HEAVEN's.

WHEN Lyu opened his eyes, all around was so dark that for some time he thought he must be dreaming and yet, although he soon made sure that he was wide awake, the darkness was so dense that he could not see his hand; his head felt dizzy and ached, and his arms and legs very sore, as if he had been beaten while asleep without knowing it. Then he endeavored to get up; but in the effort his head came violently in contact with some hard substance, that, what with fright and pain, he fell, covered with a cold sweat, where he lay for some time, wondering where he could be. He then tried to crawl out of bed, carefully putting one foot out first, which instantly touched the floor: this frightened him; for he then knew that he must be lying on the ground. Where then could he be, if not in his own bed? Again he tried to think; but as no light broke upon his mind, he crawled along the floor, and again struck his head against the side of the room, if room it was; but it was not; for he could touch both walls at the same time. After recovering from the second blow, his next attempt was to stand upright; but no sooner did he do so, than the house, room, or whatever it might be, gave a sudden jerk, and down he fell again. Trembling with surprise and fear, he then felt that he was being moved along, and the thought struck him that he must be in a wagon, travelling over rough ground, for the jolting had increased. Lyu was not the kind of boy to give way to fear; he therefore began to think, and, remembering that he had once been kidnapped, felt convinced that he must now be in a very similar predicament. Then his ideas became more lucid; and he thought of the Feast of Lanterns, the bonze, and the wine house, and no longer doubted that the priest was at the bottom of the mischief.

The room gave a sudden and greater jolt, and a glimmer of light played a few feet before him, perceiving which he crawled gently towards it, and felt some rough cloth, which gave way to his hand, and, by means of the stream of light which flowed through, he saw that he was in a covered cart, and felt sure he had been kidnapped; however, cautiously peeping through the aperture, his fears became verified; for there, on a mule harnessed to the cart, sat the bonze, rolling his beads and muttering his pagan prayers.

Lyu determined, if possible, to make his escape at once, and, retreating to the back of the cart, tried the awning. It gave way to his hand; but to make an opening sufficiently large to pass through was no easy matter. A little patience and perseverance, however, and he managed to drop from the cart without the knowledge of the bonze, who still went slowly onwards.

But no sooner did he touch the ground than his knees bent under him; they were too weak to support him, and he fell. On looking around, what was his horror to find that he was in a strange, wild, mountainous country, far from any human habitation! and he discovered that the jolting had been occasioned by the ascent of a rugged mountain, up which they had been travelling.

The wind was biting and bleak, the clouds black and angry, foreboding a fearful storm; there, in the far distance, he could perceive the fortified towers of the Great Wall of China.

This wall, which is one of the wonders of the world, was built more than two thousand years ago, by the Emperor Chi-hoang-ti, to keep out the hordes of wild Tartars who were continually endeavoring to conquer the country. It is the most ancient monument of human labor in the world, except the Pyramids of Egypt; it is 1500 miles long, and built over the highest mountains, through the deepest valleys, and across the widest rivers; it is wide enough to allow six horsemen to ride abreast on its summit without touching each other. At regular distances it is supported by strong fortified stone towers: when carried over steep rocks, where no horse can pass, it is about fifteen or twenty feet high; but when running through a valley or crossing a river, not more than thirty.

You will better understand the immensity and wonder of this work when I tell you that a calculation has been made that it contains more than sufficient bricks and other building materials to erect all the dwelling houses in England and Scotland, and this without calculating the materials in the towers which support it, and which alone would be sufficient to erect a city as large as London, great as it is. It has been further estimated, that, if the materials of this great wall were converted into another wall of twelve feet high and four feet thick, it would be long enough to surround the whole globe; but what is perhaps the most wonderful is, that it was begun and finished in five years.

Now, notwithstanding that the Emperor Chi-hoang-ti (who, as his name expresses, was the first sovereign of all China) could do what, very fortunately, no king can do nowadays, compel millions of people to work like slaves without other pay than their mere food, he must still have been a great man to plan and execute so vast an undertaking; yet, great as he was in some things, he was very contemptible in others; he was vain and ambitious, and wished not only to make his name immortal, but to be handed down to posterity as the founder of the Chinese empire; and the only obstacle to this foolish and wicked wish being the existence of some millions of books containing the histories of the emperors who had reigned before him, like the Caliph Omar, he ordered every book in the empire to be publicly burned; and so strictly was this order carried out, that vast numbers of learned men and book-writers, who valued those records more than their lives, were put to death for endeavoring to save them from the flames.

It is, however, to be regretted that the Caliph Omar, who, by burning the great library of Alexandria, shut out so much knowledge from posterity, did not as signally fail in his object as the great Chinese tyrant, who, notwithstanding all his power and cruelty, could not prevent people from hiding a vast number of copies of different great authors under

the floors, and in secret places, where they remained
till he had himself been burned in the funeral urn, as
his memory also ought to have been.

Notwithstanding the terrible situation in which
Lyu was placed, weak, ill, and alone, in the midst of a
mountainous country, a storm impending, and starvation staring him in the face, he felt joyful at having
outwitted the bonze, who kept slowly on, guiding the
mule round a ledge of the mountains. When the
cart disappeared, he made an effort to stand, but finding himself too weak, he was obliged to crawl on hands
and knees, and, although they bled from contact with
the rocky ground, he kept crawling till he reached the
entrance of a long, narrow cavern in the mountain,
through which he could perceive a glimmer of light.
as if from the other end.

No sooner had he entered the cavern than the
clouds darkened, the short grass around stood bristling
with the wind, which now blew a hurricane, and to
protect himself from the cold he crawled farther into
the cavern to save himself from the hailstones, which
in that part of China are frequently large enough to
strike a man to the earth; but O! the wind, as it
whirled through the cavern with a low, muffled roar,
like the bellowing of a herd of bulls, and burst out at
the other opening, with the explosion of a volcano, as
if with savage joy at its escape, cut the poor boy to
the very soul, made his teeth chatter, limbs tremble,
eyes burn, and benumbed his whole body; still he
was undaunted, and crawled onwards, when, O joy!
he fancied he could distinguish the sound of something
human, and he shouted as loudly as his weak voice

would permit; the shout rang through the cavern, and lasted so long that he fancied it laughed at him; but hope was in his heart, and he kept onwards till he heard — yes, really heard — the trampling of feet, and in the darkness could just make out the form of a man. This gave him strength; he stood upon his legs; a minute more, the man clutched him by the arm, and Lyu became frantic with joy at the relief. But, alas, poor Lyu! the man spoke: the voice made his heart sicken, for it was the bonze. To be again in his power — it was too much for the boy, weak as he was; and he fell senseless to the ground.

When he recovered he found himself in a small cave in the rock by the side of a blazing fire: the bonze was standing by his side attentively watching him. Lyu shuddered. "My mother, my home, my good father! where am I?" said he, pitifully.

"Think not of them, young Dragon, but take this," said the bonze, pouring some spirit down his throat; then warming some rice over the fire, he gave Lyu a hearty meal, after which, feeling refreshed, he said, "Tell me, O bonze! in what can a poor boy have harmed you, that you should steal him from his home and friends?"

"Know, then," said the bonze, "that henceforth thou hast no father, mother, nought but me, who, however, will be a parent to thee, or otherwise, according to thy merits."

"I will die first, wicked priest," said Lyu.

"Tut, ungrateful! thy new father has saved thy life, and will that of thy mother also, from the wrath of the justly incensed Son of Heaven. Art th-

of the accursed Miao-tse, each of whose heads is
valued at fifty taels?   What should prevent my gain-
ing the silver?" said the bonze.

"Then betray me at once, wicked priest, for I will
be no son of thine," said Lyu.

"It is not thy destiny, my son: thou art reserved
for the service of the living Buddha, of whose temple
thy father is a humble slave, as even thou art mine."

"Thy slave, priest?" said Lyu, with horror.

"It is so destined, boy; but let thy tongue be silent
and the porches of thine ears open, and I will tell thee
all," said the priest, continuing.   "First know how it
happened that thou art here. Hieul has long been
my friend and brother, and in his troubles he told
me that, being many years younger than his brother
Tchin, he had every right to expect to inherit his
money, and that of this he was certain, till Tchin returned home, bringing with him yourself and your
mother as his own children. From the moment that
you entered the house, Hieul determined but to wait
for a fortunate day to effect thy ruin; that day arrived
when the silly Sang, in a fit of temper which bespoke
her to be no civilized daughter of the central land,
poured into the listening ears of Chang that you were
of the accursed Miao-tse. Hieul had but to whisper
this into the ears of the nearest mandarin, and your
heads would have rolled on the ground like worthless
gourds: this, however, would have removed the roof
from Tchin's house, and perhaps have drawn upon
Hieul the black waters of despair, which always
deluge the habitations of the harborers of rebels; he
therefore sought the counsel of the police mandarin

Ki-lo, who trembled at the danger in which his friend Tchin stood, and sent him away, when he applied to me for advice. I became plunged in contemplation and the gods poured their counsel into my unworthy ears, saying, 'The boy Lyu must renounce the faith of the barbarians, and become the servant of Fo.'"

"Never, wicked bonze!" said Lyu.

"The lamb has no choice when in the claws of the wolf; attempt to escape from me, and Tchin and your mother, undutiful son, shall be immolated at the shrine of the emperor's wrath."

"No, no — kill me, if you will, but not my mother, not my good father Tchin," replied Lyu, despairingly.

"Then listen, boy; I had promised the Grand Lama of Kounboum to procure a boy, of fair looks, who might prove an ornament to the priesthood of sacred Buddha, and therefore agreed to purchase you of my brother Hieul."

"This is not true, priest: Hieul would not listen to the wronging of Lyu Payo, who has been so affectionate and kind to him."

"My words are those of truth, son; Hieul sold you to me, and received the taels."

"Wretched Hieul!" exclaimed Lyu, bitterly.

"Be not ungrateful, my son, for what Hieul did, he did to save the life of Tchin; as for Sang, she will be sold at the first opportunity to some travelling merchant who may be looking out for a wife."

"Never, priest! my mother still believes my father to be alive."

"Wher I had agreed with Hieul I followed you about at the Feast of Lanterns, took you into the opium shop, gave you a powerful sleeping potion, and removed you the same night. It is four days since, and you are a hundred miles from the city of Pekin, and many months' journey from the holy Lamasery of Kounboum, to where we proceed. Follow me, and you shall yet again see your mother; attempt to escape, and I have but to show the wolf-dog to the first passing Tartar or Chinese to have him sent in a cage to Pekin."

"Then do so at once, vile priest, for I would die a thousand times rather than be thy slave."

"And suffer your mother and Tchin to be placed in an iron cage, or pounded to death in a mortar?" said the priest.

"No, no—all but that," shrieked Lyu; adding, "will nothing else satisfy you but my desertion of the only true God?"

"Nothing, son," said the priest, sternly.

"Then I *will* die, priest," said Lyu, determinedly.

"And sacrifice thy mother, undutiful son?" added the bonze.

"Even so, priest; any thing but desert my God, and so be unworthy of either my mother or my father's noble race."

"Said I not that thou wert a young Dragon boy? Well, all the better. What if I let thee follow thy own faith, leaving it to Fo to alter thy heart?" said the priest.

"And save my mother and the good Tchin?" said Lyu.

"Yes, if thou wilt follow me for four years," said the bonze.

"Let me think, father," returned Lyu; and he rested his head upon his hand, and pondered deeply. If his mother were sacrificed by any selfishness of his? but he dared not think of that—a life of slavery would be preferable; and he said,—

"Priest, if you do not attempt to force me to thy stupid idol, I will follow thee for four years, on the word of a Miao-tse, who is too brave to lie, even to save his life."

"I believe you, my son; it is but reasonable: we will now burn incense," replied the priest.

"I believe not in such wickedness," said Lyu.

"Silence, boy! interrupt not my devotions," said the priest. Pouring some incense into a small tin vessel, he then knelt down, counting his beads, and watched, without speaking, for at least an hour.

That night Lyu slept with the conviction that he had done his duty; but the excitement, the drugs that he had swallowed in the wine, and the weak state of his body, threw him into a fever; and for many, many days, he lay in that cave, hovering between life and death. The bonze tended him night and day, giving him to eat and to drink. The medicine he made from the ginseng-root, which he bought from some wandering Tartars.

The fire he kept alive by means of argols, (a kind of dried dung,) which he gathered from the mountain-side; and, when Lyu grew strong enough to eat animal food, the bonze would take his bow and arrow and go in search of a yellow goat or wild mule, and, after preparing it with all the skill of a butcher, roast it over the argol fire. All this care and attention was very extraordinary on the part of a man who had behaved so vilely to Lyu; but then God always plants some good feelings in the very worst of bosoms.

At length Lyu regained his strength, and the bonze told him. he was about to test the value of his word: that his watching had rendered him unfit to proceed on their journey without a long rest, during which time he begged of the boy to keep a good lookout for any rambling thieves who might attempt to steal the mule.

Then, after partaking of a hearty meal of goat's flesh and a draught of the same liquor he had given to Lyu, he fell into a deep sleep.   For hours Lyu watched his now helpless enemy, and, but for his pledged word, might have effected his escape; when, however, the argols had burned out, it became very dark, and, to keep himself awake, he crept towards the mouth of the cave, but stumbled against something on the floor, and, putting forth his hand, it lighted upon the Book of History he had purchased at the Feast of Lanterns, and his heart leaped with joy.

Now, if he had but a light, the time would pass away merrily, but he knew not how to obtain one; so, with the book in his hand, he went out of the cave. There again it was pitch-dark; there was no moon, no stars, nothing but the moaning and rustling of the in-visible winds, and the howling of distant wolves, who, for all he knew, might be dangerously near, which alarmed him for the safety of the mule, whose snorting might attract their attention.

At this moment he saw something which glittered and shone like a star; as he went nearer and nearer the glittering became more distinct.   He stooped to examine it. Joy! joy! he had found a glowworm. What a capital lamp it would make, he thought; so, taking it into the cave, he laid his book open upon the floor, and, by placing the insect upon the top of the page, he could distinctly read. So, laying himself at full length on the floor, he amused himself with a story headed, "Hope *for the unfortunate and lowly.*"

"That people, however lowly or unfortunate, may learn patience and take encouragement from the wonderful histories of the two great emperors Tait-song and Tait-sou."

"In the reign of the last emperor of the Tsin family, there was born, in the city of Nankin, a poor boy, named Lieou-yu; his parents died and left him an orphan, and, but for the care of an old woman, who took compassion on him, and brought him up as her own son, he must soon have died from want and starvation. As soon as Lieou-yu was old enough, he learned to make shoes; and if the people he made them for had only known what was in store for him, the proudest of his customers would have been glad to have made shoes for Lieou-yu; however, he was so idle and careless, that all who knew him said that he would come to no good, little thinking, at the same time, that they were speaking so irreverently of the future Emperor of China. For a long time the boy earned his miserable living by selling shoes about the streets, without concerning himself much about his condition in life; until he happened to attract the notice of a military officer, who had stopped him to make a purchase, and, being pleased with his replies to some questions he had asked him, proposed that he should become a soldier. As fighting was an occupation better suited to his taste than shoemaking, Lieou-yu at once accepted the offer; and, having been introduced into this new scene of action, he displayed so much courage and ability, that he was promoted till he became chief commander of the forces; and in that capacity rendered such important services to the emperor during a serious rebellion, that he was elevated to the rank of chief minister of state. By this time he had become very ambitious, and, like all ambitious people, was not content to stop at any point while there was a higher one to attain; and therefore took advantage of the prevailing disaffection towards the reigning family, and, having made himself exceedingly popular, seized a favorable opportunity of aspiring openly to the throne; and, by the aid of a powerful party, compelled the emperor to abdicate in his favor. Such was the remarkable career of Lieou-yu, who was proclaimed emperor in the year 420, by the name of Outi, and was the first sovereign of a dynasty, or family, called 'Song;' and thus was the empire taken away from the native princes, and was again returned to them in a similar manner, as shown by the history of the boy 'Choo.'

"There was a poor laborer in Nankin who had a son named Choo — a lad whose constitution was so delicate that he was quite unfit for hard work. His father, therefore, placed him in one of the monasteries to be brought up by the bonzes, with a view to his becoming a member of that order. Choo, however had no taste for so inactive a life; and, growing stronger as his years increased, he enlisted as a common soldier in the imperial army, and distinguished himself so much by his great bravery and talents, that he was promoted, step by step, till he reached a very high rank, when he married a lady of great fortune and influence, whose family was among those who wished to overthrow the Tartar government. Choo soon imbibed the same notions, and was made general-in-chief of the patriots; and, as soon as it was known that the famous General Choo was at the head of the insurgents, thousands of people joined his army, who then marched to Pekin, drove the Emperor Shunty from the throne, and proclaimed Choo Emperor of China by the title of Tait-sou in 1366; and this was the commencement of the Ming dynasty, which was again overthrown about three hundred years afterwards by the present reigning family. 'So was it,' continued the historian, 'that these two poor humble boys, by not repining at their position in life, but by patience, good conduct, bravery, and seizing opportunities when they occurred, became Emperors of China.'"

Lyu was greatly interested in these two stories; they consoled him under his misfortune; "for, no doubt," thought he, "Heaven has great good in store for me if I endeavor to deserve it; indeed, who knows but that some day I may find my mother's people, the brave Miao-tse? who even now may be waiting for some great leader to rise up, and show them how to drive these Tartars out of the country again, like the great Tait-sou." So, building castles in the air, he watched through the night, sometimes dozing, sometimes reading, but never going quite off to sleep, for he had too much honesty and resolution to break his plighted word even to an enemy.

CHAPTER X.

"LOOKERS-ON MAY BE BETTER JUDGES OF THE GAME THAN
THE PLAYERS."

REFRESHED by his long sleep, and pleased with
Lyu's watchfulness, the bonze began to prepare for
the journey; the mule was harnessed to the cart, the
various little things packed, and they proceeded slowly
along the ridges of the mountains, till towards evening, when they entered upon a wild prairie, and were
highly pleased to perceive an encampment of wandering Tartars. This consisted of six large huts,
each of which was about seven feet high, and shaped
like a sugar-loaf, the frame being formed of wooden
trellis-work of crossed bars, and made to fold up and
expand like an angler's portable seat.

This wood-work was covered with strong, coarse
linen, the door was low and narrow, and a beam placed
across at the bottom to form a threshold, which took
so much space from the small opening, that, in passing
in and out, the Tartars were obliged both to raise their
feet and bend their necks. The chimney consisted simply of a hole in the roof. The scene, though simple,
was amusing to Lyu, who had never before seen one of
these portable villages. For a great distance around,
sheep, cows, goats, and camels were grazing, attended
by boys and women; there were also a great many
large watch-dogs, which barked at the approach of the

travellers. The noise of these animals aroused the attention of the Tartars, who no sooner saw the bonze, than, with all the good-heartedness of their simple-minded race, they prayed him to accept their hospitality, and, leading them into one of the largest of the huts, placed before them a good meal of roast mutton and tea, which I need not tell you they greatly enjoyed after their day's journey. The interior of the hut was divided into two equal portions, the left for the men, and the right for the women of the family. In the middle stood a trivet, ready to receive a great iron caldron that stood at hand. On the opposite side, facing the door, was a small sofa with two pillows, ornamented with plates of gilt copper; several small stools were arranged about the room, and against the side of the hut a chest that served as an altar for a copper image of the god Buddha; this queer little divinity had a silk scarf round his neck, and was sitting cross-legged, with nine vases, made of the same metal, before him, ready to receive the rather earth-like, than god-like, offerings of water, milk, butter, and meat, which the Tartars make daily to his copper god-ship, whose little pagod was rendered complete by a small library of six or seven of his sacred books, each of which was carefully enveloped in a wrapper of yellow satin, and laid before him. The walls of the hut were hung about with goats' horns, which served as hooks for beef, mutton, and vessels contain-ing butter, bows, arrows, and matchlocks.

Such was the habitation in which Lyu and the priest that night took up their lodging by the side of a roaring fire. At daybreak they were awakened by the barking of the dogs and the voices of men and women apparently in anger, and, on going outside, found that, in consequence of some of the cattle having disappeared during the night, the best horsemen of the tribe were preparing to mount their horses, but in a terrible state of doubt as to where or what part of the country they should scamper in search of them.

When the bonze made his appearance, the Tartars bowed their heads to the ground, and cried, "O, holy man of prayer! the children of the plains received thee hospitably, giving to thee and the little priest the best of their tents wherein to rest thy wearied limbs, and the choicest meats and tea wherewith to appease thy hunger and thirst; but now they are in trouble and seek thy aid. While they slept the dogs ceased to watch, and the animals have been driven or strayed the gods only know whither. The children of the plains therefore seek of thee, whose knowledge of hidden things must be beyond all limit, to direct them where to search for the animals."

This was a windfall for the artful bonze, who saw a means of practising on the simplicity of these nomads to his advantage; he bade them rise and collect eleven dried sheep's droppings, which he arranged in a line, and, seating himself on a mound of earth, muttered some mysterious words; he then placed them in rows, counted them over and over again, and then rear-ranged them in threes, and sat for some minutes in deep contemplation; after which he rolled his beads over, arose, and, shaking his head, said, " Alas! my good children, there must have been some wickedness in thy tent, for the gods have failed to assist my divinations." The Tartars uttered cries of disappoint-ment, and again prostrated themselves on the ground, craving his intercession with the gods.

As the wily priest intended to make the most of the favor, he was some time before he acceded to the second application; however, when he did, the people arose, the horsemen ran to their horses, and stood bridle in hand, in readiness to act upon receipt of the first intelligence from the gods. He then procured a few bricks of tea, packets of rice, and butter, which he took into the tent to offer to the little copper god. A full hour elapsed before he came out again, with slow and solemn steps, and said, " The anger of the god is appeased; my children's cattle will be found one hour's ride to the west."

A fact the Tartars might have divined for them-selves, if it had occurred to them that to the west of their tents a plentiful crop of luxuriant grass was to be found, and to which in all probability the animals had been led by their keen scent. The instant the words escaped the priest's lips the horsemen sprang into their saddles, and, by returning with the truant animals in much less than the specified time, proved that the bonze had made a good guess.

As the bonze determined to beat out the favor to the extent of its limit, during the absence of the horsemen he continued to mumble some mysterious words before the funny little cross-legged god; and when the caval-cade returned and found him still at his devotions, the simpletons gave a series of double knocks on the ground with their foreheads, thanked him for restoring the cattle, and begged of him to name his own reward.

As to get them to this point had been his object, the bonze drew a long face, and pointed out to his affectionate children the impossibility of journeying through deserts and mountains with a mere mule-cart, and told them that, as they were rich in flocks and herds, they could not better please the god Fo than by contributing a camel to his priest's necessities. The people made wry faces at this, (for camels are valuable animals,) but so satisfactorily did he show them the benefits they would ultimately obtain from heaven for aiding a priest who was on such good terms with the lord of their pagan heaven, that the Tartars not only gave him a camel, but a store of salted mutton, goat's flesh, tea, milk, and rice-cakes.

Having thus artfully supplied his wants for some time to come, the bonze blessed the encampment and prepared to depart. The camel was brought forward, holes pierced through its nostrils for the guiding-reins, — an operation that caused the poor creature to roar lustily, — and made to kneel upon his fore-legs, when the bonze mounted, telling Lyu to take the mule-cart; and, as he was obeying, a Tartar boy ran up to him with a bow and a quantity of steel-headed arrows, saying, " Will the little bonze accept this gift from his younger brother, that it may serve as a mark of the Tartar boy's friendship, and protect him against the wolves?"

As Lyu was really a very good shot with an arrow, I need not tell you how joyfully he thanked the warm-hearted boy for the present.

For many days they travelled, without meeting a human being, through a wild, mountainous country;

at night they took shelter in caves or under the shelving edges of rocks, the one sleeping while the other watched with bow and arrow in hand, and kept alive the blazing fire, for the twofold purpose of warming them and keeping off the wolves.

Although wild and desolate, the land was typical of the history of nations, for in the midst of these mountainous regions, now abandoned to the elements and wild beasts, they would every now and then approach the partly buried signs of a former civilization in the shape of remnants of stone towers and implements of both peace and war, all of which proved to them that they were treading on the ashes of a past and long-forgotten fortified city.

It was in one of these ruined towers that they one night sought rest and shelter; it was a melancholy place, wild and miserable, like the country around, yet grand in its very desolation; and though once the castle of a great chieftain, then serving only as a secret and occasional haunt for some of the robbers so numerous in the wild districts of the empire. The lower portion was so ruinous that it seemed scarcely capable of supporting the cavernous-looking upper rooms.

As the lower rooms were covered with muddy, stagnant water, in which rats and reptiles had taken up their abode, they were compelled to seek shelter in the upper; but then the staircase or steps had disappeared entirely — a misfortune the bonze and Lyu remedied as follows: As soon as they had provided for the comfort of their animals, by placing them in a small outbuilding, they found some large stones, which they placed one on the other till the pile was sufficiently high for them to clamber up, when they found themselves in a large, stone room, lighted by two loopholes; at one end there was a narrow stone staircase, which led to a chamber above. The walls were so damp that the interstices between the stones were filled with dark, slimy moss, in which were crawling and writhing, toads, snakes, and long worms — a sight that made them shudder; however, as their first object was to make a fire, the bonze again descended, but soon returned with a quantity of dried grass, by means of which they kindled a fire.

7

CHAPTER XI.

THE blaze and smoke made the snakes, worms, and other creatures curl and creep towards the loopholes, through which they endeavored to make their escape with the greatest possible speed. When they had dislodged the greater part of this vermin and made the place tolerably comfortable, they brewed some hot tea; but had scarcely sat down on the floor when they heard a moaning noise above them; and the bonze, who, although a rogue, was no coward, ran up the narrow staircase, followed by Lyu, into the upper room, where, to their surprise, they saw a man sleeping by the embers of a nearly extinguished fire; but so savage a being Lyu had never before seen. He appeared to be about six feet in height, but unequally distributed, the greater part being disposed of in the formation of a pair of long, large-boned legs; the chief portion of his trunk was taken up by a pair of immense shoulders, from which, at the top of a tall, chimney-like neck, shot out a small, round head. From his shoulders nature had hung two tediously long bones terminating in hands large and strong enough to grapple with a Titan. So far he had the appearance of a great pair of tongs in a man's skin: like his face, his knob-shaped head was covered with lon~~g~~, red hair, as shaggy as the coat of a Skye-terrier, and fell over his forehead and slate-colored eyes like a cluster of moss over a ruined wall.

The moment they entered the room, this savage-looking object awoke, and, perceiving the two travellers, sprang at the bonze, who, fortunately, was quick enough to catch hold of him by the arms. "Would my brother fall like a beast of prey upon a man of prayer?" said the latter.

"The words of the bonze are good; what dust was in thy servant's eyes that he could 'not see a man of prayer who sought not to harm him? but he is poor, and without a brick of tea or an ounce of flesh to offer," said the man.

"Will my brother join us? the teapot is still on the fire in the lower room," said the bonze.

"Thy servant is grateful, holy bonze, and will humble himself to the dust for mistaking thee for a soldier of the terrible queen, whom the fiends burn!"

But still suspicious as to the stranger's real character, the bonze made him proceed before them to the lower room. When the man saw the blazing fire and smelt the aroma of the tea and rice-cakes, his eyes glistened with anticipation, and he said, "Thanks be to Fo, the sight is agreeable, for thy servant has not tasted food this moon, and has been hiding like a deer from the hounds: truly, it is a vile affair to be hungered." When he had satisfied the ravenous craving of his appetite, he said, "Did the holy bonze mistake his worthless servant for a wild beast or a thief, that he clutched so tightly?"

"Nay, brother; it was for fear that thou mightest mistake me for an enemy," replied the bonze.

" Truly, it was so, for thy servant has many ene
mies; but would the holy bonze open his ears to his
story ? "

" Nothing could better please us, brother," replied
the bonze. .

At this reply the man, becoming more familiar in
his style, said, " Know, then, that I was born in Leao-
tung; my respected father was raised to the rank of
a mandarin of a city of the second order for his great
skill in the sciences, and enjoyed the honor and emol-
uments springing therefrom, till, from the dishonesty
of one of the clerks, a deficiency happened in the
accounts of his office, when the viceroy of the province cut the button from his cap, and sent him into
confinement. This cruel and unjust usage, as my
friends may suppose, utterly ruined our family, and
left me no resource but to join the imperial ginseng-
gatherers."

" Will the son of the mandarin pardon me for ask-
ing him the particulars of this wonderful ginseng, of
which I have heard so much ? " said Lyu.

" Know, then, my young brother, that this pure
spirit of the earth is a plant with a white, knotty
root about as thick as one's little finger, and grows in
the shape of a fork; the branches are green, and it
produces red berries. So rare is this plant, that it is
to be found only in the mountains of Leao-tung; and
as it is a certain cure for every known disease, and
not only tends to prolong the age of man, but is, at
the same time, a provocation of sound health, it is
used by all the physicians and great men in the empire, which makes the plant so valuable that the Son

of Heaven has seized upon it as a profit for himself and his Tartars; ten thousand of whom he permits every year, in the season, to gather it, paying them weight for weight in pure silver, on condition they each first give *him* two ounces for the permission to gather it; so great is the revenue that he derives from this plant. When the army of ginseng-gatherers go to search for it, in order that no Chinese may intrude or trespass upon their privilege, they encompass the whole province with palisades, under the charge of a guard of soldiers, and if they catch any prowling Chinese they imprison him for years."

"Truly it must be a wonderful plant, and China a happy nation to alone possess it!" said Lyu.

"Ay, my son, such has long been the belief of the Celestial people; but of late years it has been found by a people who have no emperor, in a country they call America, and brought to the trading city of Canton, on the sea-coast, in large quantities. But to proceed with my own history. Being of Tartar blood, I obtained permission to join the gatherers, among whom I proved one of the most successful; for I had completed a thorough scientific education under my learned father, and also, to my curse, I learned the art of detecting the presence of gold in the earth — a talent that was soon called into use, as you will find.

"One evening, after my day's work, on the very borders of the province, my love of botanical discovery led me beyond the palisades. These once passed, I strolled through the mountain, and soon met a large number of men — outlaws from debt and ruined tradesmen — proceeding into the kingdom of Ouinot, where it had long been reported that gold was to be found in large quantities hidden beneath the surface of the mountains; finding this to be the case, I laughed, and told them that no man knew better than myself where gold could be found, but that it was not in Ouinot. However, this only made them the more determined to keep me with them; so after a long and painful journey, on which my companions (who, like most gold-diggers, were of the worst and most abandoned classes) supported themselves by robbery, we arrived in the wildest regions of Ouinot, where, leaving the others to search for themselves, I examined the earth at particular spots, and, greatly to my surprise, found not only signs of gold, but the ore itself; still I would not tell my companions, who, not being able to discover a single grain, departed; but, securing a specimen within my vest, I returned to Leao-tung, and made my secret known to a few friends and neighbors. I might as well have told the whole empire, for in a very short time my secret floated wherever the winds rustled among greedy men.

"The whole province became mad with lust for the metal, and expedition after expedition started for Ouinot, which very soon swarmed with thousands and thousands of diggers, who, under my directions, riddled the mountain like a sieve. But, alas! when was it in the history of man that murder did not tread upon the heels of gold-love? Still, although the country abounded with the metal, it was but the few who succeeded in finding it; among the latter was myself. Those who were unsuccessful soon tired of digging, and commenced to plunder the whole surrounding neighborhood, sparing neither men, women, nor children.   So alarming did this state of things become, that a large body of soldiers were sent against us, but we were too strong for them; even the king himself trembled on his throne at our power and numbers, for success had made us bold; and moreover, our numbers had received considerable additions from robbers, outlaws, priests, and discharged soldiers from all parts of the empire; and but for one circumstance, I believe that this new nation of diggers would, in a short time, have become powerful enough to have subdued the whole empire: that one circumstance was as follows:—

"The queen had to pass near the mines on her annual pilgrimage to the tombs of her ancestors; the miners gathered together and beat and killed her guard of soldiers, robbed her majesty of all she possessed, and then let her depart with a few attendants.   This was our crowning crime; for on her return she so taunted the king with his cowardice for permitting the kingdom to be so overrun with robbers, that he sought and obtained the assistance of a neighboring king, and marched with a large army against us.   We met the royal armies; and, as there were twelve thousand of us, we boldly fought them for three days; the royal troops, however, proved too strong, and we were beaten. Not content with beating us, the Tartar horsemen rode mowing us down like long grass, till they had slain the greater part; large numbers of others they drove into mines and caves, fastened up the entrances with stones, and left them to destroy each other or die of starvation and thirst; some others escaped, but were soon re taken and had their eyes put out.   How I escaped know not, but here I have been for the past moon, with foul water for my drink and roots for my food."

"Thy case is indeed a hard one, my son," said the priest; "still it is the result of thy own folly, and therefore the gods may not be held accountable. But it is even now time that we sought repose."

"Then let the holy bonze seek repose, and his grateful servant will show his gratitude by keeping watch till the morning." And feeling secure in the gratitude of the miner, the bonze and Lyu lay down upon their mats and fell fast asleep. In the morning Lyu was awakened by the bonze shaking his arm, and crying, "Awake, my son: the false dog has deceived us; he is gone, and doubtless not without robbing us of our goods or our animals." On descending to the lower room this surmise was found correct, for the mule had been taken by the miner, not, however, without first politely writing on the camel's side with a piece of chalkstone, — "Thanks, holy bonze! thou hast saved the life of an unfortunate miner, — he repays you with ingratitude; he borrows thy mule but for a time; rest assured it shall be returned to thee ere long, with more than the interest of a loan-shop."

The bonze, being terribly enraged at the theft, cried aloud, "O, Fo, Fo! may the ghosts of his ancestors kick him out of their tomb when he goes to join them! But come, my son, Fo will repay us for our sufferings." Then, after taking some hot tea and rice-cakes, they both mounted the camel and proceeded on their journey.

CHAPTER XII.

"AN IGNORANT DOCTOR IS NO BETTER THAN A MURDERER.

BY nightfall they came to the skirts of the great imperial forest, where the early Tartar emperors spent so much of their time in hunting, but which is now abandoned to game and beasts of prey. As they entered the thick brushwood, a herd of startled deer scampered across their path, and they could hear the roar of tigers and the howling of wolves; Lyu's heart quavered a little at the sound; for paper tigers in books are a very different sort of a thing from the genuine article in its native regions: as for the bonze, he had travelled too frequently through such wild regions to fear sleeping even amidst the greatest dangers.

When they had ridden about five miles through the forest, they came to two high trees which stood about seven feet apart and in the middle of a wide, open space. At this spot they halted for the night; and, having secured the camel in a copse at some little distance, where the animal would be likely to be safe from the wild beasts, the bonze took from his pack a large piece of bamboo matting, and, making a number of holes, he ran a stout piece of cord along each edge; then, taking one end of the matting, he ascended about eight feet up one of the trees, and fas tened it to two branches, and, by doing the same up the opposite tree, he succeeded in slinging a capital hammock.

While the bonze had been preparing the bed, Lyu had collected a quantity of dried grass, brushwood, and dung, and spread it in a large circle around the trees. When these arrangements were completed they set fire to the fuel, which blazed to a great height, and must have been seen at a vast distance. Then, after a good meal of hot tea and cakes, Lyu clambered into the hammock, leaving the bonze to take the first watch.

Notwithstanding the novelty of his situation, which was something like a fowl in a camp-kettle suspended over a blazing fire, Lyu slept so soundly that the bonze had some difficulty in arousing him to take his turn of the watch. When he turned out of the hammock the bonze took his place, and Lyu sat down in the centre of the fire-circle, with his bow in his hand, and an arrow fixed ready for use; after some time the cosy warmth, the stillness around, and a long train of thought about home and friends, caused him to forget all about the fire; indeed it was not till the cold air chilled him that he found it had nearly burned out, and, to his horror, saw a huge tiger, with its two paws resting on the stump of a tree just without the circle; its two great eyes gleamed with hideous satisfaction at the prospect of having a boy for supper; indeed, the beast seemed to be only awaiting until the fire had burned out to make the attack.

The perspiration rolled from his forehead; he had never been in such terrible danger; therefore it was wonderful with what coolness and self-possession he gazed into the face of the beast, and, without taking his eyes off, fixed an arrow in the bow, and, pointing it at its forehead, sent the arrow into the brain of the tiger, which gave one backward leap, and rolled over dead.

Without loss of time, Lyu re-ignited the fire, and took good care that it should not go out again during his watch. The morning came, not, as you may suppose, before Lyu wanted. The bonze awoke, and praised him for his bravery, and, after a good break-fast of warm tea and boiled mutton, they resumed their journey, and for four days travelled through the great forest. On the morning of the sixth they entered a mountainous country, through which they passed till they reached a great *obo*, or altar, erected by the superstitious Tartars for the worship of the spirit of the mountain. It was about half way up, and made of a great heap of stones, the height of a mod erately high house; from the summit a number of branches of trees were suspended with strips of cloth hanging from them, on which were inscribed sacred verses. At the bottom of this heap of stones was a huge stone basin containing a great many coins, which the devotees had thrown there by way of offerings to the god. When they came in front of this obo, the priest stopped to burn incense, and then put some copper tchen in the basin with the others ; but, having so far complied with the superstition, he gathered the whole of the other pieces, placed them in his girdle, mounted the camel, and rode off, staring very solemnly at nothing, twiddling his beads, and muttering, *O-Mi To-Fo.*

Some time afterwards they came to a vast plain, where they pitched their tent; they had, however, scarcely arranged it before a bat flew across, and struck the bonze a heavy blow on the ear, when he went down on his knees, knocked his forehead a great many times upon the ground, pulled from his little pack an image of Buddha, and commenced to burn incense in thankfulness to the god.

"Know, my son," said he to Lyu, "that by means of that sacred bird the god Fo has whispered into my ear that a fortunate day is in store for us; let us now search for fuel and refresh ourselves with some tea."

While Lyu was searching for fuel, the bonze procured some water from a neighboring well and placed it in the kettle. When, however, Lyu brought some manure fuel, it proved to be so damp that it would not ignite, which placed them in a vexatious position; for, in all probability, they would be unable to procure either warmth or tea. Fortunately the bonze thought of a substitute: they would search for gray squirrels — little animals that are plentiful in those regions, and, like rats, live in holes, over the opening of which they build a dome of grass as ingeniously intricate as a spider's web. These domes make excellent fuel; and thus, by cruelly depriving these little creatures of their only and self-made protection from the elements, they obtained a plentiful supply of firing.

In the morning, when the bonze gazed round the vast horizon, he uttered an exclamation of joy, and fell upon the earth, muttering thanks to Fo. His practised eye had recognized the dim outline of a town, and that, too, long before he had anticipated. They then resumed their journey, and before night-fall reached a large and populous town of mud-built houses, where the inns were so numerous that they had no difficulty in procuring a lodging.

Thus, for the first time since leaving Pekin, Lyu had a warm bed made of thick matting placed over a fire-stove. The following day they discovered, from the unusually cleanly appearance of the streets and the gay dresses of the people, that preparations were being made for the great festival of the loaves of the moon. On that day all the moon-worshippers were dressed in their best clothes, and were going to the houses of their different friends and acquaintances with presents of money, and to interchange with each other cakes of various sizes, on which were stamped the image of the moon, with a hare crouching amid a group of trees. The Chinese relate the following legend of the origin of this feast: " An emperor of the Tang dynasty, being led one night to the palace of the moon, saw there an assembly of nymphs playing on instruments of music, and on his return command-ed persons to dress and sing in imitation of what he had seen." Little did these simple Tartars know of the tragedy that had been played upon their ancestors by means of this festival, and which, as it is an im-portant event in the history of the Chinese and their *first* Tartar conquerors, I will relate to you, as it is told by two recent travellers: —

About the year 1368 the Chinese were desirous of destroying the government of the Western Tartars, which had then been established about one hundred years; for this purpose some Chinese patriots organ ized a vast conspiracy throughout the whole empire. This was arranged to break out at one and the same moment, on the 16th day of the month, when each Chinese family was to massacre the Tartar soldiers billeted upon them by the government. The signal was given by letters concealed in the cakes which it was usual to present to each other on that day; and so secretly was this managed, that, when the appointed time arrived, the Chinese patriots succeeded in murdering nearly the whole of the Tartar army. Yet to this day the Western Tartars are so ignorant of this episode in their history, that they innocently celebrate the anniversary of this massacre of their ancestors.

In this town our travellers remained for some weeks, during which time the bonze made many attempts to cheat the people out of coin or goods; and in some instances it was no easy matter, for, notwithstanding their great veneration for the priest, they had quite as much love for their goods.

One day as the bonze and Lyu passed a large house belonging to a man of rank, they perceived a woman sitting at the door, beating her breast and crying very loudly. The bonze asked the cause of her grief, and, in the midst of sobs and cries, she told him that her master was lying dangerously ill, and no doctor could be obtained.

"Show the priest of Fo to thy master, and he will work miracles in fighting the fiends with which he is possessed."

This caused the woman to clap her hands with joy, and beg that he would follow her to her master's bedside.

The cunning bonze then felt the wrists of the sick man, looked for some time as nonsensically mysterious as some English doctors, and said, "Surely, my brother is possessed with a tchutgon, a fiend of rank and good position, who is working in his stomach; yet, by the blessing of Fo, will his priest either frighten or persuade him to leave the house."

"Will the man of prayer tell his servants how this may be attained?" said the woman.

"Know, then, my sister, that it is a gentlemanly fiend of high position, a mandarin in the lower world, and that every thing must be prepared for his departure in a manner suitable to his exalted rank."

"True, O learned bonze! but what will this great demon require? Say, and it shall be done," said the woman.

"Then, as soon as it has become dusk, my sister must put in the outhouse at the back of the mansion a handsome dress, with a warm outer garment, in case the fiend may take cold on his sudden exposure to the air; and a fine horse, ready saddled and bridled, upon which he may ride home without stumbling."

"Truly these things shall be done, holy man," said the sick person, giving the order to the woman. After this the bonze assumed a look of great seriousness, tore up some paper into very small pieces, and writing the name of a drug on each, put them in water, and rolled them up into pills, which he made the poor man swallow. He then lighted some incense before the image of Buddha, and, while it was burning, prayed vehemently. This lasted for two hours. When he had concluded, he went out of the house and returned with three more priests, all of whom brought drums, which they beat and clattered till the poor patient nearly lost his sense of hearing. When they discontinued the drumming, the bonze placed his ear to the man's stomach, and pretended to hold a confidential kind of conversation with the gentlemanly fiend within. The result was, that, providing every thing suitable to the travelling of a fiend of such a station in demon life was ready, he promised to quit the body at midnight.

The bonze then left the house with the blessing of the family, who fully believed in the whole of this mummery. Lyu longed to punish the wicked priest for his imposture; he dared not, however, speak, for he feared, as he believed, that it would injure his mother. The next morning the woman made her appearance at the inn, and informed the bonze that her master was better; the demon had evidently left, and as evidently had taken the horse and dress from the outhouse.

Now, whether these poor people really believe in this nonsense, or whether they consider it as a means of paying the priest-doctor, it is difficult to say; but as scenes like this are very common among them, it is most probable that the people are simpletons and the priests rogues. That the man got well that night was of course a mere chance, but even had he died the bonze would have persuaded his friends that it was a still greater proof of the good of his prayers, for not only had the devil left, but the patient had gone to a state far better than the one he had left behind him.

The greater portion of the next day the bonze was absent: but when he returned he borrowed from the landlord of the inn a pair of scales, and measured two hundred taels in silver, by which Lyu guessed that the bonze himself must have been the gentlemanly demon, and that he had received the silver in exchange for the horse and rich clothes that had been placed in the outhouse by the sick man's servants.

After this transaction they left the mud town, and for many days travelled after their usual style, at times seeking shelter and repose in caverns, at others under their tent. At length they came to the foot of a great mountain, the summit of which seemed to pierce the very clouds. The bonze clapped his hands together with joy; when this had subsided he dismounted, and tied the animal to a stake in the earth; he then opened his pack, and astonished the boy by producing a number of large balls of thick silk cord, pulled off his gown, and, with Lyu's assistance, rolled the silk round his head, arms, legs, and body, so tightly, and in such quantities, that he looked like a man made up of bobbins of silk, through which no sword or lance could pierce. Having done this, he walked, or rather waddled, up the mountain, followed by Lyu; about half way they came to a wide ridge, along which they walked for about half a mile, which brought them to what looked at first like an immense cleft, but which proved to be a valley running between the mountains and dividing it into two portions, each of which was surmounted by a double peak, something like a bishop's mitre.

Near the top of one of these was a large brick building, supported and adorned with figures of men, lions, elephants, tigers, and Buddhist idols; there was a low door near the centre, guarded on either side by two colossal dragons of stone; when they approached the door the bonze knocked his head on the ground in idolatrous worship, and muttered his prayers: but so tightly was he bound with silk, that, once down, he could no more rise than a lamp-post could make a bow, or the stone dragons stretch their legs and wag their tails; so Lyu helped to stand him on his feet. At that moment a flight of rooks passed over, and the bonze trembled with fear, and cried, " Is thy servant, O Fo! unworthy, that thou sendest birds of evil omen at the very threshold of my great purpose?" The perspiration rolled from him, and he sent Lyu back for his porcelain wine-bottle. When he returned, the priest was trembling in every limb; however, he could open his mouth; so Lyu poured the liquor down his throat, and his courage being restored, he ventured nearer to the door of the building, ordering Lyu to remain behind a projecting angle of rock till he should call.

The bonze then applied a key to the lock, and the door rolled upon its hinges with a heavy, grating sound. Then Lyu heard a great noise, like the twanging of a thousand cross-bows, and a heavy fall on the ground; and, in the midst, the voice of the bonze, when he ran from his resting-place, and found the bonze laying on the ground like a gigantic pincushion or a frolicsome porcupine, with arrows sticking in every part, from the top of his head to his feet; in fact, a radius of arrows, of which his person was the centre; and at once Lyu comprehended the full meaning of his whim for binding himself around with silk, for otherwise his body must have been pierced in a thousand places.

Lyu pulled out the arrows, taking care not to touch the heads, which were poisoned, and, by unwinding the silk from his body, set the bonze agoing again like an ordinary human being.

Looking into the interior of the building, Lyu uttered an exclamation of terror; the bonze had profaned the sepulchre of a Tartar king, with whom had been buried large heaps of gold and silver, regal robes, precious stones, and many other things that his subjects supposed he would require in the next life; but, worst of all, there stood around the tomb of their royal master double rows of boys and girls, who had been suffocated with mercury, in order to preserve the freshness and ruddiness of their complexions, and make them look as if they were alive.

The bodies of these unfortunate children were standing upright, some holding the pipe, others the fan, the vial of snuff, and other things ready for the dead tyrant's use. When the king had been buried, for the protection of the treasure, his officers had, according to an ancient custom, made a bow capable of discharging an immense number of arrows, so that, at the opening of the door, it would be certain death for any one who approached; and these were the arrows that the cunning bonze had so cleverly provided against. When free from the silk the bonze entered the tomb, commanding Lyu to follow.

"No, wicked priest, I would die rather than desecrate the ashes of the dead."

"Fo forbid, my son! I seek but a portion of this gold and silver for the use of Buddha, who, some years since, directed his servant's steps hither for the

purpose of attending the dying moments of one of
the priests who assisted at the entombment of the king,
and from whom I received the key; but no information of the secret bow; doubtlessly he intended
should be immolated on my duty to Fo."

"Rather on thy avarice," said Lyu.

"No, boy; not so; or Fo would not have whispered
the ancient custom in my ears, in order that I might
be prepared to defeat its murderous object. Follow
me, boy, and I will set thee free."

"For my life — no, wicked man! besides, you dare
not set me free with this secret. O, why, why did
you let me know it?" said Lyu, bitterly.

"Fear not; I have sought this tomb at the command of the living Buddha himself, and must do my
duty; but go, obstinate boy, seek the camel, and prepare for our departure."

I need scarcely say that Lyu quickly obeyed, and,
about an hour afterwards, the bonze joined him, bearing a large quantity of gold and silver, which he concealed in the packages on the camel; then mounting,
they travelled at the greatest possible speed, for the
bonze was anxious to reach some large town, the resting-place of a caravan to which he might attach himself, and thus be saved from the chances of meeting
robbers.

CHAPTER XIII.

"LOVE OF GAIN TURNS WISE MEN INTO FOOLS."

THE bonze rode silently and thoughtfully for a great length of time, as if consuming with anxiety for the safety of his ill-gotten wealth; what if robbers should attack him? true, they had not as yet met with any, although they had travelled so great a distance through a very wild country. Then, however, he had but little to lose; now he had wealth enough, not only to give a portion to Buddha, but to make himself of importance among his order. These thoughts and fears caused him great anxiety, and made him strike the camel's sides with his pointed stick till the beast howled with pain; but to little purpose, for no earthly power will increase the methodical steps of these useful and patient animals. As for Lyu, he was too much occupied in thinking of the vile practices of the priest, and the cruel chance which had robbed him of his home and parents, to care for his taciturnity. By midday they reached a large valley, through which ran a small river, on its journey as tributary to the great Hoang-ho. By the side of this river the bonze stopped, and, looking round as far as his eyes could reach, said, "Now, my son, we will seek some refreshment; we shall stand in need of it before nightfall; and here we are safe; for, as far as the human eye can pierce, we are free from strangers. Look, boy," he added, trembling with fear for the safety of his property. Lyu stood up on the camel, and gazed around the horizon.

"Do you see any signs of human habitations?" said the bonze.

"I know not, father, except those specks on the ridge of yonder mountain or cloud, whichever it may be, which appear no larger than tea-bricks," said Lyu.

The bonze then stood up on the camel, and, having examined the objects pointed out, said, "Ay, son, thine eyes are like those of the eagle; it may be a Tartar camp; look, it is surely in motion, for the specks become smaller and smaller. Look again, boy."

Lyu obeyed; and whether from the moving of the objects themselves, or the darkening of the distant clouds, it seemed to be as the bonze said, for the speck had become nearly invisible.

"Stay, my son, stay; I will try," said the bonze, who threw himself at full length on a mound, placed his ear to the earth, and listened for some minutes. "It is, it is," he said; "I heard the sounds of human movements; but still we have nothing to fear; the specks disappear, do they not?"

"Yes," said Lyu.

"Then we are safe," said the bonze, the perspiration rolling down his face.

"What should you fear more than hitherto?" said Lyu.

"The wolf fears not till the sheep is in its mouth, and the tiger on its trail to tear the prey from its teeth."

"But if the wolf could hide the sheep beneath its skin, even as you can the gold beneath your robe, father, would it fear?"

"True, boy, true," said the bonze; "out of your mouth comes the wisdom of the living Buddha. But now," he added, "let us refresh ourselves."

They then prepared their meal, and the bonze, who continued to look round the horizon, appeared more satisfied. After the meal he opened his pack and gave Lyu some arrows pointed with steel; placing one of these on his own bow, he walked to the side of the stream, and, crouching down so as to hide as much of his shadow as possible from the water, watched till a large fish leaped upwards, and, before it could again touch the water, the arrow passed through its body.

"See, boy," he added; "this is my only protection. Before I assumed the habit of Buddha I took the second military degree; hence the result. Can you twang your bow? Did my brother Hieul ever teach thee the art, for which he himself was once famous?" Now, the use of the bow and arrow had been one of the few good things that Hieul had taught Lyu; therefore he answered in the affirmative, merely saying, "I dare not try with you to kill a leaping fish with the arrow; but I will try one of those vermin," said Lyu, pointing to some huge water-rats that were running in and out of their holes on the opposite bank of the stream. He then put an arrow in his own bow, and in an instant transfixed one of the rats to the bank.

"A young dragon, a young dragon!" said the bonze; adding, "now, my son, with these bows we need not fear robbers." They again mounted and journeyed in the direction of a mountain as full of high peaks as would be a city of church steeples. It was nightfall ere they reached it; the clouds had become very dark, and the air close, sultry, and unfit for the lungs of man. Not a blade of grass moved, the sand rose upwards in columns of dust beneath the feet of the camel, and Lyu and the bonze were almost choked; till the perspiration rolled from their foreheads, the camel stretched out its long neck and hung its tongue from its mouth to catch the slightest breath of wind; foxes and goats started from the long grass, and mules ran into the defiles of the mountain, seeking shelter from the threatening storm. The bonze stopped at the foot of the mountain to search for a place of shelter; but, finding none, he cried, "We are lost, we are lost; for no human being can live throughout this scourge of Fo! Go up the mountain side, my son; search, search!"

Lyu jumped from the camel and climbed the mountain's side: in the mean time the clouds arose, and the wind blew in such fearful gusts, that the very hills themselves seemed to be toppling over; then came terrific claps of thunder as loud as if the world was being hewn asunder and re-distributed; the lightning played among the hills and across the plains, now backwards, now forwards, as might volcanoes if vomiting forth their rage at each other; then the rain fell in torrents, and huge hailstones, one of which nearly struck the bonze from his camel. Then, shivering and trembling, he got beneath the camel for shelter, and prayed to Fo resignedly, for he never expected to survive the fury of the storm.

"Here, father, here, — we are saved!" said Lyu, running from an opening, which was, fortunately, not only near at hand, but large enough to admit the camel.

Leaving the animal just within the entrance c^f the cavern, they proceeded to examine their retreat. It was an opening in the mountain. About half way down they discovered a narrow pathway, along which they proceeded till they reached an open space or corridor, lit from above. At the end of the cavern they found, to their surprise, several large rooms cut out of the rock, and each supplied with a window, a furnace and fireplace, a luxury that the Chinese themselves never enjoy, and stone seats; moreover the roof was ceiled, and the walls covered with plaster.

Overjoyed at their fortune in finding such comfortable quarters, they took possession of one of the rooms, lighted a fire, dried their clothes, and made some hot tea. Lyu could not but express his astonishment at such dwellings, and wonder how they could have got into the middle of the mountain; the bonze explained to him that they were now in the wild country of the Ortous Tartars, where he had little doubt that some Chinese agriculturists had emigrated, in the hope by persevering industry to cultivate the wild district, which would indeed have been to have made bread out of stones, and that they had chosen the interior of the mountain as the best place of shelter, for it had the advantage of being warm in winter and cool in summer; but, failing in their endeavors to cultivate the land, they had gone in search of some more fertile spot, leaving the snuggeries they had made with

such great labor for the abode of either beasts or men,
who might be fortunate enough to discover them in
time of need.

In one of these rooms they found a large quantity
of millet-stems, oats, and straw; so, having given a
portion to the camel, they made up their beds, and
endeavored to forget their dangers in sleep, not, however, before the bonze had made the doors secure
against thieves, who, he seemed to think, might find
him even there, for, as he said, the gods sometimes
give the identical thoughts and chances to different
persons at the same moment. However, the bonze
was so restless and uneasy about his money, that he
could not sleep, and so he told the story of these caves
to Lyu.

"You must know, my son, that the great emperor
will not permit any of his own people, the Tartars,
to cultivate the earth, for it would attach them to one
spot, and make them unfit for war; no, it is his heavenly will and policy that all the men of his own
Tartar race should be soldiers; he therefore pays
each man a regular sum of money each year to be in
readiness in case the Chinese people should rise up
in rebellion against the Mantchu government.

"As they have this money to live upon, they have
nothing to do, in time of peace, but hunt and look
after the herds of horses and other cattle on the
mountains and hills. Such being the will and command of the emperor, the Tartar kings, his tributaries,
have ever strictly forbidden their people to cultivate
any portion of the country.

" Now, a few years ago, when there was a famine in China, a few Chinese agriculturists came to the Ortous in a very humble manner, and sought permission from the Tartars to cultivate a little land, on condition that every year after harvest they should furnish them with a certain quantity of oatmeal; and for a time they kept to the conditions: these Chinese, however, soon began to encroach upon the simple Tartars, and invited a great number of other families to come and join them. This they did, and took possession of what land they chose, and, after they were settled, laughed at the Tartars, who asked them for their rent of oatmeal; but not only did they do this, but they turned thieves, and stole the Tartar cattle which happened to stroll near their caves.

" Now, all this so enraged one of the Tartar chiefs, that he assembled his brethren, and said, 'You see that these Chinese not only take away our land, steal our cattle, but curse us; therefore, my brethren, as they will not act like brothers, but like thieves, we must expel them.' Upon this the assembly went to the feet of the king, and told him; and his majesty, after reproaching his people for permitting the Chinese to cultivate the land against the law, issued an order for them to leave the Ortous; and as they laughed at the king's order, the Tartars armed themselves with lances, mounted their horses, and drove their flocks and herds upon the cultivated lands of the Chinese while the crop was standing; and the Chinese, though they stormed and swore, were obliged to leave the country at once. And this, my son, must be the

very spot, and these the houses inhabited by them."
After this story Lyu fell off to sleep, and became as
busily engaged in his dreams as "rare Ben Jon-
son," who dreamed that he saw thirty thousand Turks
and Tartars fighting a pitched battle on his great toe.

CHAPTER XIV.

"HE WHO COULD SEE ONLY THREE DAYS INTO FUTURITY MIGHT ENRICH HIMSELF FOREVER."

AT daybreak the bonze aroused Lyu, and they went together to feed and prepare the camel for their day's journey; but, to their great surprise, on opening the door they found the cavern filled with smoke, and, on reaching the spot where they had left the camel, found that the smoke proceeded from a large fire, near to which sat a man with a large bowl of tea before him; the sight of this stranger so alarmed the bonze that he instantly put his hand upon the knife which he carried beneath his robe.

"Welcome, brother! sit down by the fire," said the man, without lifting his eyes from the ground.

"Nay, brother," said the bonze, "we would be far on our journey before nightfall, and must take our departure at once."

"Pardon, O holy bonze! thy unworthy servant, who must have dust in his eyes, or he would surely have paid the respect due to a man of prayer," said the man; adding, "indeed, holy bonze, I sought shelter here from last night's storm, and even now proceed on my journey; should our paths turn to the same direction, your servant would gladly travel in the shadow of thy robe."

"We seek the distant and holy town of Keun

loam," said the bonze; "which way journeys my brother?"

"It is a far-distant, lonely, and dangerous journey, and beset with the children of the Golden Bee, who would scarcely respect thy cloth, holy priest," replied the man.

"Does my brother utter words of truth? Is that robber-tribe abroad then?" said the bonze, with alarm. "But we have no fear, brother; I have a strong arm, a keen eye, and good weapons; moreover, the young dragon here is brave," said the bonze.

"True, holy bonze," said the man, "but thy dog of a servant journeys to the sepulchre of Rache Tcharin, to sacrifice at the tomb of his ancestors, and for that purpose seeks but to join a large caravan of pilgrims, who journey to the grand feast to-day, near nightfall."

"True, brother; and now I remember the age of the moon, I know that you speak words of truth. But know you where to meet this caravan of holy people? for I would fain join them," replied the bonze, now quite satisfied, and rejoiced at the chance of having such a guide to the caravan.

"It is well, holy bonze," said the man, who then went with him and Lyu to the foot of the mountain, and from a hidden nook in the rock brought forth a fine Tartar horse, on to which he leaped in an instant. The bonze and Lyu mounted their camel, and as they rode along they could not keep their eyes off the animal.

"I would not break through the rules of civility, my son," said the bonze, "but thou must either hold a good rank, or have had a fortunate day lately, to own such a valuable beast."

" Thy servant has seen service in the armies of the Lord of Heaven within the last twelve moons, and been rewarded unduly with a small command," replied the Tartar soldier; for such he really appeared to be.

This reply seeming satisfactory to the bonze, whose suspicions had been aroused, they rode on for some time in silence.

" Do we not keep too near the mountain?" said the bonze.

" It is not so, holy bonze, for some two miles hence we shall reach a defile which will take us within a mile of the caravan; nay, if there is not dust in your servant's eyes, he can now see them approaching round yonder hills. See you not the tops of the lances of the guard?" said the soldier, pointing to a distant spot to their left, and which seemed to be a hollow ravine of the hills, above which could be distinguished a few moving lance-heads.

" You have rendered an unworthy servant of Fo more beholden to you than thou art aware, my brother; and now it would beseem us to show our gratitude to Fo, by relieving his children. Come, son, let us send some horses to those poor travellers, who may be lost in these desolate regions."

" Send horses!" said Lyu, with surprise; "how, father? surely we have but a camel."

" See," said the bonze; and he stopped the camel near the verge of a hill, and pulled a number of small pieces of paper from his gown, on which were drawn the *figures of horses;* having muttered some prayers over them, he threw them into the air, saying, "as these blessed papers fly, they will become changed by

Buddha into horses and camels for the aid of wanderers who may catch them." The bonze did not see that some of the paper horses had fallen into the lap of the Tartar soldier, who put them into his breast without speaking a word. As for Lyu, ridiculous as was the superstition, he did not laugh, for he now remembered to have heard that it was commonly practised by the Tartar lamas or bonzes.

Having thus exhibited this charity towards unhappy wanderers, they rode on some few miles till they reached the promised defile; at this spot the soldier rode close to the bonze and Lyu, and so they proceeded till they reached a narrow spot, with cavernous-looking openings on either side.

"We should not be far from the place of destination, brother; and yet I hear not the sounds of an approaching caravan."

"Fear not, holy father," said the soldier; adding "ah! what have we here?" As he spoke, three rough-looking Tartars sprang from each side of the road.

"Welcome, holy bonze!" said the men, prostrating themselves before him, but so that neither could pass.

"Why do my good brothers thus shower their favors upon those who would pass on their journey?" said the bonze, placing his hand upon his bow.

"My bowstring is cut, father," said Lyu, with surprise, holding up his bow, and exhibiting a severed string.

"Why seek your arrows, my friends? you would not surely injure these poor men?" said the Tartar soldier laughing.

"What would you ask of us? are you robbers? would you plunder a poor priest of Fo?" said the bonze to the soldiers, apparently not noticing the Tartar's speech.

"We are poor, holy father, and require money," said one of the robbers; for robbers they were.

"We are tired, holy bonze, and want camels to aid us," said another.

"We would save thee the trouble of carrying thy package, holy father," said another. While speaking, they surrounded Lyu and the bonze, and lifted them from the camel.

"Did I not tell you, holy bonze, that there was danger to be feared from the children of the Golden Bee?" said the soldier, unfastening his loose dress, and disclosing beneath the full dress of a Tartar chieftain.

"Speak not, thou sacrilegious, thieving Tartar dog!" said the bonze.

"O, O, sacrilege! holy bonze; if the children of the desert merit death for borrowing from a priest of Fo, what does he deserve, who, forgetful of the respect due to the dead, dares plunder the tomb of a king?"

"Pounding to death in a mortar, great chief," said the Tartars, pointing their lances at the heart of the bonze.

"Not so, my children," said the chief, waving his hand. "We will not injure this man of prayer, but set him free without the anxiety of guarding his wealth of gold and silver — a treasure which we, my children, have so long waited for, but dared not touch while within the walls of a tomb. Shades of our ancestors forbid!"

"Will the great Tartar say how he became possessed of this secret?" said the bonze with humility, now that he felt safe from personal harm.

"The cravings of the holy father's curiosity shall be satisfied," said the Tartar; adding, "that mountain tomb contains the ashes of a king with whom our people had long been at war; even the treasure buried with him was taken from us at the sacking of one of our encampments. For years we have prayed both day and night to regain it, but dared not break a tomb; indeed, my holy father, it was unnecessary, for we knew that, of the many priests who attended at the funeral, one would some day be led, by his avarice and cunning, to pass the magic arrows. Now come forth, Ali Khan, and let the good priest know to whom we are indebted for his agreeable company."

As the chief uttered this command, a man stepped forth from among the crowd of soldiers, in whom, to their astonishment, the bonze and Lyu at once recognized the miner who had robbed them of their mule.

"Welcome, welcome, holy and most hospitable bonze!" said the miner.

"Thou miserable villain! thou ungrateful tortoise-egg!" exclaimed the bonze.

"These are hard words, my father, for I did but borrow the mule to help me on my escape from the cruel Queen of Ouinot, and which even now awaits you in this mountain."

"My brother, then, is but just; but will he further say by what magic power he learned my intended journey to the king's tomb? for surely I have not uttered a word to living man," said the bonze.

"My father slumbered well," replied the miner, "while I watched; he is more cunning than his tongue; for, surely, while he slept he spoke his anxiety about the tomb-treasure; and poor and wretched as was thy servant, he could but tremble with horror at the desecration of a tomb, and hastened here to the great chief that he might prevent the crime."

"It was then, father," interposed the chief, "that we were overjoyed to think that the gods had at last listened to our prayers, and sent the priest we had been so long waiting for," said the chief; adding, "then I placed a man in a secret spot to watch the tomb; and no sooner had the holy father penetrated the sacred resting place of the royal dead, than he hastened to me with the information, when I rode to meet you; that meeting took place in the cave. The rest is fully known to the holy bonze."

The bonze bit his lips with vexation at having been so outwitted; but fear for his life made him reply, "Fo is great; it is my destiny: yet surely the great chief would not plunder a wandering priest of his camel?"

"The children of the desert plunder not good bonzes, yet they must even borrow the beast, for surely thou stolest it from a simple tribe of Tartars, my kinsmen; the mule thou shalt have for the boy to ride. The holy bonze is rich, and can make horses of paper. See, take thou these; for, as thou knowest, they will help thee on thy way, even as much as the poor travellers to whom thou sentest so many," replied the chief, giving to the bonze the pieces of paper that had fallen on him. "As for the mule, it is returned to thee for the boy's use alone; so let not thy legs cross its back within a hundred days' journey of these hills, or perchance an arrow may strike thee to the earth. Now, my children, be it your care that the holy bonze quits not our mountain hills without receiving your hospitality." As he spoke the Golden Bee received his long lance from a page, placed it in its rest, and rode away laughing at the notion of a wily bonze having been outwitted by a simple Tartar.

That night they spent with these wild Tartars, half soldiers, half robbers; but who, to do them justice, treated both Lyu and the bonze hospitably, though, in strict accordance with their chief's order, they started them the next morning with nothing but their tent and the mule: having accompanied them a few miles, they then bade our travellers farewell, much to the relief of the bonze, who had to bear their gibes and jests, which were all the worse for being covered with mock veneration for his cloth.

The bonze was now put to his wits'-ends how to live in so wild a country without the means even of hunting the wild game with which it abounds; however, you may be pretty sure he would not starve for want of schemes, and he pondered as they travelled. Had this robbery happened to them while in the mountains or the plains they must have starved; they were, therefore, fortunate to find themselves on the banks of the Hoang-ho, one of the largest rivers in the world, which rises in the Thibetian mountains of Koko-noor, and, after passing through the whole empire, empties itself into the sea near Canton

It was by the side of this great river, wearied and

hungered, and without the hope of procuring food, they pitched their tent the first evening of their departure from the Tartar's hold. Early in the morning they were delighted to find large flocks of ducks floating about on the stream, (a water plantation of immense gourds;) but so wild that they could not approach within a hundred yards of them. The bonze, however, had made up his mind to make a meal of some of them, and sat down on the bank to ponder on the means. In a few minutes he arose joyfully, and saying, " Fo is great," stripped off his clothes, and plunged into the river.

So long did he remain under the water that Lyu began to fear he was drowned. The bonze, however, was not born to be drowned, and he startled Lyu by suddenly putting his head up near the bank where he was standing, and came on shore with one of the gourds in his hand, which he had cleverly managed to pluck without disturbing the birds. In a very short time he scooped the gourd hollow, leaving a hole sufficiently large for his head; then, cutting two small holes for his eyes, he placed it on his head, looking very much like a man in a diver's helmet; again went under the water, and swam in the midst of the ducks without disturbing them, as they could not tell the difference between the gourd that held the head from the others.

By this means he astonished the birds by taking hold of their legs and pulling them under the water, and, having caught six, he swam ashore, and soon after dressed one of them by the fire which Lyu had with difficulty managed to kindle, and thus obtained a rough but tolerably good breakfast.

At length, after travelling some distance along the banks of the river, they came to a ferry, where, by a little persuasion and the gift of two of the ducks, the ferryman took them across to the other side.

CHAPTER XV.

RICHES COME BETTER AFTER POVERTY THAN POVERTY AFTER RICHES."

THEY were now in the province of Kan-sou, and, as they approached a small town, a short distance from the river, the bonze muttered prayers of gratitude to Fo for once more placing them in a land of good things. The town was very small, but thickly populated, and apparently full of people who did little else but eat and drink, for the streets were crowded with strolling eating-shop keepers, offering for sale numerous kinds of ready-dressed food. " Thank Fo, my son, that we are once more in a civilized land, with every thing around to warm and comfort us ; but, alas ! we are without money, and might as well be buried in a rice-tub, with our mouths sewn up. May the souls of those Tartar dogs be made to inhabit the bodies of snakes. May their lands be covered with grasshoppers, and their herds die of the murrain, the tortoise-eggs ! "

" Shall we sell the mule ? " said Lyu.

" No, my son; for we shall soon again want the faithful animal. But see, yonder is the inn of the ' Twelve Civilities ; ' we will seek shelter there."

" But we have not a single tchen, my father," said Lyu.

" Fo will not desert us in our hour of need," replied the bonze, entering the inn. "Will my worthy brother," said he, addressing the landlord, "have pity on two wandering bonzes, who have been despoiled of their goods by Tartar thieves?" But before he could reply, a courier, with a white button in his cap, rode up to the inn, and, pushing the people aside, cried aloud—"Make way, make way for the ray from the rainbow, the great mandarin Loo-foo and his suite, who is on his way to the province of Set-chuen to take command. Make way, make way for the great government pedestal!" And the courier finished by laying his whip stoutly about the bodies of the people, who ran in all directions. Then came the government column himself: and a very stout column he was, seated in a gilded sedan, which stopped at the inn-door, when the landlord prostrated himself at full length, and performed the kow-to, by knocking his forehead nine different times on the ground.

"What would the Son of Heaven's stupendous representative wish of the most insignificant of his humble servants?" said the landlord, without rising.

"Erect thy trifling body on thy bamboo legs and hear?" said the mandarin. "Let thine eyes be bathed in the sunshine that emanates from the countenance of the greatest of lords," said the courier, whipping the man till he stood up.

"It is the duty of a mandarin to see that justice should be administered, slave," said his greatness to the innkeeper.

"It is an excellent and most wise maxim, thou moon-and-star-like viceroy of the great Sun of Pekin and the rest of the earth," said the innkeeper.

" Myself, the father and mother of a large province, cannot do this on an empty stomach: therefore see, thou short measure of a landlord, that this town be skimmed of its best, that the fountain of justice be not soured by my wrath, like milk by the thunder of the heavens, and let thy speed be like that of an imperial arrow on its flight to the back of a running rebel. Respect and obey."

" Thy words, which have flowed like honey from thy dragon mouth, shall be obeyed," said the landlord, running off to prepare refreshment for the great man.

" Who are those two vagrants that dare to throw their snakes' eyes in our countenance ? "

This allusion was to Lyu and the bonze, who had been innocently looking on the scene.

" Nought but two vagrant, half-starved bonzes, seeking charity, most glowing ray of a rainbow," said the courier, who, being a Tartar, entertained the greatest awe for the priesthood. Not so the mandarin, who, like most Chinese of rank, regarded the whole order of bonzes as vermin.

" To be duly administered," said this very mortar among great guns, " the government of the province must be cleansed of idlers and vagrants. Bestow upon each of the insects fifty correcting blows with the bamboo." So saying, this very tangible ray from a rainbow hobbled out of his sedan, and prepared to walk into the inn through two rows of attendants.

Previous experience having taught the bonze that in all such cases as the present the most advisable course was to make the best of a bad job he quietly submitted to be taken into custody; not so Lyu, who indignantly cried,—

"Hear me, great lord, for justice sake!"

"What would the little worm ask in the name of justice?"

"To be free, great lord; I am not a bonze; indeed I am not.   They are all rogues."

"Ah! my little paper tiger; hast thou not heard that a good rat will not injure the grain near its own hole?   But if thou art not a bonze, what, in the name of the principal relations, art thou then, that I should befoul the maxim that impartial rigor and example are the best means of governing?"

"A Christian — a Christian — great Lord."

"A Christian?— well then," said the mandarin, curling his long moustache, "we will be partial; bestow upon this short weight one hundred blows of the bamboo."   So saying, the fat pedestal of the empire hobbled into the house like a young hippopotamus with the gout, and the servants seized upon Lyu and the bonze, and, throwing them upon the ground, beat the soles of their feet till they were very sore.

Lyu bore this cruelty bravely, determining, if ever he reached his mother's people, to make the mandarins pay for such tyranny; it was, however, some consolation to think that he had received the extra punishment for his courage in admitting that he was a Christian.

As for the bonze, he bore it very patiently, merely exclaiming, "it is wise to submit to destiny;" adding, "it is Fo's will, my son, that we should be immersed in misfortunes, like a leaky house in rainy weather."   They were then put outside the walls of the town; when, sorefooted and hungry, they rode on the mule till they came to a wood, where they slept beneath some trees, with the tent-covering loosely thrown over them, for they were too weak to pitch it properly. The next day they fed upon dried roots and nuts, which they gathered by the roadside. On their way, Lyu begged of the bonze to save him all this misery, and permit him to make himself known at the next town, where he should probably find some merchant to communicate with Tchin, who would not only pardon, but send him a reward.

The bonze replied by threatening to give the whole family over to the mandarins if he again mentioned the matter; Lyu therefore could but resolve to bear his miseries as best he might, and wondered whether the boy Choo had gone through so many difficulties before he became emperor; but his greatest trouble was being associated with such a thorough rogue, although, in justice to the bonze, I must inform you that he was neither better nor worse than the rest of his order, nor did he do any thing, however ridiculous or wicked, that was not commonly practised by the bonzes in general, who, by the by, are not so much worse than a great many people in England, who live as much by their wits, and that, too, without the excuse of ignorance or the darkness of paganism.

When they came to the gates of a small village, the bonze picked up two large sharp-pointed stones, and held them beneath his gown till he reached the middle of the principal street, when he placed his back against the wall of a house, and, to Lyu's astonishment, beat his head till the blood ran in streams

like water through a colander, all the time crying,
as he did when Lyu first saw him in the cage, that Fo
had ordered him to sacrifice himself for the sins of the
villagers.

The simple-minded people soon flocked around, and
threw copper coins at his feet, which he collected together, and, going to a small inn outside the village,
hired a lodging in the stables, where they resided till
the bonze had put his head in repair, and could make
his reappearance in public, when, as the last exper-
iment was too painful to be repeated at the next village, he tried another plan. This was to purchase a
large iron chain from a blacksmith, which he fastened
to his neck and feet, and pretended to drag along with
great difficulty, setting up the same cry as before about
suffering for the sins of the people. These villagers,
however, being wiser than the others, he obtained but
sorry sympathy and very few coins; so he proceeded
onwards till they came to a farmyard well stocked
with ducks, pigs, and other animals. The farmer's
wife was busily engaged with the live stock, when the
bonze, after gazing at her for a minute, went up to a
cage where two fine, fat ducks were put up for fattening, and, falling down before them, began to moan so
miserably, that the woman believed him to be out of
his wits.

"Who are you, O, holy man," said she, "who seem-
eth in such grief before these fattening ducks?"
— Quack, quack, screamed the ducks, as if in answer
to their mistress.

"Wherefore, O, unfeeling woman, have you fastened up these aged people?" cried the bonze.

"What words are these?" said the woman. "Is .he holy father mad, or has he been drinking, that he calleth these ducks people? surely they are but ducklings." — Quack, quack, said the birds, unfolding their wings, and fluttering with fright at the continued moaning of the bonze.

"Does not the daughter of the soil perceive that the birds are speaking their own sacred language to the priest of Fo? Is the dust in my daughter's eyes, that she cannot see the joy they are exhibiting at the sight of their son?" said the bonze, moaning bitterly.

"What words are these, O bonze?" said the poor woman, half frightened. — Quack, quack, quack, said the ducks again, as if to impress their mistress wi'h the real character of the bonze.

"Would my daughter kill these aged people, since they are put in this cage for fattening?"

"Truly will I, holy bonze, for the village mandarin has ordered them for a great feast he gives to-night; but pray do not call them aged; for if they prove tough, my husband will be bastinadoed as a cheat."

"O, O, O!" screamed the bonze; "I shall die with grief; for know, woman, that these apparent birds contain the souls of my venerable parents."

Lyu could hardly contain himself for laughing, and longed to proclaim the imposture to the poor woman, who dared not doubt the words of a bonze. "Since the man of prayer has discovered that these birds contain the souls of his venerable relations, — and, indeed, now I think of it, they have always seemed to me too sensible for ducks, — they shall not be killed," said the woman.

"My daughter is benevolent; but can she answer for her husband, who may not believe in the truth? Surely thou wouldst not kill a priest of Fo with grief at the danger of his venerable parents?"

At length, after many more protestations and lamentations, the simple woman became persuaded to resign her ducks, and the bonze, being overjoyed at the recovery of his venerable parents, carried them tenderly to an inn in the next village, hired a room, and, cannibal-like, made an excellent supper off one of them.

In this manner, and by means of the exhibition of the iron chain, the bonze travelled some months through the great province of Kan-sou. Another and more profitable trick was to trace upon a large sheet of paper several circles one over the other, and in the middle to execute a carefully drawn image of Fo. When finished it was placed in a handsome box; and whenever he heard that a funeral was about to take place, he would visit the relations of the deceased and sell it to them as a passport from this world to the next for the soul of their relative.

For this passport well-to-do people would give two or three taels, (about ten or twelve shillings,) and not complain of the expense, as they believed it would insure the deceased a happy voyage. Such for months proved the means of existence of the bonze, and, what is more terrible, such is the state of ignorance of vast portions of one of the most intelligent nations in the world.

You can imagine the misery of Lyu at being associated with the practices of such degrading and wicked superstitions, and how he longed to breathe a portion of his knowledge of Christianity into the ears and hearts of these foolish pagans:— once the opportunity occurred.

The bonze and Lyu were living at an inn in a small town in the province of Kan-sou, where he would frequently leave Lyu while he went to vend his passports, or try some other nefarious means of making money. Well, it so chanced that one day a pensioner of the emperor's, who was living at the same inn, was taken dangerously ill, and, thinking he was about to die, prayed that a bonze might be sent for. Now, the innkeeper, not being able to find our bonze, thought Lyu would do as well, and begged of him to go to the bedside of the sick man, who, unable to see that it was a mere boy by his side, cried, " O, holy bonze, this punishment is dreadful, and more than I can bear; is there no means of escape ?"

" From death, do you mean, brother ? " said Lyu.

" No, no," said the sick man; " it is not death that I fear, but that I should pass into a horse, a mere beast of burden, hereafter; for the bonzes, who are well instructed in what passes in the next world, have assured me that out of gratitude to the emperor, who has so long given me a pension in this life, I shall be obliged to serve his majesty after death, and that my soul will certainly pass into a post-horse, to carry despatches out of the provinces to court; for this reason they exhort me to perform my duty well when I shall have become a horse, and take care not to stumble, wince, bite, or hurt any body; besides, they direct me to travel well, to eat little, to be patient, and by that means move the compassion of the deities, who often convert a well-behaved horse into a great mandarin. It is this that I cannot think of without trembling; I dream of it every night, and, sometimes, when I am asleep, I think myself harnessed, and ready to set out at the stroke of the rider. I then awake in a cold perspiration and in great concern, scarcely knowing whether I am a man or a beast. Alas! alas! what will become of me when I am a horse in reality? It is therefore that I am resolved to become a Christian; for they tell me that those of that religion are not subject to these miseries — that men continue to be men in the next world the same as this. O, holy bonze, may I not do this?"

It was then that Lyu informed the sick man that he was no bonze, but a Christian, and knelt down by his bedside, and, with the vehemence of his strong heart, opened to him the truths of Christianity, and told him, as well as he could, the beautiful story of the Saviour's life and death, till the man's eyes beamed with delight and belief.

"I know," said he, "that your religion is hard to be observed — at least for so old and confirmed an idolater as myself; but if it were still more difficult I would still embrace it, cost what it might."

From the moment the man was relieved from the apprehensions occasioned by his miserable belief in the wretched stories of Buddhism he began to recover; and when Lyu quitted the village he left behind him at least one Christian, and that proved some consolation to him in the midst of his troubles.

CHAPTER XVI.

"LARGE FOWLS WILL NOT EAT SMALL GRAIN."

On leaving this village they passed through a romantic valley between mountains of red and yellow ochre, and, as they started early in the morning, they reached the first military station by nightfall; this station was a very warlike-looking affair, built of wood, whitewashed, and plastered over with pictures of fierce-looking war-gods and fabulous animals, like those in the arms of the English nobility and gentry.

These stations are very numerous throughout the empire, being, in fact, erected at about every ten miles distance, and used in times of peace as barracks for armed soldiers, who are supposed to perform police duties, and protect the people from robbery.

Each station has a high tower attached, and also a large room, which is hospitably set apart for benighted or wearied travellers. In war time the towers are used as telegraph stations, from which, by an explosion of fireworks, signals may be communicated from station to station throughout the whole of China, and, by this means, large bodies of troops may be drawn from different provinces, and speedily concentrated upon one spot. Of the efficiency of this mode of signalling, the Chinese relate an anecdote, which will strongly remind you of the fable of the " Boy and the Wolf."

10

"The wife of one of the emperors, having taken it into her head to have a frolic with the soldiers, persuaded her husband to order the alarum signals to be made the same as if an enemy were in the capital, for he would then find whether these boasted signals would really bring the troops to the capital. The foolish emperor complied, and the signals passed like wildfire to the different provinces; the governors took the alarm, and, in a very short time, marched their thousands and thousands of troops up to Pekin — of course, very much to the disgust of the soldiers, who were greatly amazed to find that they had been called together for the capricious whim of a woman; however, as they dared not complain openly, they returned to their different stations full of indignation.

" Shortly afterwards the Tartars really invaded the capital; this time the emperor ordered the alarm signals in grave earnest; but, throughout the whole empire, not a man stirred from his post, believing that the empress was again at her frolics; so, for want of assistance, the Tartars destroyed the city, murdered the imperial family, and set up their own chief as emperor. Thus the empress had to pay very dearly for her fun."

Lyu and the bonze, having ensconced themselves in a comfortable corner of the travellers' room, purchased a lump of coarse tea, made up into the form and size of one of our common house bricks, and called by the Chinese a tea-brick, and made themselves very comfortable over a bowl of this pleasant beverage.

They had not been seated long before another traveller arrived with his wife and family, which consisted of six persons, whom the bonze invited to take tea; and, in a conversation, he found that the man was a tradesman who had just quitted forever his native place, (Vou-si,) a village about five miles distant.

"Has my brother received some office under government, that he should thus leave the rich Vou-si, where the rice is as plentiful as the sand of the desert?" said the bonze.

"Not so, holy father; but the luxuriant fields and the profitable trade are of less value to thy servant than the wife and children of his bosom, with whom he is now leaving the abode of his ancestors."

"What manner of words are these? Surely it is but the spring time; the weather has been beneficent; Vou-si is celebrated for the productiveness of its land and the prosperity of its people; moreover, the fields are rich with seeds, and the god Shin-nung promises an abundant harvest to the husbandman."

"The words from the lips of the man of prayer are pearls of truth and gems of wisdom, yet must thy servant quit his native and beloved hills if he would not have his children sacrificed to the wrath of the gods, and leave no descendant to sacrifice at his tomb," said the man, mournfully.

"Surely my elder brother can't be a dog marked by the mandarins, and fleeing from the justice of the laws?" said a soldier.

"The suspicions of the courageous tiger of war (may he be promoted!) are not just; for his brother is as free from crime as the Son of Heaven himself."

After fencing in the true Chinese fashion with polite words for a considerable time, the man asked,

"What dust can have closed the ears of the tiger of war and the man of prayer, that they have heard not the terrible prophecy?—'Ou fou, ou kioung, huc-man-chan, kou-man-tchouan,' 'Next year there will be neither rich nor poor; blood will cover the mountains, bones will fill the valleys.'"—And he trembled as he repeated the prophecy.

"Who were the ill-omened rooks that poured such dirt into the ears of the people of Vou-si?" said the soldier.

"Has the soul of a dead goose passed into my brother, that his ears will hold such foul rice?" said the bonze.

"Is thy servant a dog, that he should doubt the words of the inspired diviners, or is he wiser than his generation and the fathers of his tribe, that he should alone be an unbeliever when all believe—the aged as they go to their tombs, and the infants as they begin to walk from their cradles? No, it is truth; and thus thy servant quits his native place," replied the man; and, as all attempts to shake his faith in this terrible prophecy proved fruitless, they discontinued the subject, and drank the spirit of the rice till they fell senseless on the floor; not by any means an uncommon termination to social parties in China.

As for Lyu, he had very little sleep that night, for, although he did not believe one jot of the prophecy, he had heard of the terrible desolation that sometimes occurred on the hills, and, moreover, knew that it was the intention of the bonze to make a long sojourn in the village of Vou-si.

The next morning the travellers departed on their respective routes—the Vou-sian towards the Yellow

River and Lyu and the bonze towards Vou-si, where they arrived about midday. The village was built about half way up the declivity of a mountain; above it, for hundreds of feet, the hill-side was luxuriantly cultivated with rice fields, which rose in great beauty, in a series of huge, verdant steps, cut one above the other, like a colossal staircase, to the heavens.

The valley beneath was covered with long grass, so verdant that it lent a distinct hue to the variegated sky, which shone with a pure, ethereal light. The village had been built in the early ages, when the constant irruptions of the Tartars on frontier towns and villages kept the inhabitants in perpetual dread. To guard against these robbers the houses had been erected in a double row of about a mile, but serpentined, so that their backs, by presenting numerous angles and abutments, served as a species of rude fortification; at each end of the village there was a strong gate, capable of resisting an enemy ignorant of the use of cannon; but, unlike our villages and towns, the path ran down the centre instead of the sides.

Our travellers had been journeying many months, and it was now early spring. The sun shone over this peaceful and prosperous village in all its glory; but what gave additional enchantment to the scene as they reached the gates was the sound of various musical instruments, and a long procession that was issuing forth to pay honor and glory to Shin-nung, the divine husbandman.

As Lyu stood by the gates, and thought of the prophecy, and of the Vou-sian's assertion of the terror of the people, he could not help smiling at his foolish fears, for never was there a happier or more social-looking crowd assembled together. Lyu moved aside for the procession, which came in the following order: First, twenty men carrying great poles, from which hung colored lanterns, and large cards inscribed with the names and titles of the god; then a band of musicians, with trumpets, clarinets, flutes, and hand-organs, filling the air with delightful sounds; then a village mandarin in his state dress of gorgeous silk, carried in a gilded sedan, and attended by a man bearing the umbrella of state; then more musicians and mandarins; then eight stout men, in full holiday dresses, supporting a large platform of vermilion, decorated with gold, and strewn with choice exotic plants, in the centre of which sat the handsomest young man of the village, sumptuously attired, and by his side a beautiful girl, dressed with the splendor of an empress, stood in a most miraculous position, balancing herself upon two wands, as if flying; her position was so difficult and painful that two men kept sprinkling her with water to keep her from fainting. The platform was succeeded by a lantern, at least forty feet long, shaped like a dragon, with wings, body, and tail, and support-ed by eight men hidden in its body, who caused it to writhe, frisk about, clap its wings, wag its tail, and open its mouth, as if alive. A great number of hand-somely dressed youths followed with mottoed banners, attended by servants with umbrellas of vermilion and yellow silk. Then a number of men in cavalry uni-forms, mounted on lanterns in the shape of horses, which, like the dragon, were made to plunge, curvet, and kick, by men within their bodies. Then laborers, who carried lanterns wrought in the form of fruits of the soil, and shopmen with teas, dried herbs, and fruits, as offerings to the god. Then followed *literati*, or scholars, bearing banners inscribed with the sayings and doings of Confucius. These were followed by representatives of the god's own executioners, bearing various instruments of torture, which the Chinese suppose to be in use in the infernal regions. Last of all, surrounded by gongs and trumpets, came an immense chair, carrying an image of Shin-nung himself, clothed in the imperial dress of yellow satin, with a vermilion face, a gorgeous crown of gold on his head, and accompanied with all the pomp and circumstance of a mandarin of the greatest rank. As the god passed the gate of the village, the bands played, and he was saluted with a salvo of artillery that shook the village to its foundation, and would have done credit to a nation really as fierce as the Chinese affect to be.

When the procession had passed, the bonze fastened his chain to his neck and feet, gave a low chuckle, and said, "It is well, my son, for the village of Vou-si is wealthy and prosperous, its inhabitants are true children of the gods, and will not allow a servant of Fo to want rice. Let us try the hearts of those within yonder felicitous-looking farm," he added, pointing to a house a short distance before them. A woman was standing at the door, who, seeing the bonze limping along, as if in terrible agony, invited him into the house.

"See, venerable grandfather," said she, addressing an aged man, "I bring a holy bonze, worn out with pain and travel; let us welcome him."

"*Shing kwan,*" — "Pull off thy cap, holy priest," — said the old man, rising to meet the bonze.

"May the gods make thy race lengthy and productive, venerable brother, notwithstanding this thy hour of trouble!"

"Hour of trouble! O, man of prayer, what words are these, when the gods have just performed a miracle in thy servant's favor?" said the old man.

"Thy unworthy servant's memory hath failed him, for he remembers not to have heard of this miracle," said the bonze; adding, "will my venerable brother be pleased to pour these glorious words into thy servant's ears?"

"My holy brother must have been but a short time in this province, not to have heard the miracle. Know, then, that I have but one son, whose life has been passed with me till, six moons since, he happened to displease the mandarin of the village, who punished him by sending him on a long and dangerous journey, without arms and with little food. When the pedestal of my existence left me, grief at his loss threw me on a bed of sickness so severe that I was almost at my last gasp. One night I had fallen into a deep sleep, and dreamed that I was on the summit of a high mountain, when a great cloud passed over, which gradually burst, and showed to me a figure sitting on a wonderful throne made of purest snow, and streaked with vermilion fire that caused the snow to melt with the soft sound of the tones of charity and mercy, instead of the hissing sounds of fire and water; the vermilion streaks of fire arose, and sent a glory of pale blue round the head of the Mandarin of Death for it was he, who said to me, 'O, venerable man, thy destiny was appointed ; thou wert at death's portals ; but the father who has so brought up his son in the practice of filial love deserves mercy from the gods ; know, then, that thy life is prolonged for twelve more years.' When the spiritual mandarin had spoken, the clouds again enveloped him, and I awoke, and, to my astonishment, found my beloved son by my side !

" After the joy at our meeting had become subdued, he told me that when at a vast distance his heart had become troubled for his parent's safety, and he dreamed that he was in great danger. His importunities ther became so great to the governor of the province, to whom he had been sent, that he obtained permission to return : on his way, however, through a forest, his foot slipped, and a ferocious tiger rushed forth, put his paws upon his breast, and was about devouring him. Still my son was not frightened ; but, thinking of his father, said, ' I hurry to save my aged parent ; let the tiger devour me at his will, he cannot prevent my spirit from going to his aid.' When he had uttered these filial words, the savage beast took his paws from his breast, licked his face, turned round, dropped his tail, and walked slowly away, as if even the animal had been inspired by the gods with respect for filial piety. When this miracle was reported to our mandarin, that beneficent fountain of justice not only pardoned the young man, but bestowed upon thy unworthy brother two hundred taels in silver."

At the greater portion of this story the bonze curled his lip, as if in pity or scorn at the old man, whom he believed to be in his dotage ; when, however, he heard of the silver, he mumbled some prayers, rolled his beads, and gave a shriek, as if from pain caused by the weight and pressure of his chains, and said, " A miracle indeed! and the more wonderful that the gods should save thy life from the process of nature, but to take it away by other means; or have the gods added to thy years but to inflict thee with the coming sights of sorrow?" And the bonze groaned as he spoke.

" What words are these from the lips of my holy brother? surely the servant of Fo does not misconstrue the actions of the gods?"

" Have the ears of my venerable brother been closed to the words of the inspired? Has he not heard that this year 'there will be neither rich nor poor, and that blood will cover the mountains, and bones fill the valleys?' and is it not for this that my footsteps have been directed to thy especial threshold?" replied the bonze, shaking his chains and roaring with pretended pain.

" Words of truth, words of truth!" said the aged man, sadly; "I have, I have, holy bonze; and, like an unworthy wretch, forgotten them in my transient joy. O, holy bonze, is there no way of turning aside the wrath of the gods? Tell us, O priest! for thou, who art in commune with the world of spirits, must know."

" It is to ward off the frowns of the gods that a priest of Fo is present; it is to try the charity and goodheartedness of the people that I am doomed to wear this chain till one hundred taels have been bestowed through me upon Fo"

So solemnly did the bonze utter this speech that the poor old gentleman trembled with fear, saying, " Surely the words from thy lips are those of truth." Then, rubbing his head as if to brighten his intellect, he added, "Truly, it may be that the gods but instructed the mandarin to bestow the taels on me as a treasure for their own inscrutable purposes. Will, then, the holy father condescend to take charge of one hundred taels, and, with his young son, bestow upon us the happiness and protection of his presence till this terrible storm has passed over, as surely it will harmlessly with his presence ? and we will daily offer to the gods a portion of the best and worthiest produce of our fields and stalls."

Thus, by working on the superstitious fears and kind heart of the aged man, the artful bonze (who in England would have been prosecuted for obtaining money under false pretences) gained really more than he wished, for it was no part of his plan to remain for any length of time in Vou-si ; but as he could not with decency refuse, and would, moreover, be supported free of cost to himself, he put a good face on the matter, and consented.   Now that he had sufficient money, he left off cheating, and not only performed the duties of a domestic chaplain in the household, but made himself useful in many other ways.   The family consisted of the old man, his son, and son's wife.   One of the useful acts of the bonze was to make a very neat and ornamental square coffin for the old man, and another for his son, both of which were placed in a very prominent position, and kept with great pride in the hall of ancestors ; and, strange as this may appear to you, there are few prudent persons in China who do not comply with this ancient custom if they can afford it.

Shortly after Lyu and the bonze had taken up their abode at the old farmer's a little boy was born, and the bonze went about with his father to a hundred different neighbors and friends, begging from each person a few copper coins; and when they had procured them from these various families, they purchased an ornament in the shape of a lock, called the "hundred families lock," and hung it round the child's neck. This process the Chinese term locking the child to life, and further believe that, by some mysterious influence of the many families who have contributed to its purchase, it insures the attaining a good old age — a very different mode of life-assurance from that practised in England. The bonze also manufactured in silver a Ky-lin, a fabulous animal, which it is believed never existed but at the birth of the great Confucius, and therefore is so holy that, if tied round the neck of a baby, it will insure promotion and good fortune for life.

As for Lyu, he was really more comfortable than he had been since leaving home, for, with the exception of being compelled to pass as a young bonze, he did pretty much as he liked; his time was chiefly passed in the mountains and forests with the young farmer, who took considerable pains to improve Lyu in riding and shooting with the bow and arrows; indeed, before he had done with him, Lyu could gallop up and down the highest mountains or pierce the eagle on the wing with ease.

So the summer passed, and the people were very happy, for the crops promised to be more luxuriant than usual; but, as the season advanced, there was a great want of rain, the land became parched and dry, and the vegetation faded and withered day by day. Then the Vou-sians grew alarmed, and began to meet in groups, and talk to each other of the terrible prophecy. Numbers sought the bonze, and induced him to offer up prayers for rain to his miserable little god of copper; and as none came without an offering of coins, he soon grew rich beyond his hopes.

One morning, however, the sun, which had risen in summer glory, became suddenly dimmed: the people began to tremble with fear, and came out in troops to the hill-sides to watch the gradual approach of a black cloud, which seemed to be riding on a sea of humming-birds, and covered half the heavens. As it spread slowly and slowly for hours, till it had become dark as night, the humming became greater and greater; the people were nearly suffocated for want of air, and sought relief from water; but, alas! it was so foul and fetid they dared not drink; at length a low, moaning wind moved the foliage, as if choking nature was making a last effort to breathe, for it almost instantly subsided. Still the drooping spirits of the people revived, a flicker of light appeared across the horizon — that again was but an unavailing effort of nature to burst asunder the cloud, for the heavens became darkened by one of still deeper hue, which hid the sun from the panting earth. As the darkness increased the humming dulled their hearing; it was scarcely louder, but larger and thicker; it filled more space, comparable to nothing but the distant rumbling of thousands of muffled drums The multitude gazed upwards with awe, then shrieked with one voice, for the very sky seemed to be descending. It came nearer and nearer; the people fell upon their faces—all but one white-bearded old man, who stood upon a piece of high ground, as Noah might have done among the rising waters, the only human being erect, who cried at the top of his voice—"Arise! arise! my children, or you will be suffocated: the Hoang-chow are upon us! to the engines! to the engines!"

The people arose—the old man spoke truth; the country was deluged with locusts, that spread like a demon mantle over hill and dale, on house-top and doop-step, on every blade of grass—the air was full of them; and at last the earth was so thickly strewn, that, as the people walked and the cattle galloped here and there with fright, they struck them up like living clouds. At the voice of the patriarch, however, the villagers brought their rakes, spades, and fire-engines, and made every effort to destroy the insects. They might as well have attempted to sweep the dust from a sand mountain in a hurricane, or to have emptied the ocean with a teacup. So night fell upon these unhappy Vou-sians.

CHAPTER XVII.

"A NEEDLE IS NOT SHARP AT BOTH ENDS."

WHERE had been the bonze during the storm of locusts? Hiding, like a coward, in the house of the farmer, where he had also detained Lyu; he had, however, shut himself in his own room, that the farmer's family might not see him that night. Lyu had scarcely fallen asleep when he was aroused by the bonze, who stood by his bedside fully equipped for travelling and with a lantern in his hand. "Rise and follow me, my son," said he; "our very lives depend upon our silence and haste."

Lyu obeyed, and the bonze, shading the light with his gown, crept noiselessly out of the house and proceeded through clouds of locusts across a small field to the stables, where they found a horse and mule ready harnessed and loaded with their travelling necessities.

Having mounted, they rode slowly towards the village gate, when, to the astonishment of Lyu, the bonze pulled a key from his girdle, and coolly unlocked it. Once upon the outer side, they put the animals at full speed, and neither drew rein nor spoke till they had placed twenty miles between themselves and Vousi, and all this through dense clouds of locusts thrown up by the hoofs of their animals. As, however, they rode against the wind, the last two miles of their journey were almost free from these destructive insects.

They ascended the sides of a high mountain, and reached about mid-distance, when the bonze slackened his pace, and seemed to breathe more freely; but still keeping silent, they rode slowly till they came to some broken crags, over which drooped a cluster of willow-like mountain trees. The bonze was evidently well acquainted with the spot, for he drew aside the drooping boughs, and disclosed to the astonished Lyu an opening large enough to pass through without dismounting.

This opening led to a huge natural cavern, so long that Lyu could not see the end, through which they rode till they came to a smaller one, evidently fashioned by the hands of man, and where they dismounted, and, after a little difficulty, in consequence of the large panniers over the backs of the animals, they passed inside, when the bonze barricaded the door on the inside with a large bar that had been left by some former occupant; then, taking two sleeping-mats from one of the panniers which they had brought with them, he threw them upon the floor, and lay down to sleep without one word to Lyu as to the meaning of this sudden departure from Vou-si.

"Art thou not curious, my son," said the bonze, the next morning, "to know the cause of our hasty departure from Vou-si?"

"Indeed I am, father, but fear to ask the reason."

"Why so, my son?"

. "For fear I should hear that you have wickedly plundered people who have been so kind to us."

"No, my son, not of one tchen; all that I possess, horse, mule, food, tea-bricks, dried pork, and coins, have been either purchased or received as gifts."

"Then why this hasty flight?" replied Lyu.

"Because the gods had deserted them, and sent ruin and destruction all around; and had we remained till this morning, the people, in their rage, would have destroyed us both, for taking their money for prayers and sacrifices that have proved useless; but, foreseeing the evil day, I had long provided for our escape, even to the key of the village gate, which I obtained from the drunken keeper."

"It was a cowardly act, O bonze, to cheat the poor people of their money, and then leave them in their distress.   You cannot prosper, O priest, by these wicked means."

"It is done, my son, and therefore not reasonable to talk about it," said the bonze, meekly, as if he had been himself injured by some foolish act, instead of having robbed the simple Vou-sians under the guise of praying for them.

"But does my father believe that the people of Vou-si will not find us even here, if their rage is so great?   Besides, is it reasonable to suppose that, as this cavern has been occupied before, chance itself may not direct some one to this spot?"

"It is not so, my son, for the people believe this to be the sacred mountain, in the bowels of which the god Buddha sits cross-kneed in everlasting contemplation.   There is even a little hole, not larger than the palm of your hand, some thousand feet above our heads, through which pilgrims travel hundreds of miles to peep, and return in the full belief that they have gazed upon his face; for, although they admit that the first half hour the vision grows dim with gazing, yet afterwards the eyes become brighter, and absorb all the glory of his face. But ask no further questions: let us proceed," added the bonze, avoiding a reply from Lyu.

So well had he provided himself with money, goods, and all necessaries, that they were enabled to travel with comfort for many days, at times sleeping under the tent, at others in village inns. When they arrived at a large city, the bonze determined to exchange a portion of his bulky copper coins for an ingot of silver, and for this purpose sent one of the inn servants to fetch a money changer. The tradesman was not at his shop, but his clerk brought an ingot, very carefully packed and marked with the government stamp; when, not contented with the sum he had already so dishonestly made, the bonze tried to make a little more by cheating the clerk; so, unpacking the ingot, and weighing it, he asserted that it weighed only fifty ounces, the full weight being fifty-two. The clerk declared that, as he had weighed it before leaving home, he knew it must be correct. This caused a great deal of higgling between them, but ultimately the clerk gave in, on condition that the bonze gave him a certificate to the effect that the ingot weighed fifty ounces. After the clerk had left, the bonze chuckled to think how he had cheated him out of two ounces of silver.

Shortly afterwards the innkeeper entered, and, examining the ingot, exclaimed, "What dirt is this? Does the venerable and holy father know that to have base bullion in his possession is to merit death by the laws?"

" What words are these? O miserable innkeeper! knowest thou not that I have but this morning bought this ingot of a money changer with good coin, at its full value?"

" Then the holy father has fallen into the hands of a trading wolf, for this is no more silver than thy servant is a wine-pot," said the landlord.

" Says the worthy landlord so with truth on his lips?" said the bonze; adding, "then will I seek the mandarin, and have the rogue before him." Then, in a great rage, and with a strong hatred of cheats, the bonze went before a mandarin, with the rogue (who really had given him base metal in exchange for his good coin) before him.

The clerk insisted upon his innocence, and prayed that the great mandarin would hear a humble insect of a clerk in his own defence.

" Then open thy dog's mouth," said the polite magistrate.

" It is most veracious that I sold an ingot to the holy bonze, but then it was of pure silver. I am but a poor man, and the priest has evidently sought to ruin me by substituting base metal for my pure silver. To show that my words are true, I beg of your mightiness to have this false ingot put in the scales."

The bullion being weighed and found to contain fifty-two ounces, the clerk drew from his girdle his certificate. The mandarin examined the paper, and then said,—

" According to the bonze, who wrote this certificate, the clerk sold him an ingot weighing fifty ounces : this ingot of base metal weighs fifty-two ounces; this, therefore, cannot be the clerk's ingot; but now arises the great question, whose is it? who has really had false bullion in his possession?"

Now the mandarin knew perfectly well who was the real rogue; but, as he was a bit of a rogue himself, he ordered the bonze to be imprisoned for life for coining—a sentence the latter only managed to escape by presenting the mandarin with nearly all that he possessed. Thus a second time was the biter bitten, and his cheating, clever as it was, brought to nought.

"Said I not, O bonze, that such wicked practices could never prosper?" said Lyu, fearlessly.

"When the error is committed, the good advice is remembered too late," replied the bonze, surlily; adding, "we had better leave this city of cheating wolves at once."

Accordingly they mounted their animals, and the bonze left the town with only a few copper coins in his pocket, muttering as he rode,—

"O Mi, To, Fo! but two moons, two moons, and I am again poorer than the dust beneath my feet."

Again they travelled across mountains, through valleys, and by the side of rivers; at times sleeping beneath the tent, and at others in the out-buildings of solitary and deserted huts, which they would occasionally find, and lived upon fish from the rivers, or birds that they shot on the wing, till, at length, after many weary days' journey, they reached the road to Ili, (the Chinese Botany Bay,) where, by the way, the bonze ought to have been sent long before.

This road brought them once more to the great

wall, and then Lyu began to think of the affectionate
home from which he had been decoyed; but the conviction that his mother and Tchin were in safety consoled and sustained him, although what was to be the
ultimate result of this long and dangerous journey
Heaven only knew. Passing the wall, they entered
a beautiful province; but, as it was midwinter, the
ground was covered with snow, so that they had but
little advantage more than the good roads, and as much
coal as they required; for this province abounds with
vast and inexhaustible mines of coal. With reference
to this coal, I may as well tell you that it was in use
in China some hundreds of years before it was known
in most European countries. The celebrated traveller,
Marco Polo, of whom I have before spoken, mentions
it in the following terms: —

"It may be observed, also, that throughout the
whole province of Cathay there are a kind of black
stones cut from the mountains, in veins, which burn
like logs; they maintain the fire better than wood.
If you put them on in the evening, they will preserve
it the whole night, and will be found burning in the
morning. Throughout the whole of Cathay this fuel
is used. They have also wood indeed; but the stones
are much less expensive."

They then passed into a wild, desolate land, through
which they travelled for some hours, when towards
evening they were overtaken by a fearful storm and
hurricane; the sky became dark as midnight, and the
rain fell in torrents. This lasted for some hours, and,
as there was nothing but a vast plain, and neither tree
nor rock beneath which to seek shelter, they kept on

wards in defiance of the storm. At length it ceased, the sky became lighter, and, O joy! they could see a town before them: the sight of human habitations made them press their animals forward, and in a short time they entered it; and a more dismal sight cannot well be imagined, for, unlike any village or town Lyu had yet seen, this was composed of wretched mud huts, built in a valley, on a filthy, black soil; the gates had been thrown down, and many of the houses unroofed by the storm. Men, women, and children were running about despairingly in all directions. Still, bad as it was, it was better than the open country through which they had been so long travelling.

"Truly, father, this is a terrible place!" said Lyu.

"Built for devils, and inhabited by them, my son. No human being would have chosen such a spot of his own free will; indeed it is the country where the emperor sends those of his children who prove to be more like fiends than men — it is a city of human tigers at bay."

Lyu shuddered, for he now knew it was an offshoot of Ili, from whence the least bad convicts had been sent, in order to supply with water the mandarin's soldiers who passed through that dismal country on their way to the former penal settlement — an occupation in itself no slight punishment, as the country is so desolate and unfruitful that they are compelled to fetch all water from a distance of twelve miles.

"It is well, my son, that we have nothing but our animals, or we should be murdered by these brigands."

At that moment a man came up to the bonze, and said, —

" Would my holy father wish to go to an inn where he will be safe from the brigands?"

" Truly will we," replied the bonze; adding, "but why does my brother utter such foolish words?"

" How is this? does not the holy father know that the village is constantly attacked by runaway devils from Ili? therefore, if he does not lodge at a fighting inn, they will steal his animals, as he has engaged no one to protect them."

" My brother speaks words of wisdom; so let him lead on," said the bonze, who, being unable to pay at either, cunningly chose the best. They were both heartily glad to find themselves once more within the four walls of a house. When the landlord perceived they were drenched to the skin, he lent them some dry clothing, and they sat down by a blazing coal fire; a luxury unknown in other parts of China, where the people temper their persons to the changing seasons by adding or decreasing the number of their gowns. In the centre of the room was a large stove covered with mats, and heated beneath like a baker's oven, on which, after a plentiful meal of boiled rice and hot tea, the bonze and Lyu rested for the night, and a very comfortable bed it proved.

The bonze soon fell asleep; but Lyu, being wakeful, arose, and, gently opening the door, passed out into a large garden by the side of the house. At the end of the garden he was rather startled to perceive the glimmering of a light. What could it mean at that time of night? — possibly robbers: however, he would see. So, walking on tiptoe to the spot, he came to a small summer-house, where he could see the innkeeper sitting at a table reading by the light of a small lantern that hung from above.

Lyu felt very uncomfortable at his position, and endeavored to return as slowly as he came, but, stumbling over a stone, the noise aroused the man, who immediately caught hold of Lyu, dragged him into the summer-house, and said,—

"Why do I find the young bonze prying into my secrets? Is he not grateful for being taken into the house when drenched to the skin like a half-drowned rat? Would he injure the hand that has warmed and fed him?"

"I am no bonze, but a Christian, who has been ——but nay, I must not tell you that," said Lyu; adding, "I sought not the worthy innkeeper; chance alone led me here."

"If my young brother is a follower of Christ, why does he travel with a priest of Fo?" was the incredulous reply.

"I utter words of truth, my friend. I dare not tell my worthy brother more; but thou then art also a believer in the only true God?" said Lyu.

"Boy, speak not so loud, or we shall be overheard,' said the innkeeper, clutching Lyu's arm.

"What can the worthy landlord fear?" said Lyu.

"Death, or being sent back to Ili, if this book is seen," replied the man, placing his hand on the Bible, which he had placed beneath his gown.

"Surely the worthy landlord cannot be a convict from Ili?" said Lyu.

"Words of truth, boy, words of truth; but follow an I fear not. My story is a sad one, but it shall enter

thy ears," said the innkeeper, extinguishing the lantern; and going to the house, he led Lyu up a flight
of stairs, into a small secret room in the roof. After
fastening the door, and lighting a small lantern, he sat
opposite to Lyu, gazed in his face for a minute steadfastly, and then said,—

"Is not my young friend the same youth who
resided with the bonze at the village of Vou-si?"

"These are words of truth; but who then is my
worthy entertainer that he is so well informed?" said
Lyu, startled at the recognition.

"If my young brother keeps his ears open he will
hear. Know then," continued the landlord, "that I
lived in Vou-si, and carried on the practice of husbandry with profit, till Heaven afflicted us with that
terrible plague of locusts, which devastated the whole
country, and preceded the total destruction of that
once happy village."

"Did then the heathenish prophecy prove true?"
said Lyu.

"If my young friend is patient he will hear. For
weeks the destroying insects covered the earth, resisting all attempts to extirpate them; as fast as they
were removed, some fiend seemed to send them again
in increased showers — our only hope was the rain;
upon this we lived. The spring, the summer passed
away, and still the cry was rain, but it came not; the
starving people prayed to Fo, incense and sacrifices
were offered up in every house and temple; still it was
of no use, and yet we had hope while the frost kept
off. By this time we had become destitute, and parted
with all for grain — our clothes, our money; and last

even the houses were pulled down and sold.   Still the rain came not, and the frantic people blasphemed against their false gods, who would afford them no relief. Then came the frost, and with it blank despair; the roads had become iron, and the mountain-sides stone; no hope of harvest then; the cattle had died of disease and want of grass; hundreds of people who had fed upon roots dug from the mountain-side till the frost came, found the ground too hardened to yield even those, and they died miserably.   As for the richer people, many killed themselves, others fled, leaving the village filled like a huge burial-place with corpses; then I fled moneyless and homeless, for my wife and children had been among the earliest of the smitten. It was then that Heaven took pity upon me, and threw across my path a travelling mandarin, who, hearing my story, permitted me to join his suite, and follow him to the town of Fou-cheou in Shensee, where, after giving me a few copper tchens, he passed on his journey.

"After leaving the good mandarin I was fortunate enough to obtain some employment at an inn.   I had not been long in that service before an elderly merchant took up his abode with us; there was something about this man that drew my heart towards him, for although he was rich he appeared filled with trouble, for he would ponder for hours and hours at a time — so often, that I began to fear that, overcome with grief, he would kill himself; so, one day when he was sitting with a book before him, I could not help saying, —

"'Will the illustrious merchant condescend to ac-cept the advice of his unworthy servant? for whatever may be his troubles, he will but make those of his household the greater, if he rushes to the yellow stream by means of his own hands.' At these words the benevolent man said, 'Alas! my trouble is great for I have lost a treasure that can never be replaced.'

"'Can thy servant seek through the empire?' I replied.

"'Alas! no, no; it is my only and very dear son I have lost.'

"This only made me the more confident he would destroy himself; and I said, 'But has my venerable master no other friends, that he would kill himself for the loss of one?'

"'Kill myself!' he replied with a smile; 'no, my friend; know you not that the great God of heaven has set his face against self-murder as a heinous crime?'

"'What words are these, my master?' I replied, surprised at such a strange doctrine. 'Do not the celestial people daily quit this life in order to escape troubles?'

"'Nevertheless, my friend, it is wicked; for know that consolation under the greatest troubles is to be sought from this book alone,' he replied, placing his hands on a volume before him.

"Then, forgetting my duty in my astonishment, I asked, 'Does that book contain a single passage that will soothe the mind of a houseless, childless outcast?'

"'It is the only consolation under the heaviest of troubles,' he added. 'But can you read, my friend?

"'Thanks be to Fo, I can,' I replied.

"'Then let thy mind absorb its teaching, and you will thank Fo no more, but the true living God.'

"'But,' I said, doubtingly, 'will the illustrious stranger intrust his servant with so valuable a talisman?'

"'Even so, my friend, providing that you return it on the first day of the moon, when I shall return to this inn.'

"That night I sat up in the outhouse and read till daybreak; the next, the next, and the next, I did the same; and, by the time the stranger returned, found the consolation I sought, and had, moreover, ascended from the pitchy darkness of a coalpit into the celestial light of heaven. I had become a Christian, though, being so poor a man, I dare not let it be known for fear of the mandarins."

"And did the stranger return?" asked Lyu.

"Truly he did, my young friend; and so great was his pleasure when I thanked him on my knees for the loan of the book, and told him I had renounced Fo and his crew of idols forever, that he presented me with the volume, saying, 'But how is this, that I see a man who should have taken a scholar's degree filling such a miserable position?' I told him my story, when, forgetting his troubles for a time, he advanced me a sum of money sufficient to establish me in a tea shop; soon after he left the province, and I have never since seen him."

"But did you never discover his name, surname, and titles?" asked Lyu impatiently.

"If my young friend will wait, he will hear all. For a month or two after the good stranger had left, my business went on prosperously, till one day, in my absence, my shopman robbed a customer of his girdle and, as he felt assured that he must have left it in the shop, he returned with some *ya-yuh*, (police,) who entered my shop just as I returned, and, after a long search, discovered the girdle in my own room, where the rogue affirmed he had hidden it by my order. Accordingly I was taken before the mandarin, who, from the account I gave of myself, believed in my innocence, and ordered the wretch to be placed in the *cangue* for three moons; when, to spite me, the rogue knelt down before the mandarin and made a pretended confession that I was a Christian, and in correspondence with a secret society of rebels, banded together for the purpose of overturning the government. At this the mandarin sent the officers to search my house, where they found my Bible, and, little as it was against me, it was sufficient; for, being too poor to make the mandarin a present, he condemned me to one hundred strokes of the bamboo, and to be sent to Ili for life. It was of no use to murmur, for Christianity and poverty were crimes he could not pardon; the governor of Ili, however, finding that my crime had not been enormous, and that I might be more useful in this town, allowed me to come and establish an inn, providing that I supplied the soldiers who pass on their way to Ili with water and lodging. My young friend has now heard the whole of his servant's history."

"But the good stranger, doubtless, discovered the name of his great benefactor?" said Lyu.

"Truly did I, my son, that it might be handed down to my posterity: it was —"

"What?" said Lyu, impatiently.

"Tchin."

"My dear, dear father!" said Lyu, bursting into tears.

"This is, indeed, a fortunate day for me. But what destiny has led the son of my benefactor to travel the empire with a roguish bonze?"

Lyu told his story, and, when he had concluded, the innkeeper shook his head, saying, "Alas! alas! my young master, how miserable is destiny! So completely are you in the power of this wicked priest, that I cannot aid you. However, take the advice of thy servant. Pour not one word of this into the ears of the bonze, but serve him faithfully according to thy word, for to break thy word of honor, even to a vile man, is to make thyself as bad; follow him, and if ever you reach Kounboum, where the bonze is journeying, endeavor to discover the venerable lama, Jin Lin; give him this coin, and he will not fail to aid thee for my sake." So saying, the inn-keeper took from his neck a small string, to which was appended a curiously engraved copper coin, and, throwing it over Lyu's head, added, "In the mean time, let thy courage fail not, and thy servant will not rest until he has sent a secret messenger in search of thy venerable parent, my benefactor."

Lyu then crept back softly into the public room, laid himself down by the bonze, fell asleep, and dreamt, as you may well believe, of the innkeeper's story.

CHAPTER XVIII.

"THE MORE TALENTS ARE EXERCISED THE MORE THEY WILL
BE DEVELOPED."

THE next day the bonze set his wits to work to
discover how he should cheat the townspeople out of
their money — a matter of no little difficulty, for,
although they were as superstitious as the other
Chinese, being semi-pardoned convicts, they were in-
different to religion of every kind. Neither the iron
chain, nor beating himself with stones, would take,
for they had very little pity, and for a long time he
was puzzled to know what to do; at length a thought
struck him, and he said to the innkeeper, "How fares
it, my brother, with the health of the people in this
unhappy and gloomy town?"

"Alas, holy bonze, but ill; they die like rotten
sheep, especially at some seasons: even now there are
many of the best to do among us at their last gasp,"
replied the innkeeper. At this news the bonze was
as merry as if he had been a doctor, as it promised
him a plentiful crop of customers for his passports, for,
bad as the people might be, he knew they would jump
at any thing that showed respect for the dead. He
therefore lost no time in beating up the town for customers. In the evening he returned to the inn highly
pleased, and with a great deal of money, and said to
Lyu, "It is well, my son, that we should remain here

for some time; for know that Fo himself cannot help him who loses opportunities, and the sickness of these miserable brigands may rebuild our fortunes, and render me capable of appearing before my Grand Lama in fitting costume."

That evening there was a great bustle outside the inn, caused by the arrival of two other priests, who, first seeing that their camels were properly disposed of for the night, entered the public room, and, after performing many salutations, took the bonze aside and entered into a long conversation with him, and, from something he whispered, they stared earnestly at Lyu for some time. They then took their seats for the evening, and, to Lyu's surprise, never addressed the bonze without paying him that respect which, in China, is due only to people of a very superior rank.

When they had sufficiently refreshed themselves, the three withdrew to another apartment to hold a private conversation. When they returned, the bonze told Lyu that his brothers brought sad news from the sacred town of Kounboum; the Grand Lama was seriously and dangerously ill: he should therefore shake the dust of the town of brigands from his feet early the next morning; and, moreover, as the stove on which they slept would only accommodate himself and brothers, he had induced the innkeeper to give Lyu a portion of his own room for the night. Lyu then proceeded to the room; and after the innkeeper had supplied the priests with some warm spirits he said, "Has the son of my benefactor a keen scent and a long vision?"

"'He who could see only three days into futurity

might enrich himself forever,' says the proverb; had I possessed such power, my worthy friend would not have me here now," replied Lyu.

"It is well and wisely answered: but does not my young master know that the bonze leaves this village in the morning?"

"Truly so, and without divination, for he himself informed me that the Grand Lama is on the point of death."

"His words are those of truth; but more, my young friend; the bonze is about to make his fortune."

"Will the worthy landlord inform me how?"

"Know, then, that this priest is not the mere wandering beggar he seems, but a lama of rank, who has been travelling through the empire on a secret mission of importance. He is, moreover, a Tchurtchun, who knows all things past and to come. These two bonzes, therefore, have been sent in search of him, and, having given him the news of the Grand Lama's approaching death, he will seek to find another Grand Lama. Now listen, and thou wilt hear of a piece of marvellous pagan superstition, by which means this bonze will erect his own fortune.

"The lamas believe that the soul of their dead chief passes into the body of a little boy, but which of all the little boys in the world they cannot tell. In this difficulty they appeal to the Tchurtchun. The bonze being this Tchurtchun, it will be his business to make the discovery; for this purpose he will search village after village till he discovers some quick, intelligent boy of five years of age, whose parents he will persuade and bribe to shut him up till he has taught him to say by heart such words as ' Behold your Great Lama in me, the living Buddha!   Conduct me to my ancient lamasary, for I am its head.'

"The bonze will then proceed to the lamasary, and if the Great Lama be dead, have exact models taken of the furniture in the room in which he died, and arrange them precisely in the same fashion in the boy's apartment; and having learned also the last words of the Lama, will make the child repeat them till he knows them by heart. Having done this, he will call around him the lamas of every degree, and declare that he has discovered the identical little boy into whose body the soul of their dead chief has passed. The lamas will then make great rejoicings, and send him in great state with numerous attendants to fetch the child to the lamasary to be enthroned; and the poor little fellow, having got his lesson by heart, will chatter away about his former life, repeatedly uttering the dying words of the defunct lama, and claiming the things around him as his own, all of which will be considered such proof of his identity that he will be installed there and then under the care of the bonze, who will become the real chief and ruler of the Lama."

"Is the worthy innkeeper a Tchurtchun himself, that he should know all this?" said Lyu, incredulously.

"Their words fell into the ears of thy servant when they knew not that he was near," said the innkeeper.

"O that I could frustrate their wicked schemes!" said Lyu.

"Let not my young master attempt such a thing," replied the innkeeper, "for they would assuredly destroy him.   These words have I spoken that he might understand their wickedness and folly, and, moreover avoid being imperceptibly led into the practices of paganism, for he travels to a land where both kindness and force will be tried to seduce him : but it is deep into the third watch, and repose is needful."

When Lyu awoke, he found the bonze ready to depart ; the camel and mule were standing at the door, and, after a hasty meal, they took their departure from the town of brigands.   Twenty days' travelling brought them to a pretty little village, where they took up their abode at the sign of "The Three Social Relations."

"Now, my son," said the bonze, "it is the will of Fo that we shall become fortunate, for the gods have revealed to their servant that in this village he shall find an immortal treasure : but as the search will take a full moon, thou art at liberty to seek thine own amusements among the hills, for truly thou canst ride, fish, and shoot ; yet remember to be within the inn by the first watch of night."

As all things happened as the landlord had foretold, I will state no more than that, for more than a month, Lyu was left to occupy himself in riding, shooting, and fishing among the hills and streams with which the country abounded.   On the morning of the fortieth day of their sojourn the bonze informed Lyu, with a very cheerful countenance, that he had found the treasure and must depart at noon.

When the hour arrived, Lyu was astonished to perceive the bonze attired in a red robe and yellow cap, which he knew to be significant of priestly rank ; he

also exhibited signs of an improved exchequer, for
the camel had been exchanged for a younger and
better one, and the mule for a full-blooded young
horse.   There was also the luxury of a Tartar camel-
driver; and, moreover, he presented Lyu with a robe
of the finest cloth and a yellow cap.   However, as
the bonze did not choose to be communicative, he
asked no questions, but felt more convinced than ever
that the innkeeper had spoken the truth; and, although
they had a longer and rougher journey at one span
than they had yet passed, these alterations and additions to their travelling gear enabled them to perform it with comfort, for, besides the animal on which
the bonze rode, they were attended by a sumpter
camel, laden with a tent, two warm sleeping-mats,
and a plentiful supply of provisions.

Within a month they came in sight of Kounboum,
an immense town of religious houses called lamasaries,
and built on the declivity of a beautiful mountain,
which as they approached, they were overtaken by
some thousands of persons of all nations on their way
to be present at the festival of the Feast of Flowers,
which was to take place the following day in Kounboum.

"Kounboum," says M. Huc, a distinguished Catho-
lic missionary and traveller, "derives its name from a
very extraordinary tree, which is called the tree of
ten thousand images, and is situated at the foot of the
mountain."   The same traveller's legend of this extraordinary member of the vegetable world is very
marvellous, for it says, "that this tree of ten thousand
images is indebted for its origin to Tsong-Kaba, the

Martin Luther of Buddhism, who at the age of three became so inspired that he resolved to renounce the world and embrace a religious life, when his mother was so delighted with her holy baby, that she shaved his head, (which was as wonderful outside as in, being adorned with fine flowing locks,) and thrust the hair outside the tent.

"From this hair," the legend goes on to say, "there forthwith sprang a tree, the wood of which diffused an exquisite perfume around, and each leaf bore engraved on its surface a character in the sacred language of the lamas." A growth as marvellous as if a tree were to spring up in the middle of Hyde Park, with a story from the "Arabian Nights" engraved upon every one of its leaves. It is further related that this Buddhist reformer caused as much alarm to Chakaja, the chief-priest of the lamas, as Martin Luther did to Pope Leo X., and that he proposed to have a religious dispute with Tsong-Kaba, which he flattered himself would result in the triumph of the old doctrine. "He repaired to the meeting with great pomp, surrounded with all the attributes of his religious supremacy. As he entered the modest cell of Tsong-Kaba his high red cap struck against the beam of the door and fell to the ground, an accident which every body regarded as a presage of triumph for the yellow cap. The reformer was seated on a cushion, his legs crossed, and apparently took no heed to the entrance of the Chakaja. He did not rise to receive him, but continued gravely to tell his beads. The Chakaja, without permitting himself to be disconcerted either by the fall of his cap or by the cold reception that was given him, entered abruptly upon

the discussion by a pompous eulogium of the old rites
and an enumeration of the privileges he claimed under
them.   Tsong-Kaba, without raising his eyes, interrupted him in these terms: 'Let go, cruel man that
thou art; let go the flea thou art crushing between thy
fingers! I hear its cries from where I sit, and my heart
is torn with commiserating grief.' The Chakaja, in
point of fact, while vaunting his own virtues, had seized
a flea under his vest, and in contempt of the doctrine
of transmigration, which forbids men to kill any thing
that has life in it, he was endeavoring to crack it between his nails.   Unprovided with a reply to the severe
words of Tsong-Kaba, he prostrated himself at his feet
and acknowledged his supremacy."

When Lyu and the bonze entered Kounboum it
was crowded with pilgrims from immense distances,
who had come to attend the great Festival of Flowers:
they, however, found little difficulty in passing, as the
people made way respectfully for the bonze. As for
the multitude of priests who walked about the town
with their long red dresses and high yellow mitres, not
one passed without paying some mark of deep respect
to the bonze, who held his head so loftily, and replied
to their salutations with such dignity and hauteur,
that Lyu could scarcely believe him to be the same
dirty, cheating beggar with whom he had been so long
travelling.

After passing through the lama town they were met
at the foot of the mountain by a body of lamas, who
followed in procession. This passage up the mountain
was the most pleasant of all Lyu's wanderings, for the
sides were planted with magnificent trees, populated

with rooks, yellow-beaked crows, and chattering magpies. On both sides of them, on the slope, were the dwelling houses of the priests, as white as snow, with every here and there a Buddhist temple, painted in variegated colors, with gilt roofs and colonnades.

At distances of about every yard there were niches in which was burning incense of odoriferous wood and cypress leaves, which filled the air with delicious perfume. Some of these white houses had turrets, from which floated long streamers, on which were painted mystic characters, which betokened them to be the residences of the chiefs of the lamas: it was to one of these that they escorted the bonze.

This dwelling was large, well furnished, and moreover contained several lama servants, who made a great fuss upon the arrival of their master, and speedily supplied both him and Lyu with a meal of tea and butter, to which Lyu sat down very much pleased, but not a little puzzled to understand all he had witnessed. He now saw a beggar on horseback — where he would ride to, however, must be left to time and circumstances.

CHAPTER XIX.

"HE WHO DOES NOT SOAR HIGH WILL SUFFER THE LESS BY A FALL."

THE following day was the great Feast of Flowers, or, more properly speaking, of fresh butter; and I question whether all the dairymaids and great artists in this kingdom united could produce such a sight. The numerous flowers of spring were all sculptured in bass-relief on walls of solid butter. These walls were erected in the spaces between the numerous Buddhist temples and before the doors. I do not know whether you can picture the sight to your imagination;—yes, you may,—there are the National Gallery, British Museum, and Marlborough House;—well, just fancy the huge walls of these buildings thickly plastered with solid butter, sculptured into scenes from the history of Buddhism, in the same manner that the earlier painters pictured the history of Christianity, and you will have some notion of the sight.

Besides, there were historical and ethnological portraits of all the different races that the fresh-butter artists had ever heard of. Then there was an account of the animal kingdom done in fresh butter, exhibiting specimens of tigers, wolves, wild boars, foxes; the coats and fur of the different creatures being so admirably imitated that Lyu almost believed them to be real.

The greater part of these pictures were enclosed in fresh-butter frames, on which were sculptured representations of rare animals, desperate wars, and wonderful feats of hunting, that had happened in the neighboring deserts. The most wonderful, however, to Lyu, was a doll theatre, decorated with fresh butter, in which, on a fresh-butter stage, pieces were performed by twelve-inch actors of the same edible.

During this fresh-butter exhibition the priests performed a great many superstitious ceremonies, which would have been equally useful if they had been performed by fresh-butter priests. In the evening a grand illumination of lanterns took place, which so warmed the soluble population of gods and animals that the greater part had melted before the morning, and thus was dissolved in one day the work and labor of months; for it is related by M. Huc that three months are occupied in the preparations for this singular spectacle, the *modus operandi* being as follows: "Twenty lamas, selected from among the most celebrated artists of the lamasary, are daily engaged in these butter-works, keeping their hands all the while in water lest the heat of the fingers should disfigure their productions. As these labors take place chiefly in the depth of winter, the operators have much suffering to endure from the cold. The first process is thoroughly to knead the butter, so as to render it firm. When the material is thus prepared the various portions of the butter-work are confided to various artists, who, however, all alike, work under the direction of a principal, who has furnished the plan of the flowers for the year, and has the general superintendence of

their production.   The figures, &c., being prepared
and put together, are then confided to another set of
artists, who color them under the direction of the same
leader."

On the third morning after Lyu's arrival in Kounboum there was a great hum of voices throughout
the lamasary — priests stood in groups of twos and
threes in deep consultation, as if some terrible calamity had occurred; still no one spoke above a whisper.
At length it was announced that the Grand Lama
had finished his old life, and was about to commence
a new one.   It was the where and when that formed
the subject of the consultations of the groups of
priests, who soon determined to appeal to the Tchurtchun, or augur, to whom all hidden things, both past
and future, were known.   When they had arrived at
this determination, the groups joined together, proceeded in procession to the house of the bonze, where
they fell upon their faces before him, and humbly
besought him to reveal the re-birthplace of their
Grand Lama.   In compliance with their prayer the
bonze, with great dignity and solemnity, proceeded to
a private apartment, and, after an absence of an hour,
during the whole of which time the lamas remained
with their foreheads bent to the ground, he returned
and informed them that he had just learned by divination that the soul of their Grand Lama had entered
the body of a little boy of Sou-chen, a village two
moons' journey from the lamasary, and who was impatiently awaiting to be reinstated in his lamasary.

Hearing this, the lamas arose and left the Tchurtchun's presence, greatly rejoicing at the success of

their mission. As for Lyu, who had been compelled to bow his forehead to the earth while the bonze pretended to consult his sacred books, he felt strongly inclined to tell the superstitious lamas all he knew of the boy Grand Lama. The innkeeper's caution, however, kept him silent and thoughtful.

"It is now time that my son should become a Chabi of the lamasary," said the bonze, as soon as the deputation had left.

"A Chabi, a pupil of these foolish pagans? never, priest," replied Lyu.

"To become a pupil will not alone render you worthy of wearing the yellow mitre of a lama, boy," said the bonze, sternly.

"Thou canst not deceive me by thy trickery, O bonze, for I know thou wouldst, if possible, make me a cheating pagan like thyself," said Lyu.

"It is thy destiny, boy," replied the bonze.

"But thy own solemn promise, O priest!" said Lyu.

"The promises of mortals, my son, avail not against the will of the gods, which was long since manifested to me. I tell thee, it is for the advantage of our lamasary that thou shouldst become a Chabi, and perhaps hereafter its chiefest ornament."

"I will die first," said Lyu.

"Young people die not so easily, my son; but open thy ears, and learn thy destiny," said the bonze; adding, "I was once a Chabi in the department of medicine as well as in the study of the holy books of Buddha. I soon sought to live and die for the lamasary alone, but, to my sorrow, observed that, with the exception of my friend and master the late Grand Lama, the lamasary possessed not one pure-minded priest. No, our holy religion but served our priests as a robe with which to cover their love of ease and sensuality. Therefore, as I grew in years, the object of my very soul, the effort of my life, was to become a reformer, like the holy Tsong-Kaba. This desire soon obtained me the friendship of the Grand Lama, to whom I imparted my plans, when he told me it had long been discovered that another great cleanser, like Tsong-Kaba, should arise, but that he would be a son of the West. These words crushed my own hopes, but made me ponder day and night, till the gods, in a dream, imparted what I sought. The new reformer was to be found in the city of Pekin, in the person of a boy, descended from the far west, in China born, though not alone of Chinese birth. I poured this into the ears of the Grand Lama, who then sent me, nominally, to collect moneys throughout the empire for the building of a great temple, but really to search for this boy. I could not doubt the intelligence of the gods, and believed I should soon find him in Pekin. I started on my journey, but, although indefatigable in my search, it proved fruitless, till one day I observed your kindness to the wretched Hieul while suffering the punishment of the cangue.

"By your features I saw that you were not of the central race: this gave me hope, and I watched my opportunity; but Hieul became very ill upon his release, and I had to wait many months before I could speak with him; at length I met him where I had expected — in an opium shop, and, believing from his dissolute habits that he could entertain no feeling of gratitude, I led the conversation to you. Fortunately for my purpose, it happened to be the day on which he had discovered your real birth. He had been to the mandarin to deliver you over to the government and claim the reward for the discovery of two wolf-people; but the mandarin, being a friend of Tchin's, to his surprise, threatened to have him bastinadoed if he dared to utter such calumny against his brother; but still the mandarin was afraid of disobeying the laws, and told Hieul that, so long as Tchin was safe, he might sell the wolf-dogs, if he could decoy them away, and promised that the police should not attempt to find you, even if Tchin offered a reward. This offer Hieul was glad to accept, but knew not how to effect his purpose. Upon hearing this I joyfully offered to purchase you. Hieul would not take less than fifty taels; it was nearly all I had, but, as I knew you to be the boy I had seen in my dream, I paid him the silver, reserving sufficient only to purchase the chair in which you first saw me, by means of which I knew I could obtain a fresh supply of money. As for the means by which I have obtained money on our journey, and which you have thought so knavish, my son, they are practised by the bonzes throughout the whole empire On my return homewards, the gods, as if pleased with my success, sent me intelligence of the Grand Lama's illness, and, moreover, pointed out to their servant the child into whose body his soul would pass. Such is my story, and thy destiny, from which thou canst not escape, nor will it long be thy wish when thou art surrounded with honor and wealth. The period of pupilage will soon terminate; for, being quick of intellect, and stout of heart, thou wilt speedily grasp the doctrines of Buddha, and a command over a number of lamas will be bestowed upon thee. But remember, the eyes of the whole lamasary are open; every where wilt thou meet lamas, nothing but lamas — priest lamas, tradesmen lamas, wealthy lamas, begging lamas, and, moreover, police lamas, from whose vigilant eyes thou canst not escape. This is enough for the present; when thou hast made some progress I will inform thee further of my intentions. Such, I repeat, is my son's destiny: what has he to reply?"

If Lyu had permitted the priest to speak so long without interruption, it was because his indignation had rendered him dumb.

" Priest, pagan, coward!" said he, " have I not said that I would die rather than pray to thy senseless idols? Nay, more; I will pour into the ears of these silly people so much of thy tricks and mummeries, thy lying and cheating, that, pagans as they are, they shall drive thee into the mountains, a beggar and rogue as I first saw thee."

" Silly boy, hast thou climbed the nest of the eagle to put thy neck in his very beak? Know, my son, that the eagle loves you; for it knows that thy dragon spirit and wolfish blood have but to be enwrapped in the folds of a lama robe, to render thee all I have sought with so much labor," said the priest, smiling.

" Then are thy pagan brothers slaves that they dare not do this, or partners in thy lies and knaveries, that I could tell them nothing that they knew not already?" said Lyu.

"Learn this, my son, as a lesson, that lamas are disciplined from childhood to respect and believe in their superiors. Many things, indeed, thou mightest tell them that they know not, but nothing that they would believe from thy lips."

So enraged was Lyu that he could make no answer, and, thinking he had at last frightened him into obedience, the bonze said, "Now know, my son, that I am about to depart on a long journey to seek the holy child, the living Buddha."

"Who, like thyself, bonze, is a wicked lie, a mere village child, whom thou hast taught to utter words of which he no more knows the meaning than a chattering magpie," said Lyu.

"What words are these?" said the bonze, with astonishment.

"Words of truth, false priest! maybe they came in a dream also; but, unlike thy vision, it was of truth, and opened my eyes and ears to thy conversation with thy brother priests, and thy after cheating at the peasant's cottage, wherein the little boy has been taught to believe himself a living Buddha. I tell thee, bonze, that thy foolish idols have deceived thee in pointing to me as the reformer of thy stupid, idolatrous lamas; they have been overcome by the true God, who has sent me here to destroy by thy own means the wicked practices of thyself and crew. Yes, these are the practices which I will proclaim to the senseless lamas around me," said Lyu.

"My son utters words of dirt," said the priest, affecting not to believe him.

"Truth, priest, truth!" said Lyu, repeating to him all that the innkeeper had told him.

"What tortoise-egg has been abusing my son's ears?" said the bonze.

"An egg whose shell was too weak to confine the words of truth, O bonze!" said Lyu.

The bonze, however, took no notice of this reply, but left the room discomfited; his calmness alarmed Lyu, who now, when it was perhaps too late, thought of the innkeeper's caution.

CHAPTER XX.

"A RASH MAN PROVOKES TROUBLE; BUT WHEN THE TROUBLE COMES IS NO MATCH FOR IT."

THAT night Lyu slept soundly, for he had given vent to his long pent-up feelings, and dreamt not of the probable consequences of his incaution and bravado; indeed, he thought nothing more of the matter till the next morning, when he was awakened by two young lamas of inferior rank.

"What would the priests of Buddha with me?" said Lyu.

"Seek not to discover, but rise, perform thy ablutions, and follow," replied one of the lamas.

As it was useless to refuse, he arose, and, after a breakfast of hot tea, butter, and rice, followed them to the end of the town, where he found a procession of lamas, with several camels, prepared for a long journey. There was also a litter, carried by two mules, into which he was ordered to climb. This he refused to do, and one of the lamas gave him a letter from the bonze; the contents were as follows :—
"My son, matters of holy import call me far away from the lamasary; therefore, for thy good, I send thee to the care of some holy brothers. Trust to the lama who will deliver this and pay thee every attention. Respect this, as thou valuest the lives of thy parents."

13

Lyu's first thought was to refuse, let the conse
quences be what they might. The allusion, however
to his parents made him tremble for their safety ; so
without another word, he ascended the litter, and the
procession moved on its way.

For three days they travelled through a delightful
country, crowded with hills and groves of luxuriant
fir trees, and dotted with pretty villages. At most
of the houses the procession stopped, and the lamas
struck a large marine conch, at the sound of which
the inmates would open the door, and deposit before
them rolls of butter, cakes of rice, bricks of tea, or
salted meat, and retire without exchanging a syllable;
and so numerous were the calls that in a very short
time the procession resembled a perambulating shop
in the general provision line.

They proceeded by easy stages, and on the fourth
day reached a vast plain, without hill or tree to be
seen around the horizon, nothing but the long grass,
which the wind swept and lashed, giving it the appearance of a great restless ocean.

Towards evening they arrived at the verge of a vast
blue lake, where they pitched their tents. "Thanks
to the three precious Buddhas, we have reached the
holy lake," said one of the lamas.

"Then at last I see this wonderful sea," exclaimed
Lyu: "but why have the holy lamas brought me to
this waste of waters?"

"To-morrow my son will know all," was the only
reply, and so he retired to his tent.

The next morning Lyu found the lamas in a better
temper, and repeated his question.

"Know, my son, we have to go to yonder holy mountain," said the priest, pointing to a cloud-like spot a great distance across the waters. "There dwell the twenty pious men"

"Is that an island, and inhabited?" asked Lyu.

"It is a mere rock, my son, without one blade of grass, or a soil that will give food to man or beast. It is there that the holiest of our lamas pass their lives in contemplation, without thought or care for any thing mundane."

"But do they not eat and drink?" said Lyu, laughing.

"Doubtless, my son, it is a weakness of our nature, and for that reason we now proceed with these offerings."

While they were speaking, a shout arose among the lamas at the arrival of two men leading a camel laden with a large boat.

"Would it not be better for the holy fathers to have a boat always in readiness for them?" said Lyu.

"This lake is sacred, my son; the waters may be ploughed by none but bearers of the yearly offerings to the holy men of the rock."

"Wheu!" cried Lyu; "it must be hard to remain there twelve moons."

"All things, my son, are as the gods will," returned the lama.

While he watched them packing the boat, which would contain but one half the offerings, it suddenly occurred to him that they might intend to imprison him for life on that rock, and the perspiration rolled down his forehead; but at that moment the lama said,

"The boat is ready; would my son prefer going with us now to visit the holy island, or will he wait for our second voyage?"

"May I, then, do as I like, go or stay?" asked Lyu, with surprise at the question.

"Would my young brother have the offer made to him if he were not permitted to choose?" said the lama; and, reassured at this reply, he laughed at his fear, and jumped into the boat. The sails were hoisted; four lamas took the oars, and pulled with such vigor that in an hour's time they came within view of the island. It arose to a height of four hundred feet out of the sea, like a huge but rugged column raised by Tritons in commemoration of some grand victory over the monsters of the deep. From crooks and crannies made by the hand of nature the gray marble sparkled and shone resplendently beneath the sun. Near the sea, about mid-distance up the rock, and hewn out of the solid mass, stood a Buddhist temple. The ascent was by a huge flight of polished stairs, wrought from the rock, and which led from the portals of the temple to the very edge of the water. It was a dreary-looking structure, but so grand in its solitariness in the midst of six hundred miles of water, that Lyu became wrapped in wonder and admiration. Truly, he thought, if the pagan god Neptune ever had a palace of repose, it must have been this isolated, sea-girt, marble mansion.

When they reached the foot of the stairs, the lama who headed the party struck a gong: the sound rang so long and strong through the distance, that Lyu could almost fancy that he saw it skipping, duck and drake fashion, across the waters. In reply to the boat's gong, a sound came from within the marble temple, heavy and dull, as if the rock itself were growling a welcome.

"The gong of reception," said the head lama, ordering his companions to discharge the cargo.

When the boat had been emptied of its contents, and two lamas sent back to the shore to fetch the remaining portion of the offerings, the rest of the party entered the vestibule of the temple, where they found two old gentlemen with very little, round, bald heads, long, white beards, and attired in red gowns, streaked with yellow, who welcomed the lamas by patting the tops of their heads and muttering some very mysterious words of blessing.

After this ceremony they were conducted to a large room, the sides and roof of which were of polished gray marble, wrought and sculptured into devices, portraying the leading features in the history of Buddhism. . At the end, on a raised pedestal of marble, stood figures of the " three precious Buddhas," — the Buddha who was, the Buddha who is, and the Buddha who will be, — at the feet of which the lamas knelt and prayed, to the disgust of Lyu, who very coolly seated himself during the performance.

"What son of a demon is this that dares profane the temple of Buddha?" exclaimed one of the outwardly clear-headed old gentlemen.

"One of such few years can scarcely intend disrespect, most venerable man; but thy servant is a disciple and believer in the only true God," said Lyu.

"What words are these?" cried the chief of the old gentlemen.

" Will the venerable father cast the light of his eyes upon these characters ?" said the chief lama, presenting a letter from the bonze.

Having perused this, the old gentleman looked better tempered, and said, "It is good; the holy Tchur-tchun's characters shall meet with respect: and now, my children, we will to refreshment."

Then one of the elderly personages went into one of twenty little rooms which led from the great apartment, and brought nineteen more holy old gentlemen, as bald-headed as himself, and they all sat down to partake of the newly-arrived provisions.

After the collation the lamas retired to some other portion of the temple with the old gentlemen, where they remained for at least six hours, leaving Lyu to his own thoughts. At length the gong announced the arrival of the boat with the remainder of the offerings, and the lamas prepared to take their departure. As the lamas, however, took their leave, the chief of the old gentlemen said, " Let my children wait till I have had some converse with this youth." Then taking Lyu into a small room, furnished with a complete set of past, present, and to come Buddhas, of shining copper, a bamboo table, two chairs, and a large sleeping-mat of the same material, he said, —

" Welcome, my son, into the bosom of Buddha."

" What words are these ? Has not thy servant said that he is a follower of the true God ?"

" The fox is not of the race of the lions, nor canst thou remain in the faith of those sea-devils of the West, of whom, thanks be to Buddha, I have only heard. Surely my son knows why the great Tchur-tchun has sent him hither ?"

"He of whom the venerable father speaks is a rogue and a knave, who decoyed a poor boy from the home of his friends."

"My son's words are profane, and his heart eaten up with anger and evil thoughts; still he has courage, talents, fair looks, and learning, that may be wrought into the long-prophesied wedge, which, pushed into the vices of our priesthood, may tear them asunder."

" Does this rogue, in whom my father has such faith, utter words of truth when he swears to his false gods ? "

" Surely the great Tchurtchun may not eat his own words."

"Then why, O my father, is thy servant sent hither ? for surely, since thou art informed of so much, thou must also know that this roguish bonze, or Tchurtchun, whatever he may be, swore by his false gods not to force thy servant into his superstitions."

" He uttered words of truth, my son."

"Then why am I here, O venerable man ? "

" That thy life might not be shortened, as most truly it would, had you given utterance to the slander you so bravely threatened to pour into the ears of the lamas of Kounboum," replied the old gentleman, at the same time striking a gong which hung from the ceiling.

" Venerable father, I must go," said Lyu, determinedly.

" Thou canst not, my son."

" How, father ? " But before the old gentleman could reply, a loud sound rang through the temple. Lyu comprehened the ruse; it was the boat's gong, announcing the departure of the lamas; and in an instant he sprang past the priest into the large room, upsetting several of the bald-headed old gentlemen who attempted to stop him, passed into the vestibule and down the stairs just — in time to be too late, — for the boat was at least ten yards off. Frantic with indignation, he halted for a moment: but he was a good swimmer, and might yet catch them; so at a bound he leaped some yards into the sea, and swam vigorously. He could see the lamas in the boat shaking their hands at him derisively. Still he swam on; then his brain became dizzy; he thought of his mother, his lost father, of Tchin; the water gurgled in his mouth, his limbs failed, and he sank deep in that solitary sea, far, far away from home and friends.

CHAPTER XXI.

"A CLEVER MAN TURNS GREAT TROUBLES INTO LITTLE ONES
AND LITTLE ONES INTO NONE AT ALL."

IN a state of semi-consciousness, with his eyes closed
and his lips compressed for fear of the water, Lyu
moved his arms and legs as if still swimming, but,
striking his ankle against some hard substance, his
eyes opened involuntarily; when, although his vision
was dimmed, his brain swam, and the sound of waters .
gurgled in his ears like the mimic roaring in a sea-
shell, he saw that he was no longer in the sea, but
lying upon a thick sleeping-mat in a small hut: still
his senses were obscure, and he rubbed his eyes,
thinking it had been a long dream; but no, sure
enough there was a real fire, and by the side of it,
assiduously tending an iron pot, a real live old gentle
man, with short round legs, upon which were piled a
very round stomach, a small fat neck, and a little
round head, looking very much as if he had been
built up, in a frolic, of flesh-colored oranges. The
noise caused by his striking his foot against a tea-
board which happened to be on the mat, aroused the
old gentleman, and he said kindly, " Thanks to the
three precious Buddhas, my son is restored."

" Where am I, O venerable father?" said the boy,
in amazement.

" With a friend who saved thee from drowning," replied the old gentleman, with an affectionate smile.

" Where am I, O father ? " again asked Lyu.

" Hist, hist ! trouble not thyself, my son," he replied ; and Lyu endeavored to force his brain into thinking order. " O, I remember, I remember ! " he cried, bitterly, as it rushed through his mind that he was a prisoner.

" Hist, hist, my son ! arise, see if thou canst walk : here is thy robe," said the kind old man, handing the garment to Lyu, who arose, dressed, and tottered towards a chair.

" Thou art better, my son ; but sit while I prepare some refreshing beverage." And the old gentleman bustled across the room, his rotund proportions tottering as if they would fall apart and roll about the floor like globules of quicksilver. The meal of hot tea, cakes, and butter, soon revived Lyu's scattered wits, and he said, " Tell me, father, how is it that I am in this hut ? Surely when I leaped into the sea it was from that solitary rock, near no other land."

" Thou art still on that rock, and within a few hundred yards of the temple itself ; and in me behold the least good, and consequently the attendant on the nineteen lamas, whose whole lives are passed in the contemplation of divine things."

" Then the temple does not constitute the whole rock ? "

" Truly it does not, my son, or thou couldst not be here, you know," said the old gentleman ; and, thinking he had been guilty of a good joke, his rotundities shook like a string of birds' eggs.

" Will my father say who saved me from the sea ? "

" Truly, son, it was my unworthy self who jumped

mto the water with a couple of swimming gourds around my arms, and, catching hold of thee, held tightly till the holy brothers put aside their contemplations, and fished us both out with a landing-net; then, being too exalted to occupy themselves with aught but contemplation, they intrusted thee to my care, and I brought thee direct to my home, where thou hast been since yesterday."

"Kindly intended, but no mercy, father; for I would rather die than become a worshipper of thy foolish paganisms."

"Hist, hist! my son makes use of words as babies use swords, without knowing their meaning. Die indeed! words of tea-dust — you wouldn't like it; but fret not — no force shall be used against thee."

"If my father's words are true, why was I sent to this wretched place?" said Lyu.

"Wretched! surely this is foolish; the island is healthy, nothing to do but contemplate, and that is good, my son. Think thyself very fortunate that you have been intrusted to my care. My holy brothers are anxious that thou shouldst be taught the faith of Buddha, but, as they cannot bring their eyes down from heaven so low as upon a boy, they have given thee over to me."

"But surely my father has not answered my question: will he tell his son why he has been brought hither, if not to be forced into the faith of Buddha?"

"Hist, hist! my son's tongue was too long, and the great Tchurtchun, being too much thy friend to cut it out, sent it where it might wag, wag, wag without harm," said the old gentleman, shaking his fat sides good-humoredly.

"This is cruel, O father: am I, then, to be imprisoned for life in this hut?"

"My son may wander where he pleases, if he will promise not to jump into the sea again."

"Father, I can promise nothing, for I will escape at the first opportunity."

"Then my son must borrow the wings of an eagle, or steal my washing vessel, the only thing large enough to carry him," he replied; adding, "but hist, hist! know that thou hast a friend in me."

"A friend in a jailer! that my father should be my friend would be indeed strange."

"Strange! not at all strange, my son; for thou art recommended to me by the innkeeper Lin-Yung."

"Does my father know the worthy innkeeper then?"

"Look," said the old gentleman, holding up the copper coin that had fallen from Lyu's robe.

"Art thou, then, Jin-Lin, whom he told me to seek?"

"Truly, my son, and, moreover, his father's brother. This copper tchen I gave him as a token by which at any time to claim my aid, and, when I found it on thee, knew that thou must have done my nephew some good service, or he would not have parted with it." I need not tell you that Lyu was overjoyed at the discovery, for he now hoped to obtain the aid of the father in making his escape, and, in the mean time, resolved to make himself as comfortable as possible under the circumstances.

It was a wild, dreary place, that rock, without a vestige of vegetation — truly a place for contemplation; but contemplation was neither amusement nor employment for Lyu; he therefore passed his time in watching the sea-fowl, fishing, and reading some choice books that the old gentleman had secreted in his hut. On this rock there were nineteen other huts, inhabited by the contemplative old gentlemen, who rarely ever spoke to each other; but walked or sat with their eyes fixed upon the clouds, their arms crossed on their breasts, and muttering as if in confidential conversation with invisible personages.

It might have been a training school for mutes who were perpetually practising their profession; for if, during his wanderings, Lyu happened to meet one of these bald-headed antiquities, all he obtained from him was a stare; still he was too thankful that they left him to himself to care about interrupting their contemplations. Once only did he enter the temple; it was empty at the time, but the gong sounded, and the nineteen old gentlemen walked out of their cells, and fell prostrate before the images of the leash of precious Buddhas, where they remained muttering till the boy became so tired that he crept softly out and walked back to his hut, where his friend, the old gentleman number twenty, soon joined him, and said, —

" Why is my son so dull this evening ? "

" Truly, my father, I am very weary of this wretched place; will my father not aid me to escape ? "

" These words are idle; it would be as easy to move a mountain as for thee to leave this island."

" Are there no planks of wood, my father, with which I could form a raft that would carry me across these waters ? "

"Hist, hist! my son must be mad to dream of such a matter; let him wait patiently, and trust to the gods for an opportunity."

"Then my father *will* aid me, or at least not prevent me making the attempt?" replied Lyu, joyfully.

"I said not so, my son; but knowest thou that this sea which thou deemest so wretched is of sacred origin?"

"My father, I believe not in your foolish superstitions, yet shall be grateful to hear the fable, for doubtless it was meant for the instruction of the people."

"Then keep thy ears open, and thou shalt hear this marvel in the world's history." With this the old gentleman commenced.

"It was in ancient times, so ancient, that the gods had not long left the earth, that the people of the kingdom of the great Valley of Oui determined to build a huge temple in the centre of their land. All the people from the highest to the lowest contributed to the good work, set about it manfully, and, after years and years of labor, succeeded in raising it to a great height; and such was their joy when the work had neared completion, that they commenced festivities, and all the kingdom attended to witness the last great stone raised to the summit. Thousands of workmen were upon the scaffolding in readiness to place it in its position. The signal was given by the king's firing a diamond-pointed arrow, the windlasses were in motion, the stone moved, and after many hours was swung into its place, when immediately a sound was heard as if the heavens were cracking; the monster stone sank through the building, carrying with it the walls and scaffolding, and crushing all the workmen and numbers of the spectators. Nothing could exceed the grief throughout the land at this disaster, which was thought to be the fault of the builders and architects, who were all immediately beheaded.

"Soon after another temple was erected, but, to the consternation of the people, with precisely the same result; and again the architects and builders were beheaded, and another temple erected, which, when just about to be completed, met with the same fate. Still the attempt was made again and again, but always with the same result; till, at length, after the destruction of millions of lives and vast wealth, the design was given over, amidst great lamentations. The king then sought the aid of an augur, who told his majesty that, although he could not divine the cause of these repeated disasters, he knew that there was a great saint in the East who possessed a certain secret, and that, if any means could be found to extract that secret from him, they would prove successful in building a temple. Upon this the king sought out his most courageous and cunning lama, and ordered him to go in search of this secret.

"After many months' travelling among the eastern tribes he was returning without having attained his object; but the moment he had made up his mind to return, the girth of his saddle broke, and he fell to the earth. Seeing a small tent near at hand, he went inside, and found a venerable man deeply engaged in prayer. 'May peace be ever in thy dwelling, my brother!' said he.

"'Brother,' replied the aged man, 'seat thyself beside my hearth.'

"Having seated himself, the lama said, 'My venerable brother, an accident has happened to me near thy tent: I have broken the girth of my saddle, and have come here to mend it.'

"'I am blind, and cannot help thee,' said the venerable man; 'but in my tent are several straps, to any of which thou art welcome.'

"While the lama was making the search, the old man said, 'O brother, thou art most happy in being able to see our beautiful monuments and temples, such that the people of the Valley of Oui can never build, for their valley has beneath it a huge subterranean sea, which will sap any foundation. But tell not this secret to a priest of Oui, shouldst thou meet one, for, if it be known to one of them, the waters of that sea will quit their abiding place and inundate our beautiful prairies.'

"Imagine, my son, the astonishment of the lama of Oui at thus discovering the important secret. So great indeed was it, that he said to the old man, —

"'Unfortunate that thou art, save thyself: the waters will soon be here, for I am a priest of Oui.' Having said this, he leaped on his horse and galloped over the desert. These words fell like a thunderbolt upon the old man, who cried out to his son, who was near at hand, 'My son, mount thy horse; gallop towards the west, where thou wilt overtake a priest of Oui; then slay him, for he has taken from me my strap.'

"The young man instantly obeyed, returned at

nightfall, and found his father's tent surrounded by the people, who could not understand the meaning of the old man's lamentations and cries. 'Be calm, my father; here is what thou wantedst;' putting the strap into his hand.

"'But the priest! didst thou put him to death?' said the old man.

"'Surely I did not, for I could not commit so great a crime upon a man who only took thy strap!' said the son.

"At this the old man trembled in every limb with fear, for he saw that his son had been outwitted — the same word in their language meaning both strap and secret; he had meant that he should kill the man who had stolen his secret. Then he cried, 'It is the will of Heaven! fly, my children, with thy flocks and herds, ere the waters drown thee all!'

"The people flew; but the old man laid himself down to die.

"Day scarcely dawned when there was heard a rumbling sound beneath the ground — thousands of wells and fountains burst upwards through the earth. Then came the sound of a great earthquake, the prairies became rent asunder, more wells appeared, and the waters spread till they reached the size of this vast sea; but they touched not the mound of earth upon which the old man's tent had stood, for, like the waves, that mound rose higher and higher, till it became the rock upon which we now stand."

"A very pretty story, my father; but what became of the kingdom of Oui? Was it not a wonder that when the sea was drawn from beneath it did not

14

collapse, like an empty bladder, or tumble in, like a stone house upon a rotten foundation?" said Lyu.

"It is well for my son that he pours these profane words into the ears of a friend," said the old gentleman. "As for the kingdom of Oui, when the lama returned with the secret he found his countrymen in terrible fear at the rumbling complaint with which the bowels of their land seemed to be afflicted; for the sounds were dreadful, as if millions and millions of demons, mounted on . elephants, were rushing through the earth after each other at a fearful speed. When, however, the lama told them the story of the secret, the whole kingdom rejoiced, set to work again, and erected the grandest and most wonderful temple in the world."

CHAPTER XXII.

"THE BEST SWIMMERS ARE OFTENEST DROWNED; AND THE
BEST RIDERS HAVE THE WORST FALLS."

As you have discovered by this time, old gentleman number twenty was a kind of servant-of-all-work to the others; but he was too good-natured to care much about that. Like most old gentlemen, he had his story. When young he had been a promising scholar, and was consequently promoted to be secretary to one of the mandarins in the province of Kan-sou, and had married a very beautiful lady, with whom he lived for some years happily. It had also been his fate to become mixed up with a sect of political reformers, who, having failed in their attempt to overturn the existing government, were, for the most part, exiled for life to Ili. He had, however, made his escape, and, as his wife and family had been killed in the struggle, he sought the lamasary of Kounboum, from whence, for still greater safety, he had joined the contemplative lamas on the rock, from which he neither hoped nor wished to move.

Dreary as this kind of life was, Lyu managed to pass nearly twelve months pretty comfortably, partly by wandering about the island in search of sea-fowl and fish, and in the evenings listening to stories similar to the legend just related, and sometimes in helping the old gentleman to transcribe the books of

Buddha. Twelve moons had passed, when one morning the old gentleman said to Lyu very gloomily,—

"Does not my son rejoice in his heart that the day has again come round for the visit of the lamas with their annual offerings?"

"Why should I, my father, without they brought that which I feel is hopeless, an order for my return?" said Lyu.

"Would, then, my son feel so happy to leave his father?" asked the old gentleman, with tears in his eyes.

"Am I less than a dog that I should be so ungrateful, my father?— but—"

"Truly! truly! my son, thou art right, and I am a selfish old weasel, for the heart of the bird flutters at the hope of escaping from its cage; besides, thou hast another parent, and a mother whose eyes must be red with weeping. I wept once for wife and children; but my eyes have been dry a long, long time! for it is foolish to weep for the dead. Then I am at the narrow outlet, whilst thou art at the wide opening of life! O, my son, may thy days be more fortunate than mine!" And the old gentleman shed many tears, notwithstanding his assertion that his eyes had been so long dry. "But listen, my son. Dost thou not hear the sound of the gong? It announces the arrival of the lamas. They may bring the order for thy release. Remain thou here; I will receive them, and learn." So saying, he left poor Lyu, who began to ponder upon his chances of escape from the rock. At the thought his heart beat against his side; he walked to and fro; his brain and heart were tremulous with excitement! At length the time appeared so long that he groaned with impatience. Four hours elapsed; the old gentleman returned; Lyu leaped towards him, but the good man's countenance was blank; and sad was his disappointment as he said bitterly, "They have not brought it, O, my father?"

"No, my son; far worse! The Tchurtchun, who has now become regent, has sent orders that you must remain another year, and become a scholar in the books of Buddha."

"Never, father, never!" said Lyu, passionately.

"Can my son prevent it? Look yonder," he said, pointing from the window of the hut towards the sea, where, some hundreds of yards beneath them, the lamas' vessel was riding. "In one hour's time they will leave, and then ——"

"O, father! father! on my knees I pray thy aid! Is there no hope of escape?" cried Lyu, falling before the good man.

Gazing at Lyu for a minute, the old man said, "Thou art young and strong, my son, but hast thou courage enough to do a daring thing for liberty?"

"Truly have I, father, for any thing but to remain here."

"Then follow me," said the old gentleman, leading him some little distance from the hut to the edge of the rock. "Look down." Lyu gazed downwards; the height made him giddy. "Canst thou make the descent? — it is thy only chance."

"O, my father, would you mock me?" said Lyu.

"Not so, my son. Look: see you not a ledge some hundred feet beneath us?"

"Yes."

"Well then, that once reached, you have but to follow the path till you come to an opening which leads to within a few feet of the marble stairs; the vessel will then be within thy grasp, if thou darest to seize it. Thou art brave, my son, but art thou equal to this?"

"But how, my father? I cannot leap the height."

"Look," said the old gentleman, taking a thin, silken cord of great length from beneath his robe, and fastening one end to a huge staple in the rock; adding, "with this I often make the descent to seek for the nests of the sea-fowl; see, it has loops by which to descend."

"Thanks, father, thanks! I will do this."

"It is well, my son; but take this for thy protection," he said, giving Lyu a short double-edged Tartar dagger or sword; and adding, "when you reach the vessel fear nothing, for I have placed meat, bread, butter, and water for thy use. Now, then, the gods take you in their keeping!" So saying, he embraced Lyu, who then stuck the dagger in his girdle, caught hold of the rope with both hands, placed one foot in a loop, and began to descend; his head felt giddy, but he kept on. Not being used to this kind of descent, his foot missed the next loop, and he hung suspended by his hands, which bled from the friction of the cord. Still he bore up bravely, and, swinging by one hand alone, caught hold of a loop by the other, and so reached the ledge, which was about mid-distance between the sea and the summit of the rock, and less than three feet wide. "The gods protect thee, my son!" cried the old man, unfastening the rope, and throwing it to him. Thinking it might be useful hereafter, Lyu coiled it round his arm, and hastened along the dangerous shelving till he came to an opening. It was a dreary place, dark as midnight; however, he had faith in the old man, and continued onwards, gently feeling his way, till his progress was impeded by something that felt like a wall, which he pressed against with his whole force to see if it would give way; but it was so firm that his heart grew sick. Perhaps the old man had been playing him false, and had induced him to make the descent that he might starve to death. It was a miserable thought; but, knowing it was useless to despair, he searched diligently with his hands, and, to his joy, found an opening near the bottom of the wall, but only large enough to admit him on all fours; thus he crept through, and in about five minutes could perceive a glimmer of light in the distance; this gave him hope, and he quickened his movements. He could also hear the roaring of the sea, and the sound of the lamas' gong, but whether the first or the second he could not imagine; if the latter, he was lost. Still his heart failed him not; he kept onwards, and in another minute reached the sea opening. There, sure enough, was the vessel, with a lama awaiting the coming of his brothers. She was moored so near that but for the priest he could easily have stepped into her; however, he pondered a minute, then uncoiled his silken cord, made a loose noose, and when the lama's back was turned, Lyu crept softly forwards, threw the noose over his arms, and, giving it a sudden jerk, sent the lama rolling into the bottom of the boat, very much to his astonishment; and before he could recover from his fright, Lyu's hand was upon his throat, and the other portion of the rope twisted round his legs. At this moment the gong again sounded, and the lamas came down the marble stairs in procession. Perceiving what was going on, one of them ran forward; his foot was upon the gunwale, when, like a wildcat, Lyu leaped up, drew his dagger across the rope that held the boat, and, as the priest toppled head over heels, the vessel bounded into the sea, to the indescribable rage of the others, who stood calling out vehemently for Lyu to return; a command he was not likely to obey. As for his prisoner, Lyu lifted him on to the edge of the boat, saying, " Canst thou swim, priest ? "

" Would the young tiger take life ? " cried the trembling lama.

" Canst thou swim, priest ? " repeated Lyu.

" Even as a fish, most magnanimous young dragon," was the reply.

" Then get thee back to thy brothers," said our hero, removing the rope from his arms, but at the same time taking hold of his legs, and turning him over into the water, " and thank them for having brought me a fortunate day."

The lama swam to the stairs, and was dragged on shore by his enraged fellows; and as the vessel was driven by the wind farther and farther out to sea, Lyu bade them a merry adieu, and laughed heartily at having secured them all for at least twelve months on the rock.

Far, far above the knavish lamas — far, far above

the Temple, upoi a jutting peak of the rock, Lyu could see his affectionate old friend *Jin-Lin* waving his yellow cap, and he thought (but that must have been impossible at that distance) he could see tears flowing from those long-dried-up old eyes; but sorry as he really was at bidding farewell to the good father, it was no time for thought; so he bent the sail to the wind, caught hold of the rudder, and directed her towards the setting sun.

CHAPTER XXIII.

"KINDNESS IS MORE BINDING THAN A LOAN."

LUCKILY for Lyu, the sea was calm and placid, with just sufficient wind to fill the sail — indeed, had it been tempestuous, the vessel would have been unmanageable; for, although courageous and strong, he knew nothing of navigation. As for where he was going, it mattered little, so that he reached the land; he therefore fastened the rudder and the sail, so that the prow pointed to the west, and as she glided through the waters he examined her contents. There were rice, butter, tea, cakes of bread, a large silk gown, lined with fur, a bow and quiver full of arrows, and, moreover, an ingot of pure silver, and some copper coins. Thus his old friend had provided him with all that was necessary for a long journey, whether by desert, mountain, or forest; and Lyu felt supremely happy at his freedom, albeit it was fraught with many possible dangers.

The sun set, the last rays had faded beneath the huge night mantle — there were no stars, nor moon; all around was gloomy, then dark as chaos; still Lyu was alone upon the sea; the wind blew stronger, carrying the boat where he knew not, except that it was in a westward direction. For two long hours did he float through the darkness, each minute expecting that the wind would become too strong for his sail, which he could now neither see how to trim or tack; yet he preferred any chance rather than by loosening it to become at the mercy of the waves, which might drive him back upon the rock.

Another hour and a few small stars suddenly peeped out of the sky, as if to light him through the waves; then came some larger stars in readiness to receive the Lady Moon, who rose resplendently, when he watched the reflection of these night lights of Heaven bathed in the waters, and the fish leaping about in delight; and there not a mile before him stretched the shore, with its yellow sands glistening and sparkling as if in joy at befriending a poor, wandering boy.—The great land once more, after twelve dreary months on that lonely rock.

When he jumped out of the boat, he stamped his feet upon the ground, to feel that it was a reality; then came another difficulty—where should he sleep? what should he do with his treasure? But watching the waves steadfastly for a few minutes, he saw that the tide was turning; and knowing that the little vessel was secure in the position into which she had been thrown by the last gust of wind, he again jumped into her, wrapped himself well in the furred gown, and fell asleep. When he awoke, it was late in the morning, although a thick mist covered the earth: when this began to clear away, he could see in the distance a number of tents, which were pitched upon the border of a huge plain; it might be the encampment of some wandering Tartar tribe, or possibly of robbers; however, enemies or friends, he must seek them; so, fastening his knife in his girdle, his bow and arrows over his shoulders, and securing the silver and coins within his robe, he made way through the long grass till he reached the outer tent, where a man stood ready to mount his horse.

"May peace be within my brother's dwelling!" said Lyu, placing his hands on his forehead, and bending his head near to the earth.

"From whence comes my boy brother, that he is alone in the plains of peaceable shepherds, and armed like a robber?" replied the astonished Tartar.

"From the far East, from whence he has escaped a great danger, and now seeks the hospitable tents of his brothers of the Desert, where he would rest till he may find a caravan journeying westward."

"My boy brother is welcome, for he has doubtless escaped the thieves of the East," said the man, taking him into the tent. So great is the awe of these wandering tribes for the Lamas of the Blue Sea, that Lyu dared not tell the story of his escape from the rock indeed, it was not necessary, for, from the quality of his gown, they believed him to be a person of some rank, at least a merchant; and exhibited no astonishment when he produced his ingot of silver, saying, "My brothers are doubtless poor in silver, while I am sore-footed for want of a horse; will they sell one of their surest footed animals and some provisions?"

"The Children of the Desert know the value of the precious metal, and will exchange with their boy brother," replied the shepherd, adding, "but let him not speak words of barter till he has partaken of our hospitality."

They then went into the tent, and partook of a hearty meal of mutton and hot tea, after which the

Tartars brought a full-blooded young horse, saddled and bridled, a brick of tea, a huge leg of salted mutton, some cakes, and a thick sleeping mat; and strewing the latter on the ground by the side of the animal, said, " The Children of the plains love silver, but they would not be thieves; is my brother satisfied ? "

" The Children of the Desert are honest and generous, and seek not to take advantage of a wandering boy," said Lyu, putting the silver ingot into the shepherd's hands.

" My brother had better take to the saddle, and keep to the west, where, if he permits not his horse's hoofs to fall heavily on the ground, he will find scarce six hours hence a caravan on its way to the city of the Son of Heaven."

This news was too good not to be taken advantage of: therefore, slinging the mutton to his saddle bow, and the other packages which were in a bag over his shoulder, Lyu vaulted into the saddle, crying, " May my brother's herds and flocks be ever increasing, and may they sleep safe from the Si-fan ! " Then, with a few more words of farewell, and good wishes from the shepherds, he gave his horse the rein, and the good beast shot over the plain, mowing the long grass down with its legs as if they had been scythes. For full twenty miles Lyu rode without stopping, except for the purpose of breathing his horse, till he came by the side of a small rivulet,—the only water he had yet seen,—he then dismounted, and while the beast was laving its feet and mouth, made a meal from the cakes and salted mutton ; after which he again mounted, and could perceive in the distance, rising into the clouds, what he took to be the summit of a mountain; it was far, far away, but he would reach it before nightfall; so setting his horse into a gentle trot, he increased its speed so gradually that they soon flew before the wind; he was not mistaken, for at the very verge of the plain were two huge mountains, and, to his joy, in a deep gorge, the caravan, which he had ridden so hard to overtake. As he approached this moving town, a small party of soldiers rode up to him with pointed lances, as if mistaking him for a robber.

"My errand is one of peace, my good brothers, and I seek for permission to join the caravan, which, I believe, journeys to the central city," said he, reining in his horse.

"My brother is surely young, to be alone and armed in these wild regions," said the chief of the soldiers, suspiciously.

"My words are those of truth," said our hero, proudly, not a little vexed at the soldier's suspicions.

"The soldiers of the embassy are many and strong, and do not doubt the boy traveller," replied the chief, riding by his side till they came to the tent of some merchants, who, liking Lyu's appearance, and moreover admiring his high bearing, invited him to spend the night with them; an invitation he readily accepted, not, however, before seeing that his horse was properly provided for.

His new friends then informed him that a great ambassador was proceeding on his way from the Tale Lama, or Prince of the Thibetians, to present tribute to the emperor at Pekin, and as he was accompanied by a good guard of soldiers, large numbers of merchants had joined the caravan on its progress. "Still, my young brother," he added, "as we have but little faith in the soldiers, who, for all we know, may be in league with the robbers themselves, we are all armed to the teeth, for the caravan is too wealthy to pass through the mountains of Setchuen without being attacked."

"What words are these of the worthy merchant? Are we not numerous and strong enough to meet the brigands of the hills?" said Lyu, fiercely.

"All are not tigers who wear the skin," replied the merchant, in allusion to the Chinese soldiers, who have those animals painted on their breasts.

"But the Tartar troops are brave, and will fight to the last," said Lyu.

"Truly, my brother; but the Tartars soon leave us to await the return of the embassy, when the caravan will be escorted by Chinese troops, who are too fat to fight," said the merchant.

At daybreak this perambulating city became in motion, and, as the merchant's party intended to follow in the rear, Lyu rested upon some rising ground with them, to take a full view of the whole caravan. It was the first he had seen, and astonished him as much as it will you, when I tell you that it consisted of fifteen hundred oxen, with long, shaggy hair; twelve hundred horses, and as many camels, all laden with goods of various kinds; two thousand men, the greater portion of whom rode the camels and oxen; the soldiers, who were all on horseback, and armed with lances, swords, bows and arrows, and great heavy matchlocks, kept as closely as possible to the sedan chair of the great ambassador.

The caravan was soon in full march, and for many days travelled through valley and desert, across rivers and mountains, without meeting with any alarm. When they arrived near the borders of the province of Shen-see, as the merchants had foretold, the Tartar soldiers took their departure, and were replaced by three hundred Chinese troops, who no sooner joined than they took it for granted that their vast numbers would frighten away the brigands, and so packed their arms on the backs of camels, and commenced singing, smoking, and joking, like some officials in this country; as if they had been especially paid for that business, and no other. I beg their pardon; they had another business, and that was, after a night's encampment, to be the last to join the rear, so that they might have every opportunity of picking up waifs and strays that might have been dropped by the travellers.

Then, O the din and noise of that travelling Babel! The long, low, hideous cries of the camels, roaring of the bulls, lowing of cows, neighing and plunging of the horses, swearing of the women, hallooing, singing, and laughing of men, and the tinkling of bells from the necks of the camels, all shrouded in storms of sand and dust, made Lyu think that Babel had reappeared in a whirlwind; still it was fine fun for him as he galloped up and down the long line of procession, chatting with one, and laughing with another.

Thus they travelled for months, till they had reached the province of Setchuen.

CHAPTER XXIV.

"FOR THE SAKE OF ONE GOOD ACTION A HUNDRED EVIL ONES
SHOULD BE FORGOTTEN."

FOR six days the caravan travelled through the
Chinese province, passing towns and numerous small
fortresses, erected for the purpose of keeping the half-
civilized inhabitants in order; on the seventh day they
entered a mountainous country. The path chosen by
the leader of the caravan was a narrow valley between two mountains; and as a strange horseman was
every now and then seen on the hills, a party of
soldiers were sent forward to scout, while the caravan
halted.

They had not been absent three hours when they
returned, bringing information that there was no fear,
for no inhabitants could be found, except a few encampments of the yellow Si-fan, a harmless tribe of
wandering shepherds; and so positively did the soldiers assert this that the caravan continued its march.
By night they had reached the centre of the valley,
and the signal gun was fired for encampment, the tents
were pitched, the guard posted, and the wanderers,
for the most part, sought repose.

Lyu slept as usual in the merchant's tent; he had
not, however, lain down many minutes when he heard
a prolonged whistle, and the sound of distant tramp-
ing; then came the crack of firearms, and immediately

15

afterwards a heavy shower of arrows fell on the tents, one of which falling at Lyu's feet, he jumped from his mat, shook the merchant, and snatching up his bow and arrow, was proceeding to seek the cause of the alarm, when the tent was burst open, and Lyu's arrow pierced the arm of a Chinese soldier, who cried, "The black Si-fan, the black Si-fan!" The cry was taken up, and ran through the encampment.

Lyu and the merchants ran to their horses, leaped upon their backs, and with sword in hand endeavored to rally the paralyzed travellers. There above them, on the hill-sides, were hordes of ferocious, swarthy-complexioned soldiers, with their arrows pointing down upon the encampment, while others behind them held flaming torches of fir-wood.

Lyu and the merchants, perceiving at once that these troops were posted on the hills to cover an attacking party, who with sword and dagger had rushed upon the head-quarters of the ambassador, dismounted, rallied a few of the Chinese soldiers, and gallantly led them up the hills, amidst a shower of arrows and shot. The three merchants were shot dead, and Lyu's foot stumbling, he rolled backwards, and thus saved his life. As for the Chinese soldiers, notwithstanding the tiger painted on their jackets, they fled as fast as their legs could carry them.

Lyu soon recovered from his fall, and ran to the assistance of the ambassador. It was useless, however, for the Chinese guard had disappeared on the first attack, the tent had been ransacked, and the poor old man pierced through the heart with an arrow. By this time the men from the hill-side, who had caused fearful destruction by their arrows and matchlocks, charged down upon the remaining numbers of the caravan, and slew them without mercy.

Sickened and enraged with the terrible scene, Lyu flew at a mounted Si-fan chief, and would have killed him on the spot, but for a lance-thrust in the chest, that brought him to the earth; when he would have been despatched there and then by the Si-fan, but for their chief, who said, " Slay him not; he is no dog of a Chinese; the blood of the wolf or tiger is in him; let him be tied hand and foot."

" Thy will be done, great prince," said the men, taking hold of Lyu, adding, " but truly the tiger boy's spirit will take flight through this wound."

" Convey him to our daughter," replied the chief, hastening to another portion of the terrible field.

Faint from loss of blood and pain, the brave boy's heart sickened as he was carried through that dreadful abattoir of men, women, horses, camels, and oxen. As for the Chinese guard, they had provided for their safety by running away at the very first shot.

The soldiers of the Si-fan carried him up the mountain into a deep gorge, in which they had awaited the arrival of the caravan, and putting him on a horse-litter, proceeded through a wild country, over hills, along ridges, and through valleys, till they came to a great plain. Crossing this, they reached another chain of mountains, the tops of which were dotted with towers, brick huts, and black tents; then taking a narrow path they continued upwards, till they arrived in front of one of the largest and most strongly fortified of the towers.

The entrance was guarded by tall, swarthy men, with long, flowing black hair, armed with long lances, sabres, bows and arrows, who, when they saw the litter, crowded around it, uttering loud cries and lamentations, which, however, soon gave place to rejoicing, when they found that the wounded person was not their prince, but one of the *Kitats*, as they call the Chinese.

Lyu was carried into an apartment of the fortress, when a young girl, seeing the prince's litter, cried, "O my father, my father, hast thou been slain by the Kitat dogs!" but, catching sight of the boy, she said, sharply, "Are the slaves mad, that they bring a Kitat into the house of their prince?"

"It is by the great chief's command that his slaves lay a wounded youth at the feet of the princess of the Si-fan," said the soldiers.

"Can the great chief command his daughter to save the miserable life of a Kitat? The warriors of the Si-fan must have dreamt this, for the wolf saves not the life of the lamb."

"The young warrior is brave, and can be no Kitat, O lady," said one of the men; adding, "the words of the chief are, that the youth's wound shall be tended by his daughter, whose skill is famous throughout the hills."

Then gazing at the wounded prisoner, the princess said, "It is well; the great chief's daughter dare not disobey his commands." She then dismissed the soldiers, and having ordered her attendants to bring a silver vessel of warm water and some green leaves, examined Lyu's chest, and steeping the leaves in the water, applied them to the wound, when, feeling im mediately relieved from pain, the poor boy attempted to speak, but the princess pressed her fingers to her lips in token of silence; so all he could do was to look his gratitude.

The royal girl was young, tall, and almost fair; her eyes were dark and shaded with long, jetty lashes; her hair was deep black, luxuriant, and long, and thickly studded with little mirrors of burnished gold. She was attired in a robe of crimson damask silk, enriched by a black girdle of the same material.

After she had dressed Lyu's wound and given him to drink of the refreshing tea, she folded her arms across her breast, and, gazing intently in his face, said, —

"The soldiers of the Si-fan have said that the little warrior is no Kitat. Do, then, any but Kitat dogs wear the symbol of slavery?"

"It is true, O princess, that though long in the land of the Kitat, thy servant is not of their blood; his father's race dwell in the far-far-western sky, and those of his mother in the free hills."

"Can these be straight words?" said the princess, incredulously.

"Straight as thine own form, O princess," replied Lyu.

"Like his face the little warrior's words seem fair, and the daughter of the Si-fan will no longer doubt him; but another time she will listen to his story," said the princess, leaving the apartment.

For three days she visited him for a short time and dressed his wound, which, being no deeper than the flesh, soon became well. On the fourth, great preparations were made throughout the town for the return of the victorious prince. All the people turned out under arms, and the air was filled with the sound of gongs and brass wind instruments.

Sheep and oxen were offered up to their gods in gratitude for the victory; but as these copper and wooden deities did not descend from their pedestals, probably from want of appetite, the good things were divided amongst the people. Later in the day there was a banquet in the great hall of the fortress; the prince of the Si-fan sat upon a raised throne, surrounded by his family, including even the ladies; the warriors were seated at different tables.

Lyu was brought forth, and, to his surprise, magnanimously praised for his bravery; for some time all was noise, singing, and bustle; the prince, however, suddenly dashed his drinking goblet upon the ground, and every voice was so hushed that the fall of a pin could have been heard; the prince whispered to his daughter, and, after she had replied, he beckoned to two of his attendants, and Lyu was led to the foot of the throne, and told to prostrate himself before the chief; the prince then said, "Were we not right, when we saved the little warrior from the fate of the Kitats, and said that he was not of their miserable race?"

"The words of the great Si-fan were those of truth," said Lyu.

"It is good," replied the prince; adding, "yet was the little warrior found among the dogs; the wolf consorts not with the lamb, nor the tiger with the sheep. Let him, then, inform the Si-fan how he came to be among them."

Lyu then related his adventures from his birth
telling the name of his father's race, but simply speak
ing of his mother as a daughter of the mountains,
without naming her particular tribe.   To this the Si-
fan warriors listened with great attention, occasionally uttering words of admiration at Lyu and disgust at the bonze, but more especially at the Chinese.
When he had finished, the prince arose and said, " My
son is young and brave, and an enemy of the Kitat,
and therefore a friend of the Si-fan, whose arms are
open to receive him.   Will he become a Si-fan warrior ? "

Not a little startled at this proposition, Lyu said,
" Thy servant is not ungrateful, great prince; but his
filial piety will not permit him to settle on earth till
he has discovered his mother.   His life is in the
hands of the great Si-fan; let him do with it as he
will."

At this reply there were great shouts of admiration; for among these wild tribes filial gratitude is regarded as a chief virtue.

" It is well spoken, my son," said the prince; " thy
first duty is to thy mother, who surely must be of the
Si-fan race, to have given birth to so worthy a son.
Let the young warrior speak."

" Truly my venerable parent is not so happy, great
prince, yet is she of a no less noble race; she is of the
Miao-tse," replied Lyu.   No sooner had he spoken
than every warrior arose, drew his sword, and pointed
it at Lyu s breast; and the princess, seeing him thus
menaced, rushed through the pointed weapons, placed
her hands upon the boy's shoulders, turned her beau

tiful head towards her parent, and, stamping her pretty
foot upon the floor, cried, " How, O my father! shall
thine own guest be slain in the midst of rejoicings
and at thy royal feet?"   The movement of the princess caused the chieftains to fall backwards, but, still
clutching the hilts of their swords, they glanced furi-
ously at Lyu; when the prince arose from his seat,
drew his form to its full height, and, without uttering
a word, shook the sleeves of his robe; a signal that
the boldest dared not disobey, for it was for instantaneously breaking up the party.   When the chieftains had
dispersed, the prince beckoned to some soldiers, and
commanded them to convey Lyu to a small stone
room at the very top of the tower, where they left
him to ponder upon the meaning of this very extraordinary finale to the banquet.

CHAPTER XXV.

THAT night Lyu was left alone to reflect upon the meaning of the sudden alarm, for, with the exception of a man who brought him some thick mats for a bed, no one came near him.

The next morning he heard a great bustle around the tower, the noise of horses and men. What could it be? Were the Si-fan about to start on another robbing expedition? if so, he might find some means of escape. Some time elapsed and all became quiet, so that he could hear soft footsteps outside the door, and in another moment the princess entered the room.

"The daughter of the Si-fan seeks the little warrior in the hour of his trouble."

"Surely, O princess, thy servant is dull; he cannot understand in what he has given offence," said Lyu.

"Did he not proclaim himself a Wolf-dog, a Miao-tse?"

"Surely the daughter of the Si-fan speaks in riddles; for are not the Miao-tse and the Si-fan both of the hills — both brave, and enemies of the Kitat?"

"Alas, no!" replied the princess, speaking more familiarly; "the Miao-tse are the enemies of the Si-fan; they have long been at war together; there can be no brotherhood between them, for they have destroyed each other's towers, towns, and tents. It

is not twelve moons since the Wolf-dogs met the
Si-fan in battle and destroyed their brave warriors,
among whom were many chiefs, brothers and fathers
of those with whom the young warrior sat. Since
that time they have sworn to the gods to kill the
Wolf-men wherever they meet them ; and would have
slain thee on the spot yesterday but for their chief's
stern eye, which told his people that thou wert befriended by him.

"When, to save thy life, the prince broke up the
meeting, he called a council of nobles, all of whom
now believe thee to be a Kitat, or a Miao-tse spy,
and demand thy blood in atonement for that of their
brothers. The noble prince would have befriended
thee ; but he was too wise to break the laws, and
therefore told his children that to assassinate a stranger
who had partaken of their hospitality would be to offend the gods ; that as brave warriors they should
keep thee a close prisoner till their passions had subsided and they could sit in council on thy fate ; still
they were clamorous for thy death ; but, fortunately,
a soldier arrived, telling them a Kitat caravan would
soon pass through the hills, heavily laden with merchandise. The chief then proposed that the Miao-tse
boy should be confined till their return, and led them
this morning to meet the Kitat cowards."

"Has the chief and daughter of the Si-fan saved
their servant's life but to assassinate him hereafter ?"
said Lyu.

"Let the young warrior listen ; he has bravery, and
may save his life : the prince knows the solemnity of
his word, and dares not break it. Still when the door

is opened the bird may escape from the cage; the outside of this tower is not guarded, the inside is full of Si-fan soldiers," said the princess; adding, "take this rope; it will help thee from the window. When you reach the earth, take the narrow track to the left, and thou wilt find every means provided for thy escape. Now, begone in peace, for thou hast brought trouble on the Si-fan." So saying, the princess left the room, not, however, before Lyu had kissed her hand.

As soon as the door was again fastened, he began to examine the rope which the princess had given him. It was of silk, and full of knots and loops, like the one by which he had descended from the rock in the blue sea. To fasten it to the window was the work of a very few minutes, and, notwithstanding the great height of the tower, he descended with safety, and proceeded as directed along the path, where, at a short distance, he was delighted to find a horse, ready saddled, with a lance and sabre; a bow, and a quiver full of arrows; on the saddle bow hung a large leg of salted mutton, and a bag containing rice, tea, and cakes; but what most astonished him was a couple of large gourds tied together like swimming corks: they afforded a hint to Lyu that he was to seek safety by crossing some river; so, throwing the gourds around his body, in the event of having to ford one in haste, he vaulted into the saddle lance in hand, and was soon galloping in freedom across the mountains like a Si-fan chief. For some hours he rode pretty hard, in order to get out of the territory as quickly as possible. After some six hours he stopped to refresh himself and his horse — just one half-hour's rest, no more — and he was again in the saddle and galloping through a deep mountain gorge, along which he continued till nearly evening, when he came to a wide plain, where, a few hundred yards before him, were six mounted Si-fan on their return home. When they perceived Lyu they mistook him for one of the princess's guard, and threw up their lances by way of salute; to deceive them, he very adroitly wheeled his horse half round, shook his lance in return salute, and galloped off in another direction; but, turning in his saddle, he could perceive that the horsemen had discovered their mistake, and were preparing for a chase; therefore to place himself as much as possible out of reach of their arrows, he flung the leg of mutton and the provision bag over his back, bent his head on his chest, gave his horse the rein, and soon came to a rivulet; when the horsemen, making no doubt that they had him, gave a shout of joy. They were mistaken, for Lyu leaped across; they were, however, gradually nearing him, for he could hear them shouting, "Wolf-dog, dead or alive:" then followed a flight of arrows, which, thanks to his presence of mind, proved harmless, as they struck his shield of salted meat. -

Away he rode, till he reached a hill apparently too steep for ascent; but, determined not to be taken alive, he gave a few words of encouragement to his horse, and the noble animal scaled the hill like a wild-cat. This feat was followed by a shout of disappointment and rage from the Si-fan. Then, in the midst

LYU PURSUED BY THE SIXAU.

Page 236.

of his danger, Lyu grew venturesome, for, holding the reins in his mouth, and fixing his lance under his arm, he placed an arrow in his bow, turned in his saddle, and, in another moment, one of the horsemen fell heavily on the ground; then, with a shout of rage, the remaining Si-fan sent arrow after arrow into the provision bag. At length he reached the top of the hill, with the horsemen at his heels; before him was a wide river, and the Si-fan gave a shout of joy; but, terrible as was his situation, even then he did not despair; but rushed down the side of the hill, till within a hundred yards of the water.

Thinking he would proceed along the bank of the river, the Si-fan galloped through a fissure of the hill at some distance, and reached the bank just as his horse fell dead beneath him. They were now within a hundred yards of him, and the boy began to despair; but the danger quickening his wits, in another moment he adjusted the gourds beneath his arms, clutched the lance, and fled towards the river, placing an arrow in his bow as he ran; he had reached the edge, when another flight of arrows nearly knocked him down; but, taking advantage of their empty bows, he fired in return, and another of the horsemen lay in the dust; the remaining four, shouting with rage and disappointment, flew upon Lyu, — nearly, not quite, — for, bag and baggage, he leaped into the river, and swam by the aid of the gourds. The waters were invigorating, and he struck out into the stream; then resting upon his gourds, he saw that his enemies had dismounted and were about to jump into the stream, when, trusting to the gourds to support him, he sent an arrow, which disabled another of the party.

He swam further across the stream; fortunately, there was a floating raft of fir-trees tied together near him; making an effort, he climbed upon it, and in so doing an arrow grazed his leg; as he was now, however, in comparative safety, for the current was so rapid that it carried the raft far out of reach of the Si-fan, he coolly sat down to appease his appetite with some of the contents of his bag.

He then began to consider his position. Night was approaching, and he was in the midst of a great river, travelling at vast speed, he knew not whither; still he felt safer than on shore in the dark night, without the means of obtaining a light, and in the neighborhood of wild beasts, with which the hills and forests abounded. Besides, he remembered that the more peaceable of the hill tribes adopted this means of sending timber down from the hills to the Chinese settlements in exchange for other commodities; so, with something like a feeling of security, he lay down upon the raft, and covering himself as well as he could with the provision bag and his robe, fell asleep amid the rushing, splashing sound of the waters, and the roaring of the wild beasts from the shore.

However, the moon arose, and he could see that the river ran between two mountains, one of which was covered by a dense forest; it was a grand sight, solemn and vast, like the mind of a great man in deep thought for the advantage of his race. The fish sprang playfully about, and the moon shone upon the deep yellow sands, which sparkled like diamonds sprinkled with gold dust; then he began to wonder where he should find himself in the morning. Where was his mother? Was he ever to see her again? Yes, for the great Emperor Tait-sou had passed through more difficulties when he was a boy. That was at least some consolation.

CHAPTER XXVI.

"BY NATURE ALL MEN ARE ALIKE, BUT BY EDUCATION WIDELY DIFFERENT."

ALONE upon a few trees, on a vast river, far, far from his friends, the winds howling through the huge woods, the brave boy floated in peace, unconscious of the beasts of prey, who sniffed him from the banks, and but for the distance would have sprung upon the raft.

His troubles and trials had passed away, and he sat at home once more, between his mother and the good Tchin; he related to them the whole of his adventures, to which they listened with tears of joy and sorrow. Then his mother besought him to rest upon a couch, and he fell asleep, and dreamed that a mist arose before his eyes, which soon formed into a circle, from which arose a lama, who grasped his arm; he shrank backwards, but the lama's hand shot out from his arm, like a telescope, and followed till it caught hold of him; then a death-like coldness seized upon his heart; he could not move; then the lama's features changed to those of the bonze, who, as he stepped out of the mist circle, changed into solid ice.

The boy tried to speak, but he was speechless; his feet and fingers tingled, a glow of warmth ran through his frame, a warm hand pressed his heart, and a voice rang in his ears —

' The grasp of the frost-fiend has become loosened from the boy's heart—he is saved!"

Lyu opened his eyes in astonishment to fi: d himself in a large room, surrounded by Chinese soldiers, who had been rubbing his limbs with snow; perceiving that he was awake, they made him swallow some hot spirits, when a genial warmth passed through his frame, and he began to remember the night on the raft, and knew at once that he must have been picked up frost-bitten.

"Thanks, my warlike brothers! thanks, for thou hast saved my life," said Lyu.

"The young tiger utters words of truth, for truly the frost-fiend would have carried his spirits to the regions of snow, but for the soldiers who were looking out for the timber from the hills. But who is my young brother, that he should be in such a plight?" replied the Chinese.

"The warrior of the Son of Heaven sees but a merchant's boy before him, who, being pursued by thieves to the banks of the river, plunged into the stream, where he was fortunate enough to find the floating timber, on to which he clambered, and then fell asleep with fatigue," replied Lyu.

"The words of my young brother are doubtless those of truth, but he must repeat them to the rebel-subduing general himself, who rests here for the pur pose of chastising the wolf-dogs of the hills."

"Am I then in the land of the Miao-tse?" cried Lyu, incautiously.

"Who may my brother be, and whrt his name, sur

16

name, and titles, that he speaks with respect of these wretched vermin?" said the soldier, sharply.

"Surely thy servant hath spoken no treason against the Son of Heaven," replied Lyu.

"Of that the wolf-dog-chastising general must judge for himself, my brother," replied the soldier; adding, "in two hours thou must be prepared to meet the general's greatness."

Notwithstanding their suspicions as to the real character of the boy, the soldiers treated him kindly, and invited him to partake of hot tea and butter; after which they told him to follow them. Lyu soon found that he was in the midst of one of the numerous fortresses which the Chinese have established from time immemorial at the feet of the hills, in order to keep the wild tribes in subjection to the emperor; still he wondered to see such vast preparations for war in a time of peace, for the place swarmed with armed soldiers and pieces of artillery; but cautious of not saying too much, he held his peace until he reached the presence of the great Le.

The general's chair was placed upon a raised platform, and he was surrounded by a number of military mandarins of rank. When Lyu had knocked his forehead upon the earth nine times, the general said, kindly:

"We have heard thy tale, O youth! and believe that thou hast spoken words of truth."

"The great general is as wise and all-seeing as he is brave," said Lyu.

"But not the whole truth, boy; for thou hast withheld the portion of thy story which most concerns us. It is even alleged that thou art a Wolf-dog."

"What dog can have poured these words into the ears of the dragon-general?" said Lyu, evasively.

"Even the Si-fan vermin, who chased thee to the water's edge, like cowards, as they were, and who were brought prisoners to the camp last night. What has the young dog to say to this?" said the general.

"Nothing; for he will not deny his blood, knowing hat the great General Le is too generous to slay one who can have committed no treason against the yellow dragon," said Lyu, boldly.

The general smiled, but then said, sternly,—

"Boy, thy life is forfeited to the laws; it shall be saved upon one condition, namely, that thou guidest the war tigers of the emperor to the tents of thy race."

"Thy slave hath never seen them; but know, O general! if he had, his tongue would remain silent, for slaves only betray their kindred."

"The young tiger is brave, and the generals of the Son of Heaven can reward bravery even in an enemy. Listen, boy; notwithstanding that these vermin of Wolf-dogs have been so often chastised by the armies of the Son of Heaven, they have again dared to break out in rebellion, and much blood has been shed. It is the desire of the emperor, however, to spare the lives of his children, and, although this great army is on its march, to root the whole of the rebellious race from the face of the earth, it will remain here, and await the return of a military mandarin, whom I send with certain propositions, that may give to us the blessings of peace, and save the lives of even these vermin. The officer is prepared to depart, but he speaks not their barbarous tongue; the young Wolf-dog must accompany the envoy, and be his interpreter. Thus, instead of taking thy life, have we condescended to confer an office upon you," said the general.

"These are fair words, O general! and the command is no more than thy servant may perform," replied Lyu, who was really well pleased at the chance of visiting his mother's race.

He was then conducted back to the town, where he remained that day with his friends the soldiers; the following morning he was introduced to the military mandarin, who was to act the part of envoy, and with him set out upon their journey through the mountains. They were accompanied as far as the outposts of the Chinese territory by a body of mounted soldiers.

They had travelled for nearly three weeks across the province, sometimes on mountains tipped with snow, and at others through verdant vales and across rivers, stopping by night at some military station. Wild, romantic, and almost uninhabited, except by peaceable agriculturists, as was the greater part of the country through which they passed, it still bore remarkable traces of having once been inhabited by a numerous and ingenious people, for the fortifications, monuments, and bridges were very many, though partly in ruins.

One of these bridges was built across a rapid torrent, which divided the land of the Chinese Tartars from that of the original children of the soil; this bridge was of solid iron, and erected many hundred years ago by a conquering general, whose name was

engraven on one of its sides; on each of the banks
there was a large door built between great stone piers,
from each of which on the east bank were suspended
four immense chains, which hung by great rings
fastened to the piers on the other side, and were kept
together by smaller chains, so interwoven together as
to have the appearance of a beautiful net-work; on
this were laid several great planks of wood, fastened
to each other; the whole was covered by an elegant
roof supported by wooden pilasters. This bridge was
so light in its structure, and moreover so steep in its
approach, that they had great difficulty in leading
their horses across; when they reached this river, the
mandarin dismissed the escort of soldiers to the nearest military station, to await his return, thinking it
safer to proceed into the enemy's country without
military show.

When the escort left, the mandarin, who had been
reserved and proud in his bearing, became communicative about the strange races of the hills, of whose
habits and customs he seemed to be well informed,
although he could not speak the language.

"Truly, my young brother, these vermin are as
numerous as locusts; destroy one, and a hundred
others swarm upon the soldiers of the emperor like
startled bees."

"The tiger of war cannot deny the courage of the
sons of the hills," said Lyu.

"The courage of the vermin is as certain as their
customs are barbarous," said the mandarin, adding,
"look yonder; those are the Ping-sha-shi mountains,
and contain a tribe, who, when they marry, stick five

small flags into a bundle of grass, fastened together by seven different bands, before which the bridegroom kneels, while his friends fold their arms and bow to the earth; after which they dance and make merry: surely, it is a stupid custom! If a parent dies the eldest son remains at home for forty-nine days without washing his face. Again, if a parent be sick, they cut off the head of a tiger, and place it upon a plate, with a sword, three incense sticks, and two candles behind it, and three cups of wine in front. This they offer up to Fo: truly it is a barbarous custom. The vermin of another tribe, when about to marry, are foolish enough to knock out two of their front teeth, which they believe will avert the mischiefs of matrimony — as, truly, it must prevent them biting each other — and when one of them dies they bury the deceased in a coffin; but twelve moons after, the barbarians go to the grave, sacrifice an ox, burn incense, drink wine, remove the earth, dig up the bones, pick comb, and wash them clean, wrap them up in a white cloth, and bury them again for a year or two, when they wash and comb them once more, for they believe that if disease comes among them, it is because the bones of their ancestors are not kept clean."

It was with anecdotes such as these that the mandarin wiled away the time; and for days and days they travelled, occasionally resting in the villages of some of the wild but peaceable tribes; and many things Lyu noticed that surprised him. Wherever they met with women they found them uniformly good-tempered, pleasing, and industrious — sometimes, at the doors of their low brick huts, spinning and weaving, or in the fields on the mountain side, taking the place and occupation of men. Every where was freedom and hospitality; no hut did they pass without receiving an offering of hot tea and cakes. For the most part the people were shy of the mandarin, but with Lyu they were delighted, the more so as he could speak their language. Indeed, so different is the position of the Miao-tse women from their Chinese sisters, that in some of their villages the office of magistrate is filled by a lady.

At one of these villages they were introduced to the lady magistrate, a tall, handsome woman, who, although she wore neither shoes nor stockings, had on a robe of dried painted leaves, lapped over each other; on her head she wore a white turban, elegantly embroidered with flowers, and golden ear-rings, so long that they rested upon her shoulders; her long black hair hung in two braided tails down her back, and she sat in a chair of state, holding a beautiful fan in her hand, while an elderly personage stood behind, holding over her head a large umbrella, the badge of her rank and authority. When this lady heard where the travellers were proceeding, she told them that the journey was long, dreary, and dangerous, the inhabitants cruel and savage; and, presenting them with sufficient provisions to last some days, ordered a party of her people to attend them to the verge of her domains.

"Truly, my young brother, it is a strange sight to see women usurping the place of men! Would to Fo. however, that we could meet with nothing worse on our journey! But let us now look to our arms, for we are entering the land of devils," said the mandarin.

"Surely the tiger of war cannot fear these simple people?" said Lyu.

" Has my brother no eyes?" replied the mandarin, pointing to a dense forest that was before them, and adding, " our enemies may be twofold, men and beasts."

" My brother's caution is wise," said Lyu, looking that his bow, arrows, and sword were at hand.

For some hours they journeyed through this forest, in which the trees and brushwood were so thick that it was with difficulty they could find way for their horses; at night they came to an open glade, where they made a large fire, sat down, and warmed some tea, after which the one slept while the other watched. The next day and the next were passed in a similar manner; the day following, they came to a portion of the forest planted with choice plants and flowers, among which were strewn a great number of dead bodies, bound round with ratan cane, so close and tight that they resembled Egyptian mummies.

" By *Fo*, we are not far distant from the vermin we seek," said the mandarin, "for they are the only barbarians who thus dispose of their dead. This is one of their cemeteries. By the chief social relations, the sight is not agreeable; let us onwards."

Lyu replied by hastening the speed of his horse, and they soon found themselves once more upon the open mountains. After an hour's ride, they came in sight of a tall column, which the mandarin no sooner saw than he joyfully exclaimed, " May the divinity of war be thanked, we have reached the rebels' holes Yonder is the boundary of their territory."

When they reached the column, Lyu saw that it was of massive brass, and engraved with a sentence in Chinese characters, which meant, that all of the tribe of the SING *Miao-tse* who passed that brazen column would be destroyed.

"Does the tiger of war know the meaning of this column?" said Lyu, looking at it with astonishment.

"Like a trumpet, it is brazen and noisy, but no terror. Six hundred years ago the SING Miao-tse vermin passed down these mountains for the purpose of invading the empire, when they were met and chastised by the rebel-killing general Ma-yuen, who erected this column as the boundary which they were not to pass on pain of death. It is a boaster, my brother, a brazen stupidity; for they have passed it many, many times, even daring to attack the fortresses of the Son of Heaven himself," said the mandarin.

"Then these SING Miao-tse are the bravest of the children of the soil," said Lyu, with pride, for he knew that they were his mother's race.

"They are rats, they are tiger-cats — as plentiful as the one, and as vicious as the other," replied the mandarin; "but look, if dust is not in my eyes, their town is on yonder hills," he added, pointing to a cluster of dark objects on the ridge of a mountain not far distant.

"The tiger of war is right; but see yon hunter. By the head of the dragon, he is off his horse;" and without another word Lyu galloped at full speed down the hill.

The hunter had been in chase of a wild boar, and had wounded without killing the brute; at the moment Lyu made the exclamation, the boar, maddened with pain, had turned suddenly upon his foe, fixed his tusks in his leg, and pulled him from his horse, where he was lying with the boar upon his chest. When Lyu got within bow-shot, he sent an arrow at the beast; still it would not loose its hold; when, dismounting, Lyu ran to the rescue, and the brute, seeing a new enemy, sprung at the brave boy, who, however, was so quick in his movements, that in an instant his sword passed through its throat, and the animal rolled over in the dust; then tearing a strip of silk from his robe, he bound it tightly round the hunter's leg to stanch the blood, which was flowing profusely.

The hunter was a man of some seventy years; of tall stature and large frame; his hair was long and white as snow, and, though his face was shrivelled, his piercing dark eyes and compressed lips proved the indomitable spirit of his race. From his dress and arms, Lyu knew that he must be a personage of consequence, for his helmet was of brass, surmounted with a long feather; his body was encased in a cuirass of the same metal, highly polished, and beautifully studded with silver nails, and had greaves or leggings of the same material, but his feet, hands, and throat were perfectly bare; the sword which he still held in his hand was short, but sharp and wide; his cross-bow was made of wood and steel; a quiver of very short, strong arrows hung by his side, which, propelled by so powerful an instrument as the cross-bow, gave them the deadly force of a cannon-ball; he had also a shield, half circular in form, and painted with the head of a tiger; this, however, like the cross-bow, had fallen on the ground during the struggle.

THE HUNTER AND THE WILD BOAR.

Page 250.

" The young stranger has gained the gratitude of Lie Yaou-jin," said the old man, in the Miao-tse tongue ; adding, sternly, " but how is it that the heart of a tiger should inhabit the body of a snake? Is it possible for the accursed Kitats to send forth a brave warrior ? "

" The dust of enmity is in the eyes of the venerable warrior, for surely he is too generous to deny that courage may be found in an enemy," replied Lyu, in the same language.

" They are all cowards ; the young warrior can be no Kitat, for the tongue of the tiger fits not the mouth of the fox," said the hunter, astonished at hearing his own language spoken so fluently by a Chinese.

" The tongue of the children of the soil was taught me by a daughter of their race, who was stolen from the tents of her father by the Kitats," said Lyu.

" It is well that the young warrior has earned the gratitude of a Miao-tse, or he should not have lived after speaking with Kitat lips of the slavery of a child of the soil," said the old hunter, sternly.

" Are the old vermin's words plain to the ears of my young brother ? " asked the tiger of war, who, now that the danger had passed, rode up to them.

However, as Lyu entertained great contempt for this paper tiger, whom he believed to be a great coward, he took no notice of this question, but proceeded to help the hunter upon his horse, who, looking at the mandarin, said, " What brings the Kitat mouse to the hills ? Is he regardless of his miserable life ? "

" It was a fortunate day, O venerable man, that

brought me to thy side; yet it would never have happened if the mandarin had not been sent on a message from the great General Le to the Prince of the Yaou-jin."

" Let my young brother ask the old vermin his name, surname, and titles, and, in the name of the great emperor, command him to lead the envoy of the rebel-subduing general to his chief," said the mandarin proudly.

" What says the Kitat dog?" asked the hunter, perceiving that the mandarin was staring at him angrily.

" He craves of the venerable warrior his name, surname, and titles, and, further, that he will show him to his chief," said Lyu.

" Said the dog these words? Then command him, in the name of the golden dragon, who rules the hills, not to approach within half an hour's ride of yon town till I report his arrival to the king; for if he disobey, the dog of an envoy will have a half hundred arrows through his miserable body," said the old man sternly; adding, " but let the brave young warrior take this sword; it may serve him in need," giving Lyu the weapon. He then rode up the mountain in the direction of the town, much to the surprise and vexation of the mandarin, who fixed an arrow in his bow, saying, " Did the old vermin utter aught that should prevent my sending an arrow through him ? "

" Thou art a coward, O mandarin of war," said Lyu, snatching the arrow from his hand, and then repeating the old man's words.

" By the thunders of war the old vermin must be

the arch-traitor himself; know thou, young wolf-dog, if I had slain him, and returned with his head, I should have been promoted to a high command?"

"Words of dirt! Could a mouse slay a tiger? Thou couldst not have killed the venerable warrior except by assassination," said Lyu, indignant at his cowardice. After this the mandarin looked mischief, but spoke not, and they rode slowly onwards to the appointed spot, where they could just perceive the hunter enter the gates of the town. Shortly after they saw a widely-spread band of warrior-looking huntsmen galloping up the hill after them; the sight caused the tiger of war to back his horse with fear; Lyu, however, placed his hand upon the sword which the hunter had given him.

When the warriors perceived Lyu and the mandarin, the chief rode straight up to them, and said, in the Miao-tse tongue, "Are the Kitats so wretched that they do not know where to find death, that they rush into the jaws of the wolf?"

"They seek protection from the children of the soil in the name of the owner of this sword, whoever the venerable man may be, brave chief," said Lyu, holding the weapon before them.

When the chief saw the sword, he dismounted, and bowed respectfully before it; but answered fiercely, as if suspicious of the safety of its owner, "The token is good; but how came that sacred weapon in the hands of the boy warrior?"

Lyu then recapitulated the whole circumstance; and when he related the saving of the stranger's life, the chief kissed the hem of his robe, and besought him to follow him into the town, at the same time guaranteeing them from all harm for breaking the old hunter's command. As they proceeded, Lyu learned that the latter was a man of consequence among the Yaou-jin; and, in his impetuosity of temper, had been led to follow the boar, till he had become lost to the rest of the hunting party.

In less than half an hour the party reached the fortified wall of the town, which, from its great strength and position, seemed impregnable. When they passed through the gates, Lyu saw crowds of armed men, piles of arms, and rows of cannon; the streets were wide, and the houses built of brick; but upon the whole it looked like a fortified mews, for the apartments of the people were all placed over stables in which were kept horses, cows, and other animals.

They were conducted to one of the largest of these houses, and left in charge of a soldier, who had orders to see that they were treated with distinguished respect; the chief then bade them adieu, and galloped off with his troop.

CHAPTER XXVII.

A MAN MUST MAKE HIMSELF DESPICABLE BEFORE HE CAN BE REALLY DESPISED BY OTHERS.*

THE following day the chief visited Lyu and the mandarin, for the purpose of conducting them into the presence of the king; as they rode through the streets, Lyu discovered that he was at the very head-quarters of the rebellious SING Miao-tse, whose daring courage had been for some time past shaking the emperor on his throne, and who would listen to no terms of peace from the imperial general. The SING Miao-tse had, moreover, elected a king from among their petty princes, whom they had invested with the yellow robe of royalty and supreme power over all the other chiefs. The latter stood in the same relation to the Miao-tse king as the nobles in England stood to their sovereign in the middle ages; that is, independent princes in their own territories, but, at the summons of the king, obliged to follow him to battle with all the armed men of their tribe.

Such a show of military power, and the assumption, by the Miao-tse chief, of that symbol of Chinese royalty, the yellow robe, had seriously alarmed the government of Pekin, who had sent army after army against them without success.

The whole distance from their lodging, to the palace of the king, was lined with a double row of well-armed soldiers, who gazed with hatred and contempt upon the Chinese mandarin, whose astonishment at such an exhibition of military power among these half-savage people might be seen upon his countenance.

When they reached the entrance of the palace, two young men of rank conducted them through a row of soldiers, into a great hall, filled with chieftains, in the various military costumes of their divisions of the country. At the extreme end of the hall, a large curtain of yellow silk was suspended from one side to the other. When the mandarin was first seen by these wild chieftains, they placed their hands upon their swords, and frowned threateningly; however, without more notice than this, they formed themselves into groups, and conversed together, leaving the mandarin and Lyu to the care of the two young chiefs. When they had been in the hall about an hour, they heard the booming of a cannon, and the chiefs formed themselves into a double rank, reaching from the yellow curtain to the entrance of the building; then came another report, and they prostrated themselves on the ground, the two young men commanding Lyu and the mandarin to do likewise. The boy readily obeyed, but the mandarin refused, till they clapped their hands upon their swords menacingly. For nearly five minutes all remained prostrate, when a third report was heard, and a shrill voice cried, " Arise, children of the soil, warriors of the hills!" and all arose and bowed several times before the old hunter, whom, now the curtain was drawn, Lyu perceived sitting upon a golden chair of state, surrounded by chieftains in armor, with yellow girdles around them. The hunter, or, to call him by his proper title, the king, or golden dragon, was attired in the same dress as when he had encountered the boar, with the addition of a robe of yellow silk, which he wore over his armor — that robe which had given such umbrage to the court of Pekin. If Lyu was astonished at the discovery of his friend the old hunter, the mandarin, slave-like, trembled with fear as the two young men conducted them to the foot of the throne, where he fell prostrate, and continued to knock his head upon the earth, till the king, with a smile of contempt, said, "Let the dog of a Kitat deliver his mission from the slave general Le, who dares to threaten us with his miserable army."

When Lyu had interpreted this command, the mandarin replied, "Behold, most wise and magnificent chief—" when, however, he came to the word chief the king said, "What means the dog by Chief? Let him know that if he refuses us our titles, he shall be thrown headlong from the walls."

"Pardon, O magnificent and all-powerful king!' said the mandarin, "thy servant but uses the words of his general."

"Proceed, dog," said the king.

"Then the all-conquering and magnificent general Le, by the mouth of his slave, says, that wishing to save the lives of his good children of the hills, the Son of Heaven is willing to negotiate peace, and re quires that the magnificent king and golden dragon should meet him near the brazen pillar, on the twen tieth day of the next moon, when he will grant unto the king and his people all their ancient rights and privileges."

"Said Le these words?" asked the king hastily.

"These are the words of the great general, O king!" replied the mandarin, but getting bolder, added, "conditionally that" (and now all the chiefs bent their heads forward, and held their breath in suspense) "the powerful king throws aside his yellow robe and assumed title, and permits a garrison of imperial troops to occupy one fortress between every two divisions of the land of the Miao-tse. This is the message of the Son of Heaven to his dearly beloved children."

The speech was scarcely delivered, when at least a hundred swords were held over Lyu and the mandarin; the king arose, waved his hand, and the weapons were instantly sheathed. "The Kitat dog has spoken: now let him open his ears. The children of the soil have been belied; they are no lovers of blood, yet they love it better than slavery. They would have granted a peace to the Kitat general, if he had withdrawn his miserable rats of soldiers from the foot of the hills. The god of war has spoken: two of the sons of the king have been slain by the Kitat: they must be avenged. Back then to the Kitat Le, and tell him that, ere three moons have passed, the bones of his army shall whiten the dust of the hills. Let not the paper tiger reply, or his ears shall be thrown to the dogs. The king has spoken."

As the mandarin knew that the wolf-king was likely to keep his word, he walked backwards out of the hall, bowing all the time, and left the palace much crest-fallen at the power of his friend the vermin king; but upon the whole very glad to get away, for when they had so indignantly refused his proposition, he expected nothing less than being hewn to pieces, as one of the Miao-tse ambassadors had been some few years before, by the more civilized and polite emperor at Pekin.

When the envoy had left the hall, the king said, "Now let the brave young warrior receive the thanks of the children of the golden dragon." No sooner had he spoken than the chiefs surrounded Lyu, and showered upon him every mark of respect and gratitude; for it had soon become known that the stranger-youth had saved their aged prince from the wild boar.

"Said I not that the Yaou-jin would be grateful? Now let the young warrior claim his reward," said the king.

Then falling before the king, Lyu replied, "What greater reward could thy servant claim, O venerable prince! than a place in the ranks of thy brave warriors?"

At this reply there were exclamations of joy, which, however, soon passed into sorrow, when the king said, "The children of the soil would gladly claim thee as a brother; but, alas! they dare not admit a Kitat, for they have sworn to destroy them, as they would rats."

"Thy servant is no Kitat, O king! but a Miao-tse."

"What words are these?" said the king; adding, "we will hear the young warrior's story."

Lyu then repeated his history, which was received by the king and chiefs with a mixture of joy and sympathy. When he had finished, the king said, "Did the young warrior ever hear the name of his mother's chief parent?"

"Truly have I, venerable king, for often with tears in her eyes has she prayed for the safety of her aged parent, the chief Sing-mien," replied Lyu.

At this there was an exclamation of surprise; the aged man's eyes became suffused with tears; he fell upon Lyu's neck, embraced him, and, turning to the warriors, exclaimed, "Heaven is just, my children, for surely this brave youth is the son of my only daughter, whom I thought massacred by the Kitats when they sacked our camp and slew my brave sons."

"Art thou, then, O venerable king! the chief Sing mien?" said Lyu, with astonishment.

"I was, my brave son, till the tyranny and cruelty of the Kitats caused the children of the hills to elect me as their king," said the aged prince.

Then the warriors surrounded Lyu, and paid him homage as a grandson of their great chieftain. After this the king conferred upon him the title of chief, and gave him the command of a considerable body of men. But gladly and frankly as the warriors had welcomed Lyu, they now began to murmur; and one young chief boldly stepped forward to the feet of the prince, and said, "Can this be just, O king! that an untried warrior should be promoted to a command of such importance? Surely the law should not be broken for even the kinsman of the king."

"The words of the young chief, though bold, are wise," said the king; who then informed Lyu that by the law no officer could be appointed till he had passed the ordeal of valor.

"The chief's words are just, O king! and thy son is prepared to pass any trial the bravest of these chiefs around may suggest," said Lyu, amidst cries of approbation. The audience then broke up, and he retired with the king into the palace.

As the Miao-tse commanders wished to take the Chinese by surprise, and meet them on the hills, where they had no doubt they would soon march, the army was ordered to be ready on the third day. The succeeding day was appointed for the military trial of Lyu, and accordingly some thousands of the troops, headed by their chiefs, in full war costume, assembled at the foot of a steep, but rugged, and almost inaccessible mountain; when a young horse, bridled and saddled, from which hung a couple of stirrups made of painted wood, was brought forward.

" Will the young warrior venture to the top of yonder mountain?" said a young chief.

Lyu made no reply, but vaulted into the saddle, bent forward, with his head almost upon the animal's neck, and, resting his whole weight upon the stirrup, pressed his horse forward. The animal, feeling the weight upon his back, sprang upwards, and ran along like a wildcat till it reached the summit of the mountain. Lyu then breathed it backwards and forwards on the level ground, lifted his helmet from his head, and waved it to the warriors beneath, whose cheers at his gallant bearing rang through the air. He then sprang off the animal's back, examined its hoofs, to see that there were no smooth stones that would interfere with the spike-like nails and cause it to slip, mounted, and, throwing himself backwards, with his head almost on the haunches, and holding by his knees, gave his horse the rein, merely keeping one end loosely in his hand, and beast and rider came at full speed down the mountain-side, as if they had grown together. Then the youthful chief who challenged him, rode up, and said, —

"My brother is brave and fearless; but he must have another trial."

Lyu was then led to the verge of a deep ditch, filled with water, at least six feet wide; beyond this was about twelve feet of land, and then another ditch of little less than eight feet in width, filled with fire, the flames from which arose far above the surface of the ground, suffusing the air around with a sulphureous smoke — the sight made his heart quail; for what horse would ever pass through this? When he announced that he was prepared for the ordeal, they brought him six horses for choice, and, choosing one, he jumped into the saddle, gave full rein, and at one bound cleared the water; but when the horse reached the fire, the flames and the sulphur got up its nostrils, and it reared upon its hind legs, refusing to move an inch forward. Its rider patted its neck and coaxed; but it was of no use. So he returned, and, choosing another, repeated the attempt, but with no more success. However, he was no more to be beaten than King Robert Bruce, who, after many failures in his attempt to beat King Edward, happening to see a spider after many failures succeed in reaching its web, made another effort, beat Edward, and became king of Scotland.

Now Lyu was no less brave and persevering; so carefully choosing a little sturdy horse he had thought less spirited than the rest, he jumped upon its back, passed the water, threw his hands over its eyes, urged it forward ; and in another instant passed through the flaming gulf, half suffocated. The horse plunged and snorted, but he patted and coaxed it, again placed his hands over its eyes, pressed it onwards, and leaped both fire and water back again. As the return had formed no portion of the ordeal, he was received by the assembled warriors with vociferous cheers.

"My son is worthy to be a leader of his race," said the old chief, embracing him.

CHAPTER XXVIII.

"EVIL CONDUCT IS THE ROOT OF MISERY."

AFTER passing the ordeal of courage, Lyu was regularly installed in the command of a portion of the guard which attended the person of the king. In the course of a few days intelligence arrived that the great Chinese general, Hae-ling-ah, had appeared at the head of a great army in the mountains near Lienchow, in such a position that if he were not speedily driven back, the Miao-tse would be surrounded by the enemy, as it was most probable that General Le would advance from the opposite side. This news caused great excitement, and made them set about preparing for the immediate march of their army, and, in a few days, a body of nearly twenty thousand men were on their way to meet the enemy; but, as I am not writing the history of that terrible war, I will merely tell you that they met on several occasions, and exhibited much bravery on both sides; at last in one battle the Miao-tse destroyed the greater portion of the Chinese army with its much-lauded general, Hae-ling-ah; and, after this victory, returned to their mountains with a great many prisoners.

As the king had sworn to save no lives, the prisoners were one day brought out upon the hill-side and barbarously shot; but, cruel as this act was, it was neither worse nor more treacherous than the treatment that a former Miao-tse army received from the Chinese emperor. Terrible as was the sight to the kind-hearted Lyu, he dared not refuse to be present, for the soldiers would have thought him a friend to the Chinese, and have sacrificed him in their rage.

The prisoners had been brought out in fifties; among the last was a white-bearded old man and his wife, a woman of much younger age, both of whom struggled very hard to get away, and prayed that they might not be shot, as they were not soldiers. The Miao-tse, however, would have killed them both, but for Lyu, who, perceiving the struggle, rode up to the prisoners, who threw themselves on the ground, and implored of him to take them before the king, as he had proclaimed that none but warriors should be slain.

"Let these people be taken before the king," said Lyu to the soldiers. But what was his surprise, when they arose to thank him, to find that the woman was no other than Chang, the wife of Hieul! but, although he recognized her, and his mind was full of anxiety about his parents, and wonder at finding Chang, so far from her home, travelling with the old man, he said nothing, but took them before the king, who not only saved their lives, but, luckily for themselves, placed them at his own disposal.

Lyu sent them to his house, where, shortly afterwards, he followed, in order to learn something from Chang about his mother and Tchin. When the wicked woman was brought before him, she fell down at his feet, saying, "The young chief's heart is as good as his arm is strong what would he with his slave?"

"Let the woman Chang, the bad wife of the worse Hieul, look upwards," said Lyu.

When she looked up, and in the person of the young chief recognized the boy Lyu, whom she had so badly treated, her heart was filled with amazement, and her limbs trembled with fear. "The gods are great, and their ways mysterious; but the heart of the good Lyu Payo must still remain in the bosom of the young chief of the hills, and he would not kill his miserable slave," said Chang.

"Does the wife of the cruel Hieul merit mercy from the son of the lady Sang?" said Lyu sternly.

"The wife of Hieul, the slave of the young chief, merits nothing but death from his hands; yet hath she been punished by the gods for her wickedness," replied Chang.

"The life of the wretched Chang shall be saved; and, moreover, she shall be permitted to depart, providing she truthfully relates the history of all that happened after the boy Lyu Payo was so shamefully decoyed from his home by the priest of Fo," said our hero.

"The son of Sang is magnanimous and just, and his miserable slave will faithfully obey his command."

"Then proceed; but remember that thy life shall answer for the truth of thy story," said Lyu.

"Then know, O son of Sang! that when the last watch of the night had struck, and you did not return from the feast of lanterns, the minds of Tchin and Sang became troubled; yet as my husband Hieul had not returned, they thought both had been detained among the great crowd at the fireworks; but when Hieul returned without their son they became distracted, for the artful villain declared that you left him early in the evening to return home.

"Tchin and Sang then broke out into loud lamentations, and employed people to search the city and suburbs, and put up advertisements on all the walls about the town, offering a large reward to any person who should give information that might lead to thy discovery. But when many days passed away, Sang began to fear that her son had been drowned in one of the canals ; but then, again, as the body could not be found, Tchin made up his mind that you had been decoyed by some rascal into one of the opium-houses, and bribed the police to make the search. After some days they went to a woman who had long been suspected of keeping an opium-house in one of the suburbs, and extorted from her that a youth had stopped there one night with a begging bonze, but that both had taken their departure early the following morning — where, or in what direction, she knew not.

"This information raised the spirits of Tchin and Sang, for they now felt assured that their boy was at least on earth, and made no doubt that he might ultimately be found. Tchin, however, was acquainted with the practices of the bonzes, and feared that his son had been intoxicated with the opium, and, while senseless, carried away and sold as a slave. He then started off on a journey through several provinces, but, alas! only to return almost broken-hearted at having failed to discover even the smallest information. The shock became so severe to Sang that her life became despaired of; and, although her natural strength of body enabled her to survive, still nothing could raise her spirits. Tchin, therefore, made another journey in a totally different direction; and so many months passed away without hearing from him, that Sang became troubled also for his safety.

"It was during his absence that my wicked husband, and, alas! thy wicked slave also, began to plot the ruin of Sang; and, as we had both pretended to grieve so much for the loss of her son, she had such great faith in our honesty, that our schemes had every chance of succeeding. One day a conversation took place between Hieul and myself, as nearly as possible in these words: 'I make no manner of doubt, wife, that we shall soon have a fortunate day.'

"'How, my husband?'

"'Surely the wife of my bosom cannot doubt that the gods have removed our brother Tchin from this earth, and that thy husband has become master of his house and fortune; therefore, as Sang is young and handsome, and without relations, I can force her to marry again, whereby I shall not only get rid of the cost of her keep, but make a considerable sum of money into the bargain.'

"'It is not possible, O my husband! to persuade Sang that Tchin is dead; so thou canst have no power over her.'

"'Thou shalt see, wife,' said the artful rogue, going immediately to a wine shop, where he bribed a drinking companion to make his appearance at our house covered with dust, as if from a long journey, and declare that he had travelled across a desert in the same caravan with Tchin, that they had been attacked by the brigands and all but himself murdered; and to give a further coloring to this falsehood, the man exhibited a jewelled ring that Sang had often seen Tchin wear, and knew he much prized; but which I must tell you Hieul had secretly stolen from his brother before he started on his last journey.

"So well did the man feign the appearance of a traveller, and describe the last moments of Tchin, that the affectionate Sang fainted with grief, and although she could not for some time fully believe in the news, it became so currently reported about the whole city, that at the time and place, named by the man, a caravan had been plundered, and its people murdered, she dared doubt no longer, so gave full vent to her grief, and attired herself in deep white mourning, deeper than that worn by my husband and myself, for it was the mourning of a widow.

"In less than a month after he had promulgated this false news, Hieul became impatient to get rid of Sang, that he might take possession of the property, turn it into ready money, and depart into a distant province, for fear of his brother's return; one day, therefore, he endeavored to persuade Sang to become the wife of a friend of his, who was dying with love for her; but Sang, as if she had just begun to suspect some roguery, answered him very haughtily, flew into a passion, declared that he was a rascal, and that she did not believe one word about Tchin's death; as for marrying again she flatly refused.

"Now as neither Hieul nor myself wished to quarrel with Sang, as it would then be more difficult to carry out our scheme, we endeavored to soothe her, and by much dissembling succeeded. When Hieul and my-self were alone, he ordered me to seek a clever marriage-broker, who would arrange to sell Sang for him, and carry her off to her new husband, without much noise; but, wicked as I was, I became afraid, and he struck me to the ground and left the house in a great rage; then, had I not felt ashamed of the part I had taken, I should have fallen at the feet of the injured Sang, and disclosed all our wickedness.

" By the time my husband returned in the evening he had recovered his temper, apologized for the blow, and moreover presented me with a beautifully embroidered fan; this present made me ready to do any thing for him, so I offered to go at once in search of a marriage-broker. 'It is useless, my wife,' said he; ' the gods themselves have provided a husband for our relation Sang.'

" ' What words are these, my husband ? '

" ' Know, wife, that this evening at the wine shop I met with a merchant, who had just lost his wife, and was looking out for another; the opportunity was too good to be lost, and therefore I proposed Sang, who, I assured him, was exceedingly well-looking, and as all the company present (who were my friends and companions) protested that I was a man of truth, and moreover, well to do in the world, as I had just inherited the fortune of a brother, the merchant rejoiced at the chance, and at once concluded the bargain, by paying down fifty taels; a portion of which I have laid out in the purchase of a fan for my wife.' —— Then, O son of Sang, if thou wert to kill thy slave on the spot, I must tell thee that my joy knew no bounds," said Chang to Lyu.

"Speak the truth and thou art safe from harm, wicked woman," said Lyu, and Chang continued: "My husband told the merchant that the lady he had purchased and paid for was proud and haughty, and a great lover of ceremony; therefore he must not be surprised to find her make a great many objections at being taken away, for she would pretend to be in much trouble and misery at being forced away from the house.

"'Truly, I understand,' said the merchant; 'ladies always say no, in these delicate matters, when it is well known that they mean yes.'

"'Let my brother, however, be cautious and determined, for he will find the lady as obstinate as she is beautiful; he had better, therefore, at the beginning of the night, bring a marriage chair, handsomely adorned with flowers and candles, and carried by good stout porters, and a band of music. Let them proceed to the door very quietly, and when there, knock loudly and suddenly, when she will herself, most probably, open the door; still, however, that my brother may make perfectly sure, he had better know, that the lady will wear a deep mourning head-dress of pure white, such as is worn by widows; when she makes her appearance, let the porters force her into the marriage chair, the band of music strike up, and then she may be safely carried to the barge on the canal, as speedily as possible.'

"'But when, O my husband, is this admirable plan to be carried out? said I.

"'It is necessary, my wife, that this two-legged merchandise be carried away this very night; but as it is not well that I should be present during the transactions, I will even now take my departure, and return when they have taken her away.' As my husband uttered these last words, the little window of the room became darkened: I looked up with alarm, and although I observed nothing, said in fear, 'It might have been Sang, my husband, who may have overheard our conversation.'

"'If so, her ears could have caught none of our words,' he replied, leaving the house. I was, however, correct in my suspicions, for no sooner had Hieul left the room than she ran in, and catching hold of me by the hands, cried, 'We have been friends a long time, and are tied by the bonds of relationship; surely my sister would not ruin a childless, friendless widow!'

"'What words are these, O my sister?' (for being of the same age, we called each other sister,) I said, affecting to be astonished.

"'Thou knowest that thy wicked husband would force me into a marriage — tell me, then, O sister! if he will really persist in this cruel design.' The question was so straightforward that I scarcely knew what to say: however, recovering my presence of mind, I replied, 'Why should my sister have such foolish thoughts? Why do such silly fancies disturb her mind? for even were such a design intended, force would not be required. There could be no difficulty in the matter, for my sister would be obliged by the laws to submit. To what purpose should a person throw himself into the water before the bark is going

to be cast away!' When I had uttered this proverb,
Sang threw my hands from her, and ran into her own
room. I followed, and watched her through an aperture in the door. She threw herself upon the floor,
and began to weep and cry 'Alas! I know the
meaning of that wicked proverb. What a wretch am
I that I should have no friend to protect me from this
villain Hieul! Alas! I cannot escape. O, surely
death is better than disgrace! What have I to live
for? No! the only thing left for me is to put an end
to this wretched life!' Again I say, O son of Sang!
kill me if thou canst not bear to hear the truth," said
Chang; "but I was wicked enough to enjoy thy mother's agony, and determined to interfere only at the last
moment; so that, by saving her life, I might prolong
her misery."

"Proceed, thou wicked woman!" said Lyu, with
tears in his eyes, but with deep anxiety to hear the
fate of his mother.

"Well, then, in the wicked satisfaction of my heart,
I watched her take a long cord from a drawer, fasten
one end to a beam which ran across the room, and
make a noose in the other. Having done this, she got
upon a stool, and put her head in the noose. Then,
frightened that I had let her proceed too far, I tried
to open the door, but it was fastened inside. I endeavored to burst it open — the noise alarmed her;
and, kicking away the stool, she became suspended by
the cord. Now, terribly alarmed, I ran into my room,
and found an iron bar, with which I forced open the
door. I then found that the cord, being too slight for
her weight, had given way, and that she had fallen

upon the floor senseless. I instantly unfastened the noose; but my feet coming in contact with a piece of furniture, I fell, and in so doing, extinguished the lantern and jerked off my head-dress. At that very moment, there came a loud knocking at the door; and, knowing that it must be the merchant, I felt about for my head-dress, placed it on my head, and ran to the door to show him into my own apartment for a time, that he might not discover what had happened. No sooner had I opened the door, than the whole neighborhood seemed lighted with flambeaux and lanterns, and I was suddenly caught round the waist, lifted into the chair, and carried away, amidst the noisy sounds of gongs and other musical instruments. It was in vain that I cried out that it was not me they sought, but Sang. 'The pretty bird is wrong, for I know her by the white mourning head-dress of a widow, and surely there are not two widows in the house of Hieul.' It was then that I felt I was punished for my wickedness; in my haste I had picked up Sang's head-dress in place of my own. To inform the merchant of this was useless, for he would not believe me; and, moreover, expressed himself well satisfied with his bargain. He carried me to his barge on the canal, when for weeks we travelled till we reached Canton. But, wicked as I was, I was more fortunate than I deserved, for the good merchant has treated me with great kindness, even offering to restore me to Hieul; but truly I never wish to see that wicked man again. After living in Canton many months the merchant had business to transact in a distant province; we therefore joined a party proceeding by the same route, when we were overtaken by the

Chinese army, on its march into the mountains of Koei-cheou, robbed, taken prisoners, and made to perform the low offices of camp-servants. Thus has thy slave told the whole truth, and confessed wickedness that the son of Sang can never pardon," said Chang.

"But my mother — my mother, heard ye aught of her?" asked Lyu.

"I have since heard from a merchant of Pekin, who corresponded with my new husband, that when the wicked Hieul returned home, his rage was great at discovering the mistake; but that he sought the pardon of Sang, and, like an ungrateful wretch as he is, placed the fruit of his crimes at the feet of destiny, forgetting all the sufferings of his wife."

"But my mother — is she safe?"

"She was, O chief, and residing in the house of Hieul when the last news came some months since; she may not be now, for I fear the rascal will not rest content till he has disposed of her."

Then, remembering what the bonze had told him, Lyu asked Chang, "How it was that, being a Miaotse woman, Sang could have been of so much trouble to Hieul, inasmuch that if he had exhibited her to the government, they would have rid him of her, and rewarded him at the same time?"

"The government war not with women, neither could they interfere with a family so harmless as that of Tchin's; thou wert told this, O son of Sang, that your filial duty might prevent you from attempting to escape."

"Woman, thou hast indeed removed a load from my heart, for I will now seek no rest until I have discovered my good mother; and for thy news the son of Sang freely forgives the injury you have done him," said Lyu.

When Chang had finished her story, so great was Lyu's anxiety to see his mother once more, that he lost no time in repeating every word of it to the old king, whose delight was so great at the chance of once more embracing his daughter, and rescuing her from the Chinese, that he begged of Lyu to throw off his Miao-tse dress, take that of a Chinese merchant, and proceed immediately in search of her, making no doubt that Sang would be as glad to return as he would be to see her. For this purpose the king presented Lyu with several ingots of silver, and some jewels of value, a fleet horse, and all the necessaries for a long journey, and, further, ordered that an escort of mounted soldiers should accompany him as far as safety would permit; and I need not tell you that, sorry as he was to part from his kind old grandfather, Lyu lost no time in making preparations for his journey; and although he did not doubt the truth of Chang's story, as a matter of precaution, he left her in charge of the king till his return — an arrangement at which neither Chang nor the old merchant could complain, as they were treated with every possible respect.

CHAPTER XXIX.

"TO PERSECUTE THE UNFORTUNATE IS LIKE THROWING STONES
ON ONE FALLEN INTO A WELL."

THE next day Lyu took a formal and affectionate
leave of the old king, at the same time promising to
return when he had discovered his mother.   As for the
Miao-tse chiefs, they were so delighted with his bravery that nothing would content them but to accompany him as far as possible on his journey; for this
purpose some twenty of them obtained the king's permission, and, attended by servants, who carried their
tents and other necessaries, accompanied Lyu through
the provinces of Koei-Cheou, Quang-See, and Quang-
Tung, keeping as far south of Canton as possible for
fear of meeting any straggling party of Chinese
troops.

When they came to within fifty miles of the sea-
coast, the party halted, and made merry for three
days; on the fourth Lyu exchanged his military garb
for the dress of a Chinese merchant, took leave of the
Miao-tse chiefs, and departed alone, with the intention
of reaching some small fishing town on the coast,
where he might await the arrival of a trading vessel
on its passage to the Gulf of Pe-tche-lee, near Pekin.
After some six hours' hard riding, he came to a
small town on the very verge of the sea, and, fortunately, in time to find a junk that had just put in for

water and fish, on its passage from Siam to the mouth of the Pei-ho River.

Lyu lost no time iu searching for the captain, whom he found on the sands, bargaining with some fishermen; this officer, a short, thickset man, with fat cheeks and sunken, fishy eyes, was so deeply engaged in haggling that he did not perceive Lyu till the latter touched him on the shoulder, and said, " Can the gallant son of the ocean find room in his ship for a passenger who would go to Pekin? "

" My brother is young to travel alone, and yet seems well to do," replied the captain in drawling tones, glancing sharply at Lyu's rich silk robe and horse.

" The son of the ocean has not answered the question of his younger brother, who is willing to give three ingots of silver if the captain will take him to the mouth of the Pei-ho."

At the mention of the ingots the captain's fishy eyes grew brighter, and he said, " Surely my brother must be in his dreams to make so small an offer, for the voyage is long and dangerous. Will he not give four ingots? "

" If the noble captain does not at once accept the three ingots, there will be an end of the matter; for his younger brother's offer is liberal, and he can wait for another ship," said Lyu, determined not to be outwitted by the crafty sailor, who, really fearing that he might keep his word, closed the bargain.

Lyu then galloped to an inn at some distance from the shore, sold his horse for a small sum in silver, and returned as the captain was stepping into his boat to proceed out to his vessel. Once on board he felt rejoiced, for every hour would bring him nearer to his mother; the sailors weighed anchor, and, as there was a brisk wind, the vessel shot through the waters at a rapid pace. In the evening he was shown to his cabin—a spout-like hole, so narrow that he could not turn, and so short that his feet hung over the opening through which he had to creep in head first; but, small as it was, he managed to sleep very well, undisturbed by the rolling of the vessel.

The next morning he was awakened by an uneasy sensation in his legs, as if an effort was being made to unscrew them; and being midway between asleep and awake, he struck out, and the next moment found himself dragged by the legs out of the hole, and saw a priest standing over him, swinging an incense vessel to and fro, the smoke from which not only fumigated the whole of that part of the ship, but nearly suffocated Lyu, who said, " What would the servant of Fo with his younger brother, that he behaveth thus rudely to him ?"

" The sun has long been high in the heavens, and the young merchant's eyes have been closed, or he would have seen that the good ship is becalmed, and that the skies presage it to be lasting," said the priest.

" But what, in the name of the principal relations, can a calm have to do with me, save delaying my journey ?" said Lyu.

" Is the young merchant a barbarian, that he is ignorant that the captain and crew seek to propitiate the goddess of the sea, Ma-tsoo-po, and to beg a fair wind ?" said the priest.

Imagining from this speech, that the sailors were about to perform some of their idolatrous rites, and that it would be dangerous not to appear to comply, Lyu, without another word, followed the priest, who went into every part of the vessel, burned incense, muttered some prayers, and then proceeded upon deck, where the image of the goddess Ma-tsoo-po was sitting cross-legged, like a tailor, with a burning lamp, and several cups of hot tea before her. Every part of the vessel was adorned with pieces of red cloth, and stuck over with burning sticks of incense. The fat captain and his officers, in full uniform, stood near the image, and recited prayers to its wooden ears. This ceremony lasted some hours, and then, as the wind refused to blow, the priest proclaimed the goddess to be in a bad humor, and directed the sailors to offer prayers, roasted pigs, and fowls to the gods of the winds; and the perfume of the joss-sticks became changed for the more pleasant aroma of roast pig and fowl, which were strewn about the deck. Then the priest added some spirits and fruit, burned some gilt paper, and with the whole crew, prostrated himself before the invisible gods.

· About ten minutes elapsed and the priest said solemnly, " Let the sons of the ocean follow the spirits; " upon which the crew jumped upon their legs, and began to scramble for the viands, leaving nothing but the fragrance of roast pig to tickle the appetites of the wind deities. After they had been demolished, the sailors seized upon the tinsel-paper, and made a quantity of small boats, which they set adrift upon the sea, and watched them float away.

Then, as the winds still refused to obey, to make the

best of the matter, they left the ship to sail by herself, crowded around the compass, and fell to enjoying themselves with tobacco, opium, and the spirit of rice, and in a very little time became in such a state of intoxication, that Lyu began to fear for the safety of the vessel. However, he had yet worse to fear; for one sailor, if possible more intoxicated than the others, proclaimed that he had discovered the cause of the anger of the goddess, and until that cause had been removed, the ship would continue becalmed. Now, as every sailor was more or less a trader on his own account, and had purchased some trifling commodity at Siam for the purpose of re-selling at Pekin, and the longer they were at sea the longer they would have to wait for their anticipated profits, this announcement made them very angry, and the more so, when the drunken man pointed to Lyu, and accused him of not joining in their prayers and offerings. The sailors surrounded the boy, and were about throwing him into the sea, when the captain spoke: " The young merchant is wealthy ; he possesses ingots of silver; let him, then, save his life by offering them up to the goddess."

" The words of the noble captain are wise; let the stranger, who has brought this calm upon us, make the offerings to the goddess," said the priest, who was as great a rogue as any among them. Glad as Lyu was to purchase his life at the price, his indignation was so great at the robbery, that had he still worn his sword and bow, not a few of the robbers would have fallen, even though with the conviction of certain death to himself; as it was, he resigned the precious metal with as good a grace as possible; after which the sailors became appeased.

For nearly a week the ship had lain rocking in a dead calm, when the winds arose, and, as she scudded along at a rapid pace, the sailors recovered their good humor, although not sufficiently so to make them return the silver ingots to Lyu. One morning when he went on deck, he found the whole crew in a state of terrible commotion at the appearance of a large junk in the distance, which seemed to be chasing them.

"What have the sailors to fear?" said Lyu to the captain, who was standing at the prow of the junk gazing through a small telescope.

"Has my brother no eyes? Can he not see in yon war-junk a floating nest of the wasps of the ocean?" — "The wasps of the ocean!" replied the captain, running off to press the sailors to add more and more canvas, that they might outrun the pirate vessel.

It was, however, of little use, for in less than an hour the wasps came within gun-shot, and sent some heavy cannon balls, which raked the vessel from stem to stern, killing at one time the priest, captain, and chief mate; and one whizzed within half an inch of Lyu's ear. When their officers were killed, the sailors relinquished every hope of saving themselves, and fell prostrate on the decks; the pirate came alongside, threw out his grappling-irons, and, in a few minutes, a hundred sea-savages jumped on board the trader; but, finding no resistance, they contented themselves with binding the sailors together two by two, and taking them aboard the pirate ship. As for Lyu, perceiving from his superior dress that he was a passenger of some consequence, they bound his arms behind his back, carried him on to the deck of their own vessel, and placed him under a guard, who stood near him with drawn sabres. When the pirates had ransacked the ship, and secured every portable article of value, they took the prisoners, including Lyu, before the pirate chief, a tall, handsome young man, whose dark, black hair hung over his shoulders, in defiance of the Tartar-Chinese law, and who wore a superb robe of rich purple velvet, and a high turban of black velvet.

This chief was seated in a chair of state, which stood upon a raised platform at the end of the after part of the deck, surrounded by his officers with drawn swords. When the Chinese sailors were brought before him, the chief bade them arise, and, after having narrowly examined each man, he pointed his hand to two of the weakest and most wretched-looking, saying, " Let the Tartar dogs receive their doom." No sooner were the words out of his mouth, than the two miserable men were seized, bound back to back, and tossed into the sea. This produced the effect the cruel chief intended ; for the whole of the prisoners, with the exception of Lyu, fell again at his feet, and prayed that the great mandarin of the wasps would save their insect lives, which, to their surprise, the chief readily promised, on condition that they would swear hatred to the Chinese government, and enroll themselves among the wasps of the ocean, which the cowardly rascals as readily agreed to.

Having thus disposed of his prisoners, the chief turned sternly to Lyu, saying, " How is this, that a Chinese dog dare remain standing in our very presence ? " This speech was a sufficient hint for the pirate crew, several of whom caught hold of Lyu, and, after considerable resistance on his part, forced him to the ground, where they held him so that he could not move. "How is this? a Tartar-Chinese dog, and yet brave? Let him open his mouth if he would save his miserable life."

"I fear neither thee nor thy ruffians, pirate, and seek death rather than the alternative of joining thy villanous band, like those wretched cowards," replied Lyu.

"The Tartar dog is young, and utters words worthy of death; yet, as he is rich and has friends who can ransom him, his life is of more value than his death," replied the chief.

"What ransom dost thou enforce, O pirate?" said Lyu boldly.

"One thousand dollars in silver," said the chief.

"Then slay me, O pirate, for I can never obtain so much."

"Idle words, O boy, for thou art, doubtless, of a respectable and wealthy family, who will rather part with their whole wealth than lose their son."

"I tell thee, pirate, that I am but a wanderer in the world, whose life is devoted to the search for his lost friends."

"Words of dirt; away with him," said the chief; adding, "if thou dost not prepare a letter, that on the first opportunity may be carried to thy friends, within six days, I will have thee thrown into the sea."

Lyu was then taken below, his arms unbound, and, to his surprise, placed in a very comfortable cabin, at the door of which a savage-looking pirate stood on guard; he was then left to his own thoughts, and terrible thoughts they were. If he did not comply with the pirate's command he had threatened to murder him; and he was sure that he would keep his word, for he knew that the Ladrone pirates were so cruel that they had become the terror of the whole of the southern coast of China. To die so young was very hard; still, what was he to do? Whom could he write to? If, as Chang had said, his mother still lived in Pekin, and a letter could be sent to her, she would make every effort to save her darling son; so he wrote a long letter, and then sought an interview with the chief, who not only promised to find an opportunity of sending the letter, but praised his bravery, and, moreover, gave him the free range of the ship till a reply should be received.

CHAPTER XXX.

"WATER IS LESS DREADED THAN FIRE, YET FEWER SUFFER
BY FIRE THAN BY WATER.

HAVING liberty to range at will over the whole ship, Lyu could observe for himself the manners of that terrible race of pirates, who have for so many years set the government of the emperor at defiance, and who, at one time, under a chief of great genius, threatened to change the dynasty itself. The discipline and order of the ship astonished him, for it had more the resemblance of a regular ship of war than a pirate vessel, and he soon discovered that it was but one of a large fleet, and its chief a man of considerable rank among them, being in fact their admiral. At the time of the capture of the trading junk, the pirate admiral was sailing in search of some other vessels of his fleet, which were cruising along the coast, for the purpose not only of plunder, but harassing the Chinese government.

About a fortnight after Lyu was taken on board, four other vessels joined them, and they sailed in concert, for it was reported that a Chinese fleet of warjunks were scouring those seas in search of them. The five vessels had sailed together for about a week, when they came to the mouth of a wide river; the captains of the four junks were then summoned to a council of war, on board the admiral's ship, and from the preparations that were made immediately after, Lyu found that they were about to attack a Chinese town, some distance up the river.

This being determined, the four vessels were anchored at the mouth, and the admiral ship proceeded alone some twenty or thirty miles, and anchored off a large town ; the chief then sent an officer, with a large boat well manned, to demand of the governor 100,000 dollars in silver. The officer was away some hours, but on his return reported that the governor was so terrified that he agreed to give half the sum demand ed, providing the chief would guarantee to protect the town for the future from all ravages of his people.

" Have the dogs any guns mounted in yonder forts ? " asked the chief, pointing to several small towers which ran along the water's edge.

" The forts are in ruins, and the guns rusted and dismounted, noble chief: it is for this reason that the miserable dogs seek to purchase thy mercy," replied the officer.

" Then back to them, and say that unless they send me the whole sum, with ten thousand more dollars for this delay, I will lay their town in ashes," said the chief.

The officer obeyed, and on his return said that the governor had agreed to his terms, but required four hours to collect the silver from the different inhabitants, and further stipulated that the wasps should not land, but await out in the river, when they would bring them the silver in their own boats.

Then, smiling contemptuously at their cowardice, the chief ordered four boats, well manned, and mounted with small guns for fear of treachery, to fetch the booty; and, moreover, gave the officer in command of the party a written document to the effect that the town had paid the Ladrones a commuted sum instead of an annual tribute, and that all officers commanding Ladrone junks were for the future to respect that town under penalty of death.

The boats then proceeded to the shore, where beneath the forts they could see the Chinese boats, some eight in number, putting off to meet them. The wasps pulled hard without fear of treachery, but, as they approached nearer the shore, the officer in command observing that the Chinese splashed their oars in the waters without moving their boats forward, misgivings passed through his mind, and he commanded the men to rest on their oars while he reconnoitred: however, so great was the impetus at which the boats were going, that the crew could not stop them till they had come within a few yards of the Chinese.

A minute after, each Chinese took up a matchlock from the bottom of the boat, and simultaneously fired a volley at the pirates, killing several of them; and before they could recover from their surprise the towers bristled with armed men, the masks fell from before the batteries, and four great guns poured a heavy fire upon them, killing nearly half of their number, and among them the commander of the party; however, when they had recovered from their surprise, one half of the remaining pirates pulled at their oars, under cover of the others, who fired into the Chinese boats.

So satisfied had the chief been at the negotiations of his officer, and with the cowardice of the Chinese governor that after the boat party had been despatched he had thrown himself upon some cushions in his cabin, quietly to await their return; when, however, he heard the booming of the guns across the water, he knew that mischief was afloat, and, going on deck, perceived the discomfiture of his men. For some minutes his rage knew no bounds, and he raved like a madman. When the surviving portion of the boat party came on board, he ordered a return to the fleet; every bit of sail was spread to the wind, and in a very short time they reached the other vessels at the mouth of the river, when, a council of war being again called, it was determined that the whole five ships should attack the town.

The next morning by daybreak the pirate fleet stood in front of the place; the whole of the numerous boats, which each ship carried for the express purpose of attacking towns and villages situated on the banks of rivers, were marshalled out, each carrying a long gun at her prow. The men were feasted with rice and salt fish, and then drawn up in rows on the decks of the ships, each man being armed with two short double-edged swords, and many with matchlocks. When they were arranged on the decks, they were sprinkled with garlic-water, which Chinese sailors believe renders them shot-proof, and harangued by the admiral, who told them that the gods had promised success, and concluded his speech by offering twenty dollars for the head of every Chinese. After this, the men gave a few wild cheers, stuck their swords securely in their belts, climbed over the sides of the junk into their boats, and caught up their oars, four men in each boat standing with loaded matchlocks to cover the rowers.

The word was given from the admiral's ship, and thirty-five armed boats went on their way to the doomed town. When they reached the shore they found a very slight show of resistance from about a hundred Chinese tigers of war, who, seeing the sea-wasps approach, fired one volley, and beat an instantaneous retreat.

All this Lyu saw from the deck of the admiral's junk, and his heart sickened at the terrible scene. The cowardly soldiers fled to the neighboring mountains, the powder magazine blew up, and in a very short time the whole town was on fire, and women and children running about the streets in all directions. The women were taken prisoners, in the hope that they might be ransomed by their friends. As for the men, wherever the pirates met them, they slew them, cut off their heads, and, in order to obtain the chief's promised reward, tied their tails together, and returned on board, some of them with as many as six heads slung around their necks. Lyu had often heard that such was the common custom among the Ladrones, but such a terrible sight it had never been his lot to see before.

After the victory every single thing of value, sufficiently portable, was taken on board the ships, and the women arranged before the chief, who examined each separately as to her chance of obtaining a ransom from her friends. Those who answered favorably were set aside; those who had no friends were secured in open cabins on the deck, to be hereafter sold as slaves;

several indeed of these poor women managed to slip through the hands of the pirates, and throw themselves headlong into the water, preferring drowning to slavery.

Ladies who had rich friends instantly despatched letters ashore by a pirate boat, bearing a white flag to show that they were peaceably inclined. The Chinese, from the hills to which they had fled, seeing this, and knowing that the Ladrones, savage and cruel as they are, still possess a savage kind of honor, ventured down to the shore, bringing the ransom money with them, and with every ransom a roast pig, or fowl, as a present to the Joss, or image god of the ship. The pirate fleet then weighed anchor, and when it reached the open sea, as the weather was calm, and nothing but a gentle breeze moved across the waters, the crews of the ships gave way to revelry and drunkenness; indeed, before night they were nearly all in a state of insensibility.

As for Lyu, he was so disgusted and heart-sickened with the scenes he had witnessed, that, unable to sleep, he walked the deck, gazing upon the bright moon and beautiful sea that lay before him. At length, tired of walking, he folded his arms, and rested against the outer wall of the chief's cabin, and began to contemplate his chances of ever seeing his mother again. A few minutes afterwards he saw a female figure stealing towards the door of the chief's cabin: surprised at seeing one of the prisoners at large, he watched her without moving, and observed that she tried the handle; the door gave way, and she entered, Lyu following her. She crept softly up to a low couch, upon which the chief of the wasps was lying, overcome with in toxication, and pulling a short dagger from her bosom, she was about to plunge it into his heart, when Lyu caught her arm, and in her fright she let the weapon fall from her hand upon the chief, who sprang from the couch, saying, " How, slaves, dare you to enter the cabin of the chief?" Then seizing the lady by her wrist, he struck a gong that hung from the centre of the cabin, which brought several sailors to his presence. By this time he had recovered from his surprise, and very plainly saw that but for the interposition of Lyu he would then have been a dead man.

" The Tartar women should be the warriors of the empire, for they possess the courage that the men lack," said the chief, smiling derisively; adding, "does my warrior sister know that she has earned for herself death by slow torture?"

" The daughter of a murdered father sought death in seeking to slay the cruel pirate," replied the lady, unabashed.

" The Tartar beauty utters brave words. What would she do if the chief she sought to slay should pardon her?" asked the pirate.

" Seek the first opportunity to destroy thee, pirate; and if she succeeded, throw herself into the sea," she undauntedly replied.

" My courageous sister will make a fitting wife for one of my brave wasps. Away with her, and as you regard your lives, treat her well, for the son of Ko- shinga wars not with the women even of the detested race," said the chief to the sailors, who gently forced her away. When the lady had been removed, the chief turned to Lyu, saying, " The young merchant has deserved well of the chief, and shall not find him ungrateful. He can be no Chinese, or he would not have saved the life of the greatest enemy of his accursed race."

" I am no Chinese, O cruel pirate, nor do I deserve thy thanks; for though I have saved the man from assassination, I would slay thee, pirate, in fair fight."

" The young merchant carries the heart of a tiger beneath the robe of commerce; and though his words are harsh, he has softened a great enemy," said the chief; adding, " did thou not say that thou wert a wanderer in search of thy friends? "

" Those were words of truth, O chief," said Lyu.

" I now believe thee; yet surely it is miraculous for one so young. Relate thy story, youth; thy name, surname, and family."

As Lyu knew that it might be of service to him, with a heavy heart he related his history from his birth ; but when he came to the fate of his father, the chief interrupted him, and made very many close inquiries as to Captain Richardson's personal appearance, and other details connected with his disappearance. These inquiries so much surprised Lyu, that he cried, " Surely the chief cannot know aught of my noble father ! "

" Ask me no questions, youth, but take this comfort to thy soul: the pirate chief for whose blood thou thirstest can and will aid thee; for he is bound to thee by double ties, — first, that thou savedst my life ; and next, that thou art of the blood of that brave, free nation of the west, and also of the Miao tse, whose hatred to the accursed Tartar dynasty is no less than my own. Open thine ears, youth, and thou wilt find that the name of Sea-thief is unworthy the descendant of a hero and king. Know that, when the illustrious and true-blooded race of Ming had been driven from the throne by the accursed Tartars, a great sea-chief sprang from the patriotic portion of the true Chinese. Yes, when the great Koshinga held aloft his banner, many thousands became alive to a sense of their disgrace, and fled to his fleet, which forever after became the scourge of the Tartar emperor, destroying his towns, sinking his ships, and sweeping his troops from the face of the earth. At length so great did the power of the great chief become, that he sailed for the great Island of Formosa, — then held by a nation from the west called Holland, — landed with twenty thousand men, fought many terrible battles, drove away the foreigners, and made himself King of Formosa.

"After his great victory he encouraged all the disaffected in China to settle in his new dominions, and kept such a great fleet afloat that the Tartar emperor ordered all of his subjects who lived near the seashore to withdraw at least ten miles inland. And even thus Koshinga was revenged, for many towns, and thousands of families who lived by fishing, were either destroyed, or joined his ships. But, alas! Koshinga died without leaving a son worthy of his name, and who, many years afterwards, sold his island to the Tartars for a title and pension for life. When the latter, however, had once resigned his power, so great was the hatred of the Tartars to his name, that they treacherously murdered him and all his family, with the exception of one son, who effected his escape to the Ladrone Islands, where he was afterwards joined by many of his grandfather's people, who elected him their chief; when his exploits along the coast became almost as celebrated as those of the great Koshinga himself. At length he was slain in fight; his power descended to his wife, who was for many years the terror of the Tartars. She was succeeded by her son, who was again succeeded by the present chief — myself.

"Now, boy, think you that I have not sufficient cause of hatred to these mongrel Chinese?" but, without waiting for a reply, he added, "enough of this for the present; the subject is painful;" and Lyu sought his cabin.

CHAPTER XXXI.

"HE WHO TOILS WITH PAIN WILL EAT WITH PLEASURE."

CONTENTED with their recent success, and loaded with plunder, the pirates made sail for the Ladrone Islands to disgorge their cargo; and no incident of any consequence took place during the voyage, except, that as they sailed through the Gulf of Tonquin, the revelry and joy of the sailors knew no bounds. The third day after their entering the gulf, the vessels came to an anchor, between two of a cluster of small islands, which, for the greater part, appeared to be inhabited by fishermen. After they had anchored, the crews were sent ashore to recruit themselves; as for the chief, he seldom or ever left the vessel.

For three days they remained at anchor, and on the fourth the crews rejoined their respective vessels; and when they were about to weigh anchor, the chief took Lyu into his cabin and said, "Did I not promise to befriend thee, brave youth?"

"The chief is brave, and therefore cannot break his word," answered Lyu.

"The messenger despatched with thy letter has returned to these islands by my command."

"What said he of my parent, O chief?" said Lyu, impatiently.

"Thy venerable parent could not be found in or near Pekin; all the household of the merchant Tchin had long since departed."

"Alas, alas! what a cruel destiny is mine!" said Lyu.

"Let my brave young friend not despair, for there is good yet in store for him," replied the chief, striking the gong; and in another instant a sailor entered the cabin, bringing with him a tall man in the mean attire of a working slave.

"What would the pirate chief with me?" said the slave, boldly.

"Restore thee to thy liberty, and —" Here the chief pointed to Lyu.

"My son!" said the slave, after gazing into the face of Lyu; and father and son became locked in each other's arms once more, after their long separation.

"O, joy! joy! Thanks, brave chief! you have indeed more, much more than repaid me," said Lyu.

"And me for my long slavery," added Captain Richardson.

"Now, no more thanks. This youth made me indebted to him for my life. The chief of the Ladrones would be indebted to no one. The debt is now repaid, or will be when I have placed you both on board some trading junk, which I will spare on purpose to take the new-found relations to their home," said the chief; who then ordered some suitable garments to be brought for the captain, and proceeded on deck to give orders about sailing, and perhaps to leave father and son alone for a time.

O, how much was talked about in that short time! But the principal matter of consequence to the reader was the captain's account of himself. His story was a very short one. When he fell into the water on the night he had saved Lyu from the kidnappers, he had been picked up by the men of the Tankea, taken on board, gagged, and, under cover of the darkness which ensued, when the lanterns were cut away from the war-junk, conveyed down the river, and then removed to a pirate-junk, which they met sailing under the guise of a trading-vessel. The pirates readily seized him, with the hope of obtaining a ransom; but, hearing of the uproar that had occurred at Pekin about the child-stealing, dared not venture to send a messenger to his friends; they therefore took him to one of the Ladrone Islands, where they made him a slave, and employed him in tilling the ground and assisting them to land their cargoes, hoping that they should some day obtain a large ransom from his friends.

Of course this history was well known to the pirate chief; and when he heard a portion of it related by Lyu, he was so struck with the chance that had placed both father and son at his disposal, that, with the chivalrous feeling that belongs more or less to all brave men, of whatever race or name, he had, as you have seen, determined to bring about this great surprise. For some weeks they sailed in the pirate-ship without meeting a solitary vessel; at last a trading-junk appeared in sight — the Ladrone gave chase, and soon overtook her, when the captain and all her crew fell upon their faces with fear; and you may judge of their surprise when the chief went on board, and offered to forego all harm and plunder providing the trading captain would take Lyu and his father to any place they might name. An offer the captain only too readily embraced.

They then took leave of the chief, the trading-junk set sail, and, after a long though pleasant voyage, both father and son arrived safely at the mouth of the Yang-tse-kiang, where they disembarked from the trading-junk, took a passage on board a canal-boat, and proceeded slowly through the beautiful country, which was studded on all sides with tea plantations; and I need scarcely tell you that, during their voyage, Lyu told his father the story of his adventures with the bonze, Hieul, and Chang. How sad and angry the captain felt at the misfortunes of his family! but melancholy as was the prospect of their endeavor to find Sang and Tchin, in so great an empire as China, the captain was brave, hopeful, and determined, and, moreover, had faith in that providence which had preserved him and his son from so many dangers; and it was with comparatively light heart that they left the boat, when within a few miles of the great city of Hang-tchou-fou.

They then hired a sedan, and in a short time came to the great lake See-ho, situated in the most beautiful spot in China. At this place they got out of the sedan, and walked to a promontory which ran jutting out into the lake, and there they stood by the side of one of the world's wonders of antiquity — a building of immense height, and celebrated as the Lui-fung-ta, or Tówer of Thundering Wind, from which, to use the words of the great Napoleon, forty-five centuries looked down upon them, smiling at the pygmy man, whom it had seen for thousands of years, rolling him-self up the hill of one generation, but to be toppled over, and to begin again, like another Sisyphus.

This tower, which is even now only partly in ruins, was built in the time of the philosopher Confucius, 2,500 years since. Where shall we all be in 2,500 years hence? Whole empires will have arisen, decayed, and become lost; nay, perhaps, the civilized inhabitants of some yet undiscovered country, may be sending out vessels of discovery to dig from the bowels of the earth monuments of that mighty England, that they will only know as we know Pompeii, Xanthus, and other cities — from books.

This Tower of Thundering Winds was on an eminence, from which, on one side, they could see the shining roofs of the houses in Hang-tcheou-fou; beneath them, sloping to a long distance, was a city of the dead, called the " Vale of Tombs." So thickly set, and so various were the forms of the tombs, that the whole vale had the appearance of a village of Lilliputian houses; then it was also strewn with an abundance of unburied coffins, and the whole, to give due solemnity to the dead, shaded with thickly-planted willows, which hung down their heads, and drooped over the tombs, as if they had been mediums of communication between the dead and the living, and were perpetually holding a whispering conversation with those at rest forever.

So solemnly beautiful was the scenery, and so fascinating the appearance of this city of perpetual repose, that Lyu and the captain determined to wander among the tombs before entering Hang-tcheou-fou. They had not walked far before they saw a man walking before a tomb sweeping away dust, pulling out weeds, and strewing sweet flowers all about. As

he turned his face towards Lyu, he recognized the innkeeper of the convict town, to whom he said, —

"Does the worthy innkeeper forget the features of
the Christian boy who travelled with the cheating
bonze?"

"May the spirits of our ancestors watch over us,
but this is miraculous," said the man, with surprise;
adding, "this is indeed a fortunate day; but what
chance brings the son of my benefactor to the Vale of
Tombs?"

Lyu then introduced the captain to Lin-Yung, and
told him that they were in search of Sang and Tchin.

"Then," said Lin-Yung, "my friends must for a
time make my house their home; for know that I
have been fortunate since we parted, and being now
blessed with abundance, may aid their search."

The captain and Lyu very readily accepted Lin-
Yung's invitation, and, having discharged the chair-
porters, they walked by the side of Lin-Yung, who
related his adventures somewhat as follows: "When
I told my young friend my story, I omitted to tell him
that I had an uncle settled in the city Hang-tcheou-fou,
who, although wealthy, had so many children that it
would have been useless for his nephew to ask his aid.
Well, some time after my young friend left the Town
of Thieves, a terrible disease took possession of my
uncle's house, and all his children but one daughter
died; then, having no son left to pay respect to his
tomb, he remembered his nephew, and made inquiries
through different provinces, till at last he heard the
story of my being exiled. He then went before the
mandarin who had ordered my punishment with an

account of the injustice done to his nephew in one hand, and a large sum of money in the other, when the unjust judge remitted my punishment, and sent orders that I should be released, and conveyed free of expense to Hang-tcheou-fou. When I reached my uncle's house, he promised to adopt me for his son and heir if I would marry my cousin; with this I could not but comply. He then proceeded on a journey, and on his return my cousin and I were married. Soon after, the good man died, and left me in possession of great wealth. It is twelve moons this day since his death; and therefore it was that I was sweeping his tomb. But we are even now at my house," said Lin-Yung, stopping before a large mansion in the principal street of the city. Having passed the court-yard and garden, they entered the large vestibule, which was supported by marble pillars, and were introduced by Lin-Yung into a small room set apart for visitors, when he left them attended by servants, who brought ewers of silver and napkins of fine cloth for their ablutions. Then another servant brought them handsome robes of silk, and informed them that his master would meet them at dinner in the Hall of Ancestors. Lyu being greatly pleased with Lin-Yung, he felt much delighted at seeing the good man surrounded with so much luxury after his long and unmerited misfortunes.

In about two hours a servant announced that his master was awaiting his guests, and the captain and Lyu were shown into the Hall of Ancestors. This was a large room, supported by marble pillars, and festooned around with rich drapery; the walls were hung with numerous marble tablets, on which were engraven the names, ages, and occupations of the deceased relatives. And as that happened to be the anniversary of the death of the last owner of the mansion, the hall was used, in order to pay due respect to his memory, for upon none but a great occasion is this room used. In this apartment three tables were spread with meats, rice, wine, and hot tea, to one of which Lin-Yung handed Lyu and his father.

"The hospitable and estimable Lin-Yung does us much honor, for surely we are about to be introduced to some of his noble friends," said Lyu, looking at the untenanted tables. The next minute a young lady was ushered into the room, and introduced to Lyu and the captain, both of whom said, "The worthy Lin-Yung is indeed honoring his friends!" much surprised at the appearance of their host's wife; for in China the ladies of the household are never presented to other gentlemen than the members of the family. After this introduction the lady withdrew from the apartment, but returned in a few minutes with — whom do you imagine? — indeed no others but Tchin and Sang.

Then occurred a scene that you may better imagine than I describe; the captain, Sang, Lyu, and Tchin were in ecstasies, for they were all equally surprised, to the delight of the good Lin-Yung and his wife, whose eyes swam with tears of joy at having been the means of so much happiness. O! there was so much love, so much joy, so much to say, so much to listen to — such a famous dinner, and so little appetite for any thing but each other's company, that — that I shall leave them alone for another chapter.

CHAPTER XXXII

"EGGS ARE CLOSE THINGS, BUT THE CHICKS COME OUT AT LAST."

So astonishing was this meeting, that they were all very anxious to know how it came about. Lyu first related his adventures to Tchin and his mother, who listened amidst smiles and tears, and not without many exclamations of anger at the villain Hieul. Then the captain repeated his story; after which Tchin said, "Now must my dear friends and children open their ears for my story," which, with the exception of the account given to Lyu by Chang, was as follows:—

"As you all are aware, after the disappearance of our dear boy Lyu, I determined to search every spot in the empire before I would relinquish hope, and, consequently, notwithstanding the failure of my first journey, I set out again, and journeyed by slow stages to the very borders of the empire, taking care to send letters by every opportunity to Sang. These letters I afterwards found must have been opened and destroyed by the villain Hieul, for they never reached their destination. Well, after two dreary years of search, I returned to Pekin; when, to my horror and surprise, I found that Hieul had sworn to my death before the proper officer, who permitted him to take possession of my whole property, which he immediately disposed of for a smaller sum than it was worth, and departed for some other province, doubtless fearing that I should return.

"Finding myself a beggar, and without home or family, I began to despond; but after a little I said to myself, Surely God must intend this for my own benefit, as, if I were still in possession of luxury, I might relax in my efforts to discover my dear child Lyt. Then I became better spirited, and went to a few friends, of whom I borrowed a small sum of money for the purpose of trading in different provinces. With this I started on my journey, and after many weeks travelling I came to the town of Tchin-Lieou; but just before entering it, I saw, near a cluster of trees, a girdle on the ground, and, taking it up, I found that it contained two hundred taels in silver, and I was wicked and ungrateful enough to think how useful this money would be to me. But then, again, I thought of the agony of mind of the person who had lost it; and, moreover, that perhaps the Supreme Being had caused it to be placed there to try my honesty, and to find out whether I merited to discover my lost son and daughter. It became very clear that I had no right to money that had been lost by some unfortunate traveller; so I determined to restore it if possible. With that intent, I placed myself near the spot where I had found the girdle, thinking it possible that the owner might return there to look for it; however, as this proved useless, I proceeded on my journey, and, after a few days, arrived at the city of Man-sou-tcheou, where I took up my lodgings at an inn. At this place there were several merchants engaged in recounting their trade adventures and other matters, when one of them said, with a very desponding look, 'Alas! my brothers, you perceive before you an unfortunate man; for a few days since I possessed two hundred taels, but lost them near Tchin-Lieou, where, as I was entering the town, a mandarin passed by with his train of attendants, and in the scuffle to get away from the in sulting soldiers, my girdle must have become loosened, and dropped on the earth without my knowing it; and it was not until night, when I went to undress myself, that I discovered my loss.'

"When the merchant related this the others all pitied him, but observed that as he was a very rich man, the loss of such a sum would not matter. My heart rejoiced at having discovered the owner of the money; and I said, 'May I ask the color of the girdle?' he replied, 'Blue.' 'Then,' I said, 'this is my brother's property.' The merchant was so delighted with the recovery of the money, and moreover at the honesty of returning it, that he begged I would accept at least one half of the money, which I steadfastly refused. At this refusal he was so full of gratitude, that he cried aloud, 'O, where may be found so much honesty and generosity! Still I dare not receive this favor without some return. My friend and brother must tell me his history.' I then told him of my great misfortunes, and particularly of the disappearance of Sang, to which he listened very attentively, and then made me travel home with him, to his house in the city of Hang-tcheou-fou, to which, out of politeness, I could not but assent. On our road, he told me that he was one of the most wealthy merchants of the city, and begged that as I had been unfortunate,

and seemed to understand mercantile affairs, that I
would accept the situation of chief clerk, which was
vacant in his establishment — a favor I accepted at
once.

" When we arrived at his house, greatly to my surprise, I found our worthy host, Lin-Yung, installed
here as his nephew; and when the merchant discovered how much I had befriended him when in distress, he increased his favor by offering me a small
partnership with him. Then came the marriage of
his daughter to Lin-Yung; and on that very morning,
as I was passing across the Hall of Ancestors, I met
a lady, one of the bride's friends; although deeply
veiled, she no sooner perceived me than she shrieked
and fainted. To give her air I lifted the veil from
her face, and saw Sang, my beloved daughter, the
mother of Lyu. My heart was too full to speak; but
I said to myself, ' Heaven has rewarded me: it is indeed true, that Honesty is the best Policy.'

" At this moment the merchant entered the apartment; and when he found out that Sang was my
adopted daughter, he said, ' My amiable friend, it is
this generous act of virtue in restoring the two hundred taels which has moved the compassion of
Heaven: it is Heaven itself that hath conducted you
hither, where you have recovered your lost daughter.
Indeed I am now uneasy that she has not been used
more kindly under my roof.' — ' O, say not such words!
for the good merchant hath treated me like his own
daughter,' said Sang, interrupting him. From that
time we all lived together as one family, till, alas!
twelve moons since the good man died," said Tchin;

adding, "my daughter Sang had better relate her own adventures." Then Sang commenced her story as follows : —

" When I came to my senses, after so wickedly attempting to destroy myself, I found the room in great confusion, and sat down for some time to gather my ideas, and at last remembered the whole of the plot to marry me against my will. When I saw Chang's head-dress in place of my own, I comprehended all that had happened, and began to fear the effects of Hieul's rage, when he returned home, and discovered the real state of affairs. It was late in the night before he came back, intoxicated with opium; he made so much noise at the door that I was afraid the neighbors would be alarmed, and, as all the servants had been purposely sent out of the way that the intrigue might be successfully carried out, I opened the door, when the wretched Hieul staggered at the sight of her he thought far enough away by that time. 'How is this, my niece ? Where is my wife Chang ?' he said.

"'Providence has turned thy wickedness against thyself, O miserable man ! for thy own wife has been taken away instead of her thou intendedst,' I said. Whereupon he raved and stamped about the floor, and made use of all the worst kind of oaths. However, by degrees he became more calm, and earnestly begged my forgiveness, saying that he had been doubly punished; for not only had he sold his own wife by mistake, but that he had since (in a few hours) lost all the money at a gaming table. Then he fell upon his knees, and begged my forgiveness, which I willingly gave, not knowing half his wickedness, and thinking he had been sufficiently punished by the loss of Chang, whom I believed he sincerely loved.

" So for many weeks we continued to live in the same house, without any thing disagreeable occurring. Hieul, indeed, appeared to feel the loss of his wife so much, that he had become a reformed man ; moreover, he was so attentive, and endeavored so much to condole with me on the loss of my darling son and the good Tchin, that each day I trusted him more and more, till once I went so far as to accompany him on the Grand Canal on a pleasure excursion, in a small covered boat he had hired for the purpose. We had been out the whole day ; it had become very dark, and I grew anxious to return home ; still Hieul continued along the canal, till the boat had passed the Great Wall, when we came in sight of a large covered barge. When he perceived this, he rested on his oars for a minute or two, and then turned the head of the boat, as if for the purpose of returning homewards. This, however, was merely a trick to save time, for he was so long in moving her around, that the barge had come alongside. Two men jumped into our boat, threw a large robe round my head, and lifted me into the barge ; carried me into the cabin, fastened the door, and left me alone for some hours. As you may imagine, my dear friends, my mind became greatly troubled at this terrible situation, for I made no doubt that the wretch had sold me as a slave ; still I believed that Providence would come to my aid, and I prayed to God more for my child than myself, and this afforded me much consolation.

" After I had been in the cabin some few hours, an old woman made her appearance, to whom I said, 'Tell me, O venerable mother, what injury I have done thee and thine, that I should merit this cruel treatment.'

" ' Thou art nothing but merchandise, daughter, to us, for thy nearest male relation has sold thee for one hundred taels; and as thou art young, accomplished, and well-looking, thou mayest turn out a profitable speculation. However, let not my daughter take this thing so much to heart, for she will be well treated.' Having made this cruel reply, the old woman set down the meat that she had brought, and left the cabin without another word.

" Again I was left to myself, and I wept bitterly as I thought of being severed from all chance of finding my son and friend; but then, as I murmured to myself the word chance, the thought suddenly occurred to me that it might be all for the best, and that this very misfortune might turn out a blessing. I became more cheerful, for I felt the light weight of hope sitting on my heart. That all this was not without reason, you will presently find. For a long time I was carried I knew not whither, and by different conveyances; till one day the old woman again came to me, and told me that we had reached our journey's end, and that I might rejoice at my fortune, for I should assuredly be happy, as I had been purchased by a wealthy merchant of Hang-tcheou-fou, the city in which we had just arrived, as a handmaid for his only daughter, who was about being married to her cousin. Then 1 thought if this old merchant and his young daughter were in possession of human feelings, that I had only to tell them my story to get released at once. But I could scarcely believe this good news, for surely, I thought, the wicked Hieul is too crafty to sell me where I might escape. Then I thought of the law which gave him the power, and hoped it might be true.

"The next day I was brought to this very mansion, and shown to the uncle of our worthy friend Lin-Yung, who, to my great delight, was so satisfied with my appearance, that he instantly completed the bargain. I took the first opportunity of throwing myself at his feet, and told him my story. As I related the fact of my only child and friend in the world being so torn away from me, the good man burst into tears; he had not very long before lost his sons and wife by a cruel disease. He raised me from the floor, and prom-ised that his house should be my home, and his daugh-ter my friend, and not my mistress. But when I related to him the wicked practices of Hieul, he be-came greatly enraged, and instantly set off on a journey to Pekin, to set the matter before the mandarins, and have Hieul punished. It was on his return from that journey that he lost his girdle and met our dear friend Tchin. The wicked Hieul had been too wary to remain near the scene of his villanies; he had sold off the property, and migrated to another and probably more distant province. How I met Tchin you have already heard. Now, I trust, our troubles are passed." So saying, Sang once more warmly embraced her husband and her son.

"Providence has, indeed, had a hand in these mat-ters, my dear children. Is it not a lesson to the avaricious and dishonest? for if I had had a blind passion for gold, and had kept the money in the lost girdle, surely we might never have become reunited," said Tchin. As he spoke there was a great hubbub near the house, and a loud knocking at the gate.

CHAPTER XXXIII.

"A HUNTER'S DOG WILL AT LAST DIE A VIOLENT DEATH."

WHEN the gate was opened by the porter, a voice was heard saying, "Is this the house of the great merchant Lin-Yung?" The reply being in the affirmative, a little, very stout, very round, old gentleman, enveloped in a large travelling robe and cap of thick silk, jumped out of a sedan, as lively as a young kitten, and to the great surprise of the servants, who were unaccustomed to such rudeness in the stately land of China, pushed them on one side, "Make way, make way, good people, for the venerable uncle of thy noble master," ran into the room, and without one of the customary forms, rushed into the arms of Lin-Yung, and embraced him heartily. Then the old gentleman's merry eyes lighted upon Lyu, and he cried, "How! by the toe of the emperor, can it be my young War Tiger, who ran away with the sacred boat of the lamas, and gave me extra mouths to feed for twelve entire moons?"

"My dear old friend, Jin-Lin," exclaimed Lyu, recognizing his old friend of the rock, as soon as the cap had fallen off, and the old gentleman had left off hugging him. He was then introduced to the Captain, Tchin, and Sang, but became very impatient till he heard a general outline of Lyu's adventures since their parting. When Lyu had again repeated his story, to which he listened attentively, he swallowed a cup of hot tea, rubbed his hands together, and, in the exuberance of his spirit, said, "Ain't I a Comedy? me a lama, one of. the twenty gong-headed old fellows at the lake? no, nothing of the sort; I am a Comedy." Yet, he added gravely, "I have much tragedy behind, as you will hear. Now open thy ears," he added: "I have already related my history up to my unfortunate connection with rebels, the death of my family," (here the Comedy shed tears, which, coming from a comedy, affected the eyes of his listeners tragically,) "and having to fly for my life; but, having been brought up a lama, I was enabled, first to pass for a hermit, and then to be elected the junior of the twenty contemplative lamas; but I have not told you, that, like my nephew, I have also long been a convert to the true faith. Surely there was not much of comedy in being tied up in a small island, and compelled for my safety to practise the foolish mummeries of idolatry; however, I did it, and it is a sin that I have to atone for, (here the Comedy again shed tears of real penitence;) but to continue my story, I should have remained exiled for life, but for my sly nephew here, who abused the laws by first bribing the different grades of mandarins of state, up to the greatest of them all, and then the minister himself, to listen to the truth of my innocence and long sufferings; would that I could bribe them as easily to give me back my murdered wife and children! (Here the Comedy shed bitter tears of memory.) The bribe must have been very great, for it succeeded, and I one day received a full pardon; for

what, I know not, except my sufferings and innocei.ce ;
and, what was more to the purpose, my liberty, and
ingots of silver sufficient to defray all expenses of
travelling; and here I am. This pardon was brought
to me by the boat whicli came to bring the offerings
to the island, twelve moons after the Young Tiger
locked the lamas up."

"Their wicked design was turned upon themselves,
my venerable father," said Lyu.

"Ay, ay," said Jin-Lin chuckling, "añd finely
they raved for some time afterwards, determining to
have revenge on the boy, and on the Tchurtchun
who had been the cause of all; however, the year
rolled round, and the lamas, who had bred a famine
in the island, returned with me to Kounboum, where
we arrived just in time to hear that your old friend,
the Tchurtchun, or bonze, having been too avaricious
to pay the people sufficiently whose child he was
about to introduce into the lamasary, they objected
to part with the little lama, and, moreover, explained
the whole imposture to the prince, who accompanied
the party to fetch the boy lama; and although he,
doubtless, knew all about it, the exposure was made
so publicly, that for his own safety his highness gave
the bonze over to the more stupid and believing lamas,
who took him back to the lamasary, degraded him
from his high rank, and confined him in a dungeon,
where, if not dead, he still remains a prisoner."

"Then the bonze has met his merits at last," said
Lyu ; adding, "would that the villain Hieul had also
met his deserts."

"Hist, my son; the ways of Providence are mys

terious; open thy ears and thou shalt hear," said the
old gentleman; continuing, "one night, when I had
nearly travelled through the whole of Kan-sou, I
took up my lodgings at a small inn; and as there
were no other travellers, I had the room to myself,
consequently sat down to enjoy a cup of hot tea, and
contemplate the change in my fortunes. I had not
long been seated before there was a great clamor at
the outer door, and the innkeeper shortly afterwards
introduced an old man and his wife, both of whom
looked hungered, wearied, and almost frozen with the
cold. As I could not but notice that they called for
neither meat nor drink, I made up my mind that
they were poor; still they had the appearance of
being far above the rank of beggars; so, not liking
them to starve while I had plenty, and yet fearing
to offend their pride, I approached the old man, and
said as delicately as I could, ' My brother and his wife
are probably beneath the cloud of temporary misfortune, perhaps even have been molested and robbed by
the thieves of the desert; if such be the case, he will
confer a favor on his younger brother by accepting
the loan of a few taels.'

" At this the old man's eyes glistened with pleasure,
and he replied, ' Truly my venerable brother speaks
the truth, and is, moreover, very generous to two unhappy wretches covered with misfortune; his kindness will indeed be acceptable, and save the life of my
poor wife, who is starving.' Whereupon he took the
money, and, as his wife lay upon the floor worn out
with fatigue, he ran into the inner apartment to fetch
some refreshment; after partaking of this, the woman

said very faintly, 'Alas! venerable and generous man, your kindness has come but just in time to save the life of a wicked wretch whom the gods are punishing for her sins, which are many and heavy.' She then told me her story, from which I knew her to be the wife of the wretch Hieul, by whom my young tiger-friend has suffered so much; but then I was astonished to find that she had another husband. Then she told me how she had been so justly punished by being mistaken for Sang, whom she had been vile enough to attempt to ruin. She then burst into loud praise of the old man, who she declared was too good for such a wicked wretch; and then further astonished me by the account of her meeting Lyu, and his goodness in saving her wretched life from the fury of the mountaineers; further saying, that, after Lyu's departure from the Miao-tse country, a party of the mountaineers took her and the old man to the very verge of their territory, where, after giving them some money and a couple of mules, they left them. Then, as the old merchant was a native of the province of Kan-sou, where he possessed some property, he determined, notwithstanding the journey was so long and hazardous, to return and spend the remainder of his days in peace; fortunately, soon after, they met a party of merchants, who were travelling the same road, but from whom they parted on entering the province. An hour afterwards they were overtaken by some robbers, who took from them their mules, money, and almost every thing they possessed, and then left them to find their way through those dreary regions on foot. For six days they had walked, sleeping by night beneath trees or hedges, and sup porting themselves upon roots and herbs till they reached that inn.

" When she had finished her story, her eyes seemed to be starting from her head, and her breath grew so short that I feared she would die, and endeavored to soothe her mind by telling her that, as she had become so sincerely repentant, her punishment had been sufficient; and after some time she slept upon the floor, covered with some robes that I obtained from the innkeeper.

" When she had fallen asleep the poor old man's eyes became full of tears, and he sobbed aloud, declaring that he should lose her, for he knew that she must die; but I soothed him, and told him that being wearied in body and mind, he was fearful and tremulous for want of sleep. To which he replied, ' My generous friend utters words of kindness,' and then lay on the floor to sleep. After this, being myself really worn out with fatigue, I adjusted my travelling mat to sleep. But I had not long laid down, when I heard a whispering near the door; one voice said, ' Art sure he has money?' then another voice replied, ' Truly am I, for he is generous, and pays well, not only for himself, but for others who have nothing.'

" Now, although fighting is not my trade, I knew that if not well prepared I should be murdered, and so catching hold of a great iron bar close at hand, I pretended to sleep. A few minutes afterwards, a man opened the door and crept towards me, holding a short sword in one hand and a small round lantern in the other. I let him get quite close, when I sprang upon my feet, and struck him to the earth with my bar, and directly began to think the act very wicked for a man of peace. The noise not only awoke the old man and his wife, but brought the innkeeper, who no sooner saw the robber on the floor, than he began to abuse me for committing murder in his house, and, moreover, threatened to send to the nearest military station to take me into custody. All this took place while the robber was lying senseless before us, and the old man and his wife stood in one corner of the room trembling with fear, for any harm that might happen to me.

"However, the innkeeper's threats were anticipated, for while he was threatening and looking very fiercely at me, some soldiers entered the room, when the innkeeper said, 'Surely it is fortunate that the soldiers have arrived, for this seemingly respectable, mock venerable-looking old rascal has just murdered a traveller who came into his room by mistake.'

"Then the officer who commanded the soldiers looked sternly at the innkeeper, and said, 'Thou dog of an innkeeper, it has long been suspected that thou consortest with thieves, and this night we have traced one to your house.' Whereupon he ordered the soldiers to take him into custody, and give him fifty strokes of the bamboo to keep him quiet. Then kicking the senseless robber, and turning to me, he said, 'Does the venerable stranger know aught of this wretch?' I told the officer what had happened, and he ordered some of his men to endeavor to bring him to; and, by throwing water over his face, in a little time he recovered, for fortunately my blow had only stunned him. The men lifted the robber upon his feet, when, seeing the soldiers around him, the cowardly wretch began to tremble and implore forgiveness No sooner, however, had he spoken, than the old merchant's wife suddenly sprang forward like one possessed, gave one long shriek, and fell at his feet.

" The soldiers in surprise turned aside, the robber knelt down by the woman's side, put his hands before his eyes to hide the tears, which, wicked as he was, fell from them, and bitterly sobbed, 'My wretched, wretched wife!' He then endeavored to arouse her; but alas! it was of no use; she had been long suffering from an internal disease, the shock had been too great, she was dead!" As the old gentleman related this, Comedy as he professed himself to be, his eyes swam with tears; but wiping them away, he continued, "The officer was so affected, that, notwithstanding his familiarity with crime and misery, he allowed his prisoner Hieul to weep by her side for some time; but then had him taken with the innkeeper to the nearest prison. Anxious as I was to get away from the place, I determined to see this wretched man before I left the province. I saw him in his dungeon, and he related to me the history of his crimes. It was as short as it was wicked. After he had sold Sang and his brother's property, he departed with the money to Canton Province, where he for some time lived quiet and retired; but his love of gambling and drinking soon returned, and in a short time he had not only lost all he possessed, but became deeply in debt; and, rather than seek regular employment, he solicited permission to join the army that was then proceeding against the rebel mountaineers. He remained with it for some time; but, either getting tired or being too great a coward, he managed to make his escape, and fled into the woods, where he worked his way, at times starving, at times begging, and at times thieving, into the province of Kan-sou. Once there, he joined a band of robbers, who had become terrible to the travellers through the province.

"This life lasted but a short period, for one day the band attacked a party of merchants,—the same party with which the old man had travelled,—and were all taken but Hieul. His companions in crime, however, gave such a description of him, and the innkeeper who for a long time had harbored them, that it resulted, as I have related, in the appearance of the soldiers at the inn, just after I had knocked him down. Thus, my young friend, you see the wicked Hieul has suffered for his wickedness, as punishment ever follows vice like its shadow."

"Truly this is wonderful, but most just!" said Tchin—"but the venerable father has not related what became of Hieul."

"He was sentenced to be pounded to death in a mortar; but, through the representations of the respectability of his brother Tchin, and a handsome bribe to the mandarin, the sentence was commuted to banishment to Ili for life. As for the old merchant, by means of a small sum of money which I gave him, he returned to his native town in safety."

At the mention of Hieul's first sentence Tchin's eyes became filled with tears, and every limb trembled; but at the commutation, by means of Jin-Lin's intervention, Tchin grasped both his hands, and endeavored to express his gratitude.

"Not me, not me!—all my sly nephew's doing; for he sent the money but two days ago with which to pay the mandarin," replied the old gentleman, chuckling.

Whereupon the whole family were profuse in their expressions of gratitude to Lin-Yung, who merely replied, "Surely, I could do no less for my benefactor; for what does Heaven endow us with wealth, if it be not to relieve our fellow-creatures?" After which, as the hour had grown very late, they retired to their respective apartments.

CHAPTER XXXIV.

"LET US FULFIL OUR OWN PARTS, AND AWAIT THE WILL OF
HEAVEN."

THE next day, when the party re-assembled, Sang
appeared so silent and dull that Lyu kissed her affectionately, saying, " Surely my beloved mother cannot be sad in the midst of so much happiness ? "

". Truly I am not so wicked as to be ungrateful to
the Almighty for the restoration of ·my dear relatives ; but neither can I be so vile as to forget that
I have an aged parent, whose mind must even now
be full of anxiety for the safety of his only surviving
child. Nay, I should not merit the blessings now bestowed upon me did I for an instant forget my duty
towards my noble and venerable parent."

At such becoming sentiments the whole party bowed
their heads in token of their deep sympathy with
Sang's filial respect ; and the gentlemanly old Comedy, notwithstanding his regret at parting with this
amiable family, proposed that the captain, Tchin, Sang,
and Lyu, should immediately proceed to the feet of
the venerable chief of the hills.

" My noble mother has but spoken my thoughts,"
said Lyu ; " for surely, even in the midst of so much
joy, I had not forgotten either my promise or my
duty to my venerable grandfather. If I have hes-
itated to propose our immediate departure for Koei-

cheou, it is because the whole province is filled with the emperor's troops, who would put us all to cruel deaths did they but dream of our connection with the great chief whom they are now endeavoring to subdue."

"Indeed our brave Lyu utters words of wisdom," said Tchin; "for it would be madness to undergo such risk. Yet it occurs to me that the generous Lin-Yung possesses a house at the Barbarian colony of Macao, where he transacts foreign trade. If he would appoint me his agent, we might all repair there at once, when my good daughter and her family would not only enjoy present safety, but be in readiness at the first announcement of peace to make their way through the adjoining provinces to the hills of Koei-cheou. What says my worthy friend?"

"The worthy Tchin's wisdom entitles him to a place in the inner council of the emperor!" said Lin-Yung; adding, "the papers necessary shall be made out this day. It is also a fortunate event that I have a cargo of merchandise now in one of my own boats, lying in the canal, and but awaiting my orders for sailing; and can I say more than that the vessel, nay, half my fortune, are at the service of my dear friends around me?"

Scarcely had they time to thank the worthy merchant for his offer when a great noise seemed to shake the very air; it was the sound of millions of human voices in rejoicing, mixed with the discordant tones of drums and brass instruments; and they all started from their seats half with fear, half with wonder.

"Surely this bodes no good for us, my dear friends

if it is what I fear; but move not from this room till my return," said Lyu, rushing out of the house.

In a few minutes he returned with great alarm depicted on his countenance; and as all arose on tiptoe with anxiety to inquire the cause, he placed his finger on his lip, saying, "Hush, hush! speak not, for thy words once wafted into the ears of the mob, will insure our instantaneous destruction." Then he added, in whispering tones, "A courier has just arrived from the hills, bringing intelligence of a great battle. The Tartars have been victorious; many thousands of our brave race have been butchered; and, it is further reported, that a body of troops are now passing through the city on their way to Pekin with Miao-tse prisoners."

"Great Heaven! can this be possible?" said Sang.

"Hush, hush, mother!" said Lyu; adding, "it is now necessary that we depart this very night. Is the boat prepared, O noble Lin-Yung?"

"It is; but dares not attempt to pass at night without a pass from the officer of the canal guard."

"Will my parents — will the noble Tchin — trust their son, who can yet save them?" said Lyu, impatiently.

"Surely, we cannot do otherwise, my brave boy; but what do you purpose?" said the captain.

"Trust me, O my father, by placing yourselves under my directions for a few short hours; but believe me there is danger every minute that you remain here, for I heard it whispered that suspicious strangers had taken possession of the house o Lin-Yung. Therefore leave the house cautiously mix with the crowd, and haste to the boat; get her moored as far out as possible, and then wait my rejoining you." Then taking a warm farewell of Jin-Lin and Lin-Yung, the brave boy borrowed a quantity of silver from Tchin, and left the house.

Great as was the sorrow of Sang at the destruction of so many of her people, it would have been greater had she known either the fears of Lyu, or the risk he was about to undergo.

When he reached the streets, he found crowds of people flocking from all quarters of the city towards the great square, to witness the arrival of the troops with their prisoners. Floating rather than walking with the stream, Lyu reached the great square, on two sides of which treble lines of armed soldiers were drawn up to keep the path clear; however, by dint of much pushing, Lyu thrust himself into the first line, indeed so near to the reserved path that one of the soldiers struck him with his bamboo cane.

After waiting a full hour, there arose a tremendous shout of welcome to a large body of cavalry, which was immediately followed by a body of foot soldiers, with tigers and lions painted on their breasts, and the character Brave on their backs; some bore banners with the emperor's crest of the five-clawed dragon; and others flags, with the words, "The rebel-subduing army of the South." These were followed by two large bands of musicians, playing upon their instruments. Then came a double column of foot soldiers, with drawn swords, between every two of which marched a Miao-tse prisoner, with his arms bound, and a chain hanging from his neck; and as these brave men appeared, the crowd gave fearful yells of pleasure, at which the captive children of the hills gnashed their teeth and looked scornfully.   Then came about a dozen horse litters, each of which contained a large wooden cage, in which, stripped of arms and decoration, clad in a simple robe of brown stuff, knelt (for the cage was too small for him to stand) a Miao-tse chieftain, with his arms bound and an iron chain around his neck, yet frowning defiance at the horse soldiers, who closely guarded him on both sides.   O, how Lyu's heart ached at the sight, for he recognized them all; they were the noblest and bravest chiefs of his grandfather's court; and when he could no longer doubt that it was the old king's tribe that had been defeated, he trembled for fear of what might follow.

When the chiefs had passed, there came a vast body of cavalry, then a company of foot guards, all with their swords drawn and faces turned towards a large iron cage, which rested upon a platform thrown across the backs of two horses; on each side of the cage, upon tall horses, rode savage-looking Tartar soldiers, armed to the teeth, with their eyes glancing upon the cage, and the thumbs of their right hands affixed upon their bows, ready for instant use.   In the midst of these soldiers rode a man carrying a yellow banner, on which was written, "*Behold and tremble at the chastisement which awaits rebellion;*" and as these banners were waved to and fro, the crowd stood tiptoe with impatience to get a sight of the prisoner.   It was useless, however, for the soldiers kept too close to the bars of the cage.   Immediately after the cage came a mandarin's chair of state, followed by its owner on horseback, and surrounded by a large staff of officers, one of whom held aloft the dragon standard, and another a banner upon which was inscribed, " *The powerful and exalted lieutenant of the rebel-exterminating General Le.*" When the cage reached the centre of the square, the lieutenant commanded a halt, while he sent an officer forward to the governor of the town, and all those who could find room to do so, fell flat upon their faces and performed the ko-tow before the emperor's representative. In about a minute, however, the people were commanded to arise and behold the consequence of rebellion; and when the soldiers moved aside from the bars of the cage, Lyu's heart beat quickly, his limbs trembled, and his brain swam; but for the pressure from the crowd he must have fallen; his doubts and fears were horribly realized, for there in the cage sat the old king, stripped of every insignia of his rank except the yellow robe which had given such terror to the government, and which in mockery he was still permitted to wear, but cut into a thousand strips, which hung from him like ribbons. He sat with his noble head bared, and the long white locks flowing over his shoulders, resting upon his hands, in a crouching form, peering into the faces of the crowd with glances that showed his spirit to be still unsubdued, like a tiger at bay.

" This then is the arch-thief himself, the cunning rat of the hills, who stole the imperial robe of yellow: truly like his fortune it is in fragments," said one of the mob.

" Let us give the rat a welcome, my brother," said another, throwing a handful of sand towards the cage.

This was too much for Lyu, who, forgetting his prudence, clutched the man by the throat, saying, "Dost thou not venerate even old age, thou coward slave?"

"A rebel, a rebel!" cried the mob, surrounding Lyu, and who would doubtless have immolated him on the spot but for the mandarin lieutenant, who, perceiving the disturbance, and finding out the cause, ordered Lyu to be brought before him, saying, "How, slave! darest thou to protect such vermin in defiance of the emperor?"

"To protect age and misfortune, most noble warrior, is the duty of all," said Lyu.

"These are bold words from the lips of a youth," replied the mandarin; but he added, well scanning his features, "our eyes have fallen on thy features before, youth."

"The illustrious lieutenant mistakes the face of his servant, who is but the son of a poor merchant, for that of another," said Lyu, with no very pleasant sensation, for in the lieutenant he now recognized the foppish, cowardly mandarin sent by the General Le as envoy to the Miao-tse king. But before the mandarin could reply the officer returned, with orders from the governor for the prisoner to be confined till the following day in the strongest prison in the city, where they were to await the arrival of another body of troops, who were expected the next day, and, for greater safety, would accompany them on their route to Pekin. As these orders were imperative and immediate, he gave Lyu into the custody of a guard of soldiers, passed the word of command, and the procession passed on to the prison.

CHAPTER XXXV.

"A HUNTER'S DOG WILL AT LAST DIE A VIOLENT DEATH."

NOTHING could exceed the misery of Lyu at the position in which he found himself by his own imprudence: not only was he now incapable of devising any means of rescuing the king, but he had placed his whole family in great danger; for he knew that the moment the mandarin's other duties permitted, he would again examine him, and, when certain of his identity, leave no means untried to discover his family, who were, at that very moment, awaiting him on the canal. However, as some hours passed without a summons from the mandarin, he began to entertain hopes that he had been forgotten, and that he might manage to bribe the soldiers on guard outside the strong-room in which he was confined. For this purpose he endeavored to attract the man's attention by thumping at the door. "What would the rebel dog, that he dares clatter in this unseemly manner?" said the soldier, entering the room.

"May the tiger of war meet with the promotion he merits," said Lyu, placing a piece of silver in the soldier's hand, and adding, "surely so brave a warrior would not be needlessly severe to an unfortunate youth, who, now that he needs but little money, would venture to offer a portion to him."

"Surely the young merchant is too open-hearted

to be guilty of treason, and therefore it is permissible
for his unworthy servant'to accept his present. Still
it is a maxim of the wise, 'that he who giveth ex-
pecteth something in return,'" said the soldier.

"Would the war-tiger earn a sum of money sufficient to purchase his promotion?" said Lyu — showing
a handful of silver to the man, whose eyes glistened
with delight.

" Truly, it is the command of Tien, that every man
should seek to advance the interests of his family, and
as the young merchant is generous, and, moreover, not
convicted of any crime against the state or the social
relations, there can be no great harm done in my leaving the door of his prison open," said the soldier, very
readily, placing the silver pieces in his girdle. He
had scarcely, however, completed the transfer of the
silver, when the officer of the guard, missing him from
his post, entered the room, greatly to the discomfiture
of the soldier, who immediately threw himself upon
his face, crying, "The villain rebel dog has been endeavoring to bribe the incorruptible, O most noble
commander." The officer, however, was not to be
deceived so easily, and would have passed his sword
through him but for Lyu, who threw himself between
them, saying, " Mine is the punishment, for I offered
the bribe." No sooner had Lyu spoken, than the
officer's face became of a deathly hue, every limb
trembled, and he shrank backwards aghast, as if he
had encountered a spirit. Then, remembering the
presence of the soldier, he said, " Back, dog, to thy
post; but get thee fifty paces from the door, while I
examine this rebel dog." When the soldier had gladly

enough scampered away, the officer said, "Who art
thou, O youth?" and, as he spoke, he removed his
helmet-cap, as if to obtain relief and aid his memory,
when Lyu, in his turn, became surprised, for there
before him, dressed as a mandarin officer, stood the
wretched, degraded Hieul; and he replied, " Lyu Payo
— thy brother's adopted son; even as thou art the
villain Hieul, who sought his ruin."

"Pardon, O noble Lyu, for the miserable wretch
has been sufficiently punished," said Hieul, falling on
his knees, and taking Lyu's hand between his own.

"Art thou repentant, O degraded man?" said Lyu.

"Truly am I, O noble boy!"

"What proof have I?"

"A blessed one, for I can effect thy escape from this
prison, at the cost of degradation, if not of life itself."

"It is not enough," said Lyu, turning from him in
disgust.

"Ask even my life in atonement of the injuries I
did thee, O noble Lyu," said the wretched man.

"Nay, I ask not that, but more; even the life of
the venerable chief who remains for one night within
these walls," said Lyu.

"Even that is within my power; for the soldiers of
the guard are for the night beneath my command.
Yet it will be ingratitude, for I shall encompass the
ruin of the mandarin lieutenant who took compassion
on me in my misery, obtained my release from perpetual confinement, and afterwards promoted me to my
present rank. Truly it will be most foul ingratitude.
Will not the noble Lyu ask my own life instead?"

"It would be useless, O degraded man; but save

that noble old chief, and not only will thy family pardon thy faults, but become thy debtors for life. For know, that he is the father of my much injured mother, Sang," said Lyu.

"The father of Sang! This is a wonderful event. The gods give me a noble opportunity of showing my repentance. Boy, it will cost me my worthless life; but it shall be done. But where, O where are Sang and my noble brother?"

"In great danger; but as I dare not trust so false a wretch, I will not tell thee, O Hieul, till thou hast in truth performed this act of repentance," said Lyu, firmly.

"O, how bitter is the punishment of such as Hieul the degraded! But thou art right, Lyu; thou canst not trust me yet. But I am impatient to restore myself to thy good esteem. In two hours, when thou hearest the tones of the second watch of the night, I will return to thy room." So saying, he left the room.

Notwithstanding these vehement protestations of repentance, Lyu had but small faith in Hieul; still, small as it was, he clung to it. Nor was he disappointed, for precisely as the bell tolled the second watch, Hieul reappeared with an officer's jacket, robe, helmet, bow, and sword, saying, "Attire thyself in this uniform. It is thy best safeguard; for the sentries as we pass will think that two officers are on guard, by way of extra precaution, now the prison holds such important prisoners." Then, with lantern in hand, but the light sufficiently shaded to hide Lyu's features, they proceeded on their way through that dreary building It was a wilderness of passages; at the be ginning and end of each stood a sentry, incessantly clapping together two pieces of sticks to keep them from sleeping on duty. Having passed through a great many of these passages, they came to another and larger one, studded with doors, within which the Miao-tse chiefs were confined, and guarded by a soldier at every door. As they passed down this passage, Hieul stopped to speak to each soldier, and pulling from beneath his robe a long, narrow skin, full of liquor, gave them to drink, very much to the astonishment of the soldiers, who could only account for their officer's condescension, from a belief that in his joy at his prospect of promotion on his arrival at Pekin, he had been drinking too freely.

At length they came to a door, on the outside of which stood a double guard, and, having given them both a large draught of the liquor, Hieul took a key from his girdle and passed into the cell, where, to his joy, Lyu found the old king; but, to his grief, still confined within the iron cage. The white-headed old warrior had been sitting in deep contemplation, supporting his head with his hands, and his elbows resting upon his knees. Upon the entrance of Hieul and Lyu he but lifted his head, and, with a scornful smile, said, "What, would the coward slaves torture a maimed tiger in his cage?"

"We come to save thee, O venerable chief," said Hieul.

"Does the Tartar rat still fear the chief of the hills, or does he seek a bribe? The Miao-tse chief possesses none of the accursed metal for which the Tartar mire, buy and sell their souls," said the king.

"Does not my venerable and most noble relation remember the promise of his daughter's son?" said Lyu, kneeling down by the cage, and lifting the helmet from his head.

"My noble, noble boy, the accursed Tartars may now take the worthless life of their worst enemy, for at the last moment he is triumphant in the nobility of his descendants," replied the old warrior, placing his hands through the bars upon Lyu's head.

"But the key, the key, O Hieul!" said Lyu, impatient to release his venerable relative.

But Hieul's face wore a blank, disappointed expression: in his haste he had forgotten the key.

"This is cruel, most cruel, O Hieul! to place the cup of liberty in our hands but to dash it into a thousand fragments."

"Pardon, O noble youth! but I will obtain it yet; remain you here till I return; stir not for your lives; the key is in the possession of the mandarin, who keeps it in his girdle; I will entice him here, by telling him that the chief is dying, and has a secret to impart; hide you in yon dark corner;" so saying, Hieul left the cell. Taking advantage of the absence of Hieul, Lyu informed the king of his plans, and once more inspired him with a wish to live by telling him that, if all prospered, in a few hours he would hold his long-lost daughter in his arms. "Haste, haste, my noble boy; for once take the coward's advice and hide, to save thy life." He had scarcely spoken, when the mandarin entered the cell, followed by Hieul.

"What would the Wolf-dog with the all-powerful

and all-victorious lieutenant?" said the mandarin, pompously walking up to the cage, but with his drawn sword in his hand, as if still in fear of the caged king.

" Had the hill chieftain tossed the cowardly dog from his town walls when he so threatened, he would not have lived to repent his mercy in saving thy miserable dog's life !" said the old king with the imprudence and temper of his race, and drawing himself up to his full height.

" Miserable vermin, I would slay thee like a rat in thy cage, wert thou not reserved for a heavier punishment, and an example for all future rebels !" said the lieutenant. " But how is this, dog ? didst thou not say the old dog was dying ?" he said, turning to Hieul, who was at that moment locking the door on the inner side. " Ah, treachery !" he added, passing his sword in an instant through the body of Hieul; but before he could open the door, Lyu sprang upon him, passed his girdle several times around his arms, threw him on the floor, and, holding his sword to his throat, said, " Silence, coward ! if thou wouldst live !" Then, trembling with rage and terror, the mandarin submitted to be so gagged that he could not speak, or even moan. Lyu then took the key from his girdle and let out the king, and then went to the assistance of Hieul. The wretched man, however, was past all human aid — he could but murmur, " Pardon, O Lyu ! Pardon from Sang and my good brother ! Tell them I have been justly punished; for even this, the only good act of my life, has been attained by treachery to yonder mandarin, my only friend." So saying he died.

Then, as every instant was of vital importance, Lyu stripped the lieutenant of his uniform, robe, cap, and arms, not forgetting the commission of office which had been given to him by the viceroy General Le; after which he lifted him into the cage, fastened the door, and, with the king, left the cell.

By aid of the darkness of the night they passed through the passages, nearly falling over the bodies of the guards, who had been rendered insensible by Hieul's liquor, till they reached the gate, where they were challenged by the guard.

"The rebel-subduing general's lieutenant and his aide-de-camp," replied Lyu unhesitatingly. The soldier bowed, and they continued onwards till they reached the court-yard, where they found the mandarin's chair and two porters. "The powerful lieutenant desires to be conveyed to the house of the officer of the canal guard, said Lyu, entering the chair after the old king.

The men, not doubting what Lyu had said, immediately obeyed. When they reached the officer, Lyu exhibited the lieutenant's commission, and demanded the watchword of the night and a boat for the especial private business of the lieutenant. The officer readily complied; and as soon as Lyu found himself and the king in the boat, he dismissed the boatmen, and, pulling lustily at the oars, they soon became lost among the dense mass of vessels, and, after an hour's pulling, reached Lin-Yung's barge, where, in the great cabin, they found the captain, Tchin, and Sang in the greatest anxiety at his long absence, and not a little surprised at the appearance of his companion. "Mother, behold your father!" said Lyu; and without a word, for their hearts were too full of joy, the father and daughter became locked in each other's arms.

When the first surprise was over, and the old king recounted the story, the family fully comprehended the bravery and talents of Lyu, who had saved them from destruction. Still they were not free from danger while so near the city; therefore they gave orders to proceed, and by the morning they had passed from the canal into the great Yang-tse-Kiang River, along which they proceeded for many days unmolested till they reached the sea, where Tchin, as the agent of Lin-Yung, engaged a small ship, into which they transferred the merchandise, and immediately set sail for the Portuguese COLONY of MACAO. And although during the whole journey the old king sorrowed and was angered at the loss of his army and his brave chieftains, his joy and satisfaction were so great at the restoration of his daughter, that he consented to live with them all at Tchin's new house; at least, until a general peace should be proclaimed, and he might in safety return to his beloved hills. That time, however, never arrived, for, some few months after their arrival at Macao, the old chief's health broke up, and he expired in the arms of his beloved daughter.

Then, as no further motive remained either for Sang or Lyu to seek the mountains of Koei-cheou, they determined to rest quietly at Macao with the captain, who resumed his partnership with Tchin and soon established a prosperous house — the more so, as Lin-Yung, who, to show his gratitude to God for the benefits he had received, resolved to devote the remainder of his life to the propagation of Christianity in their native province, resigned his business to them.

As for the mandarin whom Lyu locked in the iron cage, he was discovered the next morning, half dead with fright for fear of the terrible consequences should it reach the emperor's ears that the Miao-tse chief had escaped.   However, by means of bribing the governor of the town and the soldier who discovered him, at the cost of half his fortune, he got a report drawn up and sent to the emperor, containing an account of the king's sudden death on the road to Pekin; and the people were satisfied, for Hieul's body was substituted and buried for that of the caged prisoner.

I may also tell you that, brave and adventurous as Lyu was, he had had quite enough of adventure to last him a long time; for, although it is very fine to sit by a fireside, and talk about perils and fighting, once tried, it is soon found that " it is not all gold that glitters."   Again, it is only of the fortunate, who are lucky enough to save their lives and relate their adventures, that we all hear.   For instance, had Lyu been killed, as he might have been, in one of his earlier enterprises, you would not now have had to read " The Adventures of Lyu Payo, the Wolf-Boy of China."

THE END.